PRAISE FOR STEVEN I
GHOSTS OF WATT O'HUGH

NAMED TO *KIRKUS REVIEWS'* "BEST OF 2011"

WINNER, BEST FANTASY NOVEL, INDIE EXCELLENCE BOOK AWARDS, 2012

FINALIST, ACTION ADVENTURE CATEGORY, NEXT GENERATION INDIE BOOK AWARDS, 2012

"[An] engaging tale of Western science fiction and amazing fantasy.... Drachman pens a standout lead in the character of Watt O'Hugh. The cool hero's tale is told in charming, romping detail, from the magical adventurer's poor childhood in the Five Points and the Tomb[s], to his notorious, gun-toting dalliances in the Wild West and his wilder exploits through time itself. ... Adding legitimate historical figures, such as the esteemed author Oscar Wilde, to the fictional mix builds levels of believability to the time-traveling romp's fast-paced flavor. ... Fast-paced, energetic and fun; a dime novel for modern intellectuals."

> – *Kirkus Reviews*

"If you gave up on the feasibility of a Western/science fiction mash-up when 'Cowboys vs Aliens' tanked a few months back, give it another try. On the page, at any rate. ... Drachman revives the nascent genre with his rip-snorting, mind boggling novel ... [T]here's a lot going on in this teeming tome!"

> – Peter Keough, *The Boston Phoenix*

"Blending in elements of fantasy and time travel, ... *The Ghosts of Watt O'Hugh* is a humorous and fun adventure, recommended."

> – *The Midwest Book Review*

"Quixote-esque …. With stories of Chinese emperors, legends of magical creatures, the streets of 1870s New York and time-roaming gunmen of the Wild West[.]"

    – *The Bethesda Gazette*

"… a tale of yesteryear, evocative of Robber Barons and the old West, while ingeniously narrated from a modern perspective, courtesy of Magic and an ability to roam Time. Watt O'Hugh is a character for sure and an engaging narrator who will take you through fascinating worlds, meticulously researched …. *Watt O'Hugh* is cowboy fantasy noir and worth a read."

    – Mike Brotherton, author, *Star Dragon* and *Spider Star* (Tor Books)

" … a triumph of genre bending, a fine, literary mashup of cowboy adventure and science fiction magic that makes you wish you could meet its carefully hewn characters in real life."

    – Harold Goldberg, author, *All Your Base are Belong to Us* (Random House)

"… a vivid, fast-paced and unpredictable journey, keenly observed and lyrically presented, through the life and times of a most unusual man.

    – Helen Pfeffer, Contributing Writer, *FilmCritic.com*

"A fine writer, and a fine fellow …."

    – Raymond Kennedy, author, *Ride a Cockhorse* (Knopf)

THE GHOSTS OF WATT O'HUGH

BEING THE FIRST PART OF THE STRANGE AND ASTOUNDING
MEMOIRS OF WATT O'HUGH THE THIRD

Steven S. Drachman

ISBN 978-0-9913274-0-9

Front cover illustration and book design by Mark Matcho

Chickadee Prince Logo by Garrett Gilchrist

Visit him at www.watt-ohugh.com

Third Printing

This edition contains minor corrections from the first and second printings and a new afterword, but is otherwise identical in all material respects.

STEVEN S. DRACHMAN

THE GHOSTS OF WATT O'HUGH

STEVEN S. DRACHMAN is a restaurateur, writer and critic whose work has appeared in *The New York Times, The Washington Post, The Boston Phoenix, Entertainment Weekly, The Village Voice* and *The Chicago Sun-Times*. He lives in Brooklyn with his wife and two daughters..

THE GHOSTS OF WATT O'HUGH

Being the First Part of the Strange and Astounding Memoirs of Watt O'Hugh the Third

Chickadee Prince Books
New York

To Lan,
Liana and Julianne

PROLOGUE

I have my ghosts. In a way, I am a ghost myself.

My name is Watt O'Hugh III, this is my story, and I've tried to write it exactly the way it happened. Some conversations may be approximations. Scenes that occurred when I was not present are based on reconstruction, conjecture, and sometimes pure guesses. Maybe I don't remember every last detail properly, but I've never outright lied. I have also tried to be candid about my experiences roaming Time, even though I know that as a result of this revelation many readers will disbelieve my yarn.

I have tried to keep my story accurate by referring frequently to a journal in which I've written nearly every day of my life since the charity workers taught me to write, which is a very long time.

As I write these words, it's early 1936.

I know that I will die on my ranch in 1937 from old age and natural causes, alone, with no heirs or family by my bedside. It took me a long time to muster the courage to peek through Time at my ultimate fate, but now I know. Believe me, I'm writing as fast as I can.

My diary entry on July 10, 1863, began:

"I awoke in the arms of the beautiful Lucy Billings. May this day last forever."

That morning, more than 70 years ago, I awoke to Lucy's smile, a bright white smile on a beautiful ivory-white face. That July – July of 1863 – was the early culmination of my own Summer of Love, which occurred more than a hundred years before yours. I was twenty-one years old. Lucy and I had been together for one year and one month. I didn't mind that she was a subversive. I wouldn't have minded even if I'd known what the word meant.

"Happy anniversary," I whispered.

"What," she asked me, her mouth so close to my young ear, "shall we do today?"

And here is what we did: she took me to the horse races in Jerome Park, where, in my one good suit, I passed myself off as a gentleman, which I likewise attempted on Lucy's arm at the New York Academy of Music that evening, while her most powerful financial benefactor (and most prominent sexual beneficiary), a whiskered old man with millions to spare, sat miles above us in his prestigious box, surrounded by fawning business associates and a contemptuous, ageing wife. Lucy assumed the crinoline-garbed guise of a youthful heiress from the old country, a woman who spoke with a very light, unidentifiable accent and who would admit not to a name like "Lucy Billings", but instead to something more exotic and difficult to pronounce. I pretended to be her brother, Tomas, who didn't speak much. In reality, of course, just as I was not her brother, Lucy was not an heiress. She was born a poor girl someplace in America and invented both her pedigree and her accent. But everyone in New York City was a liar, back in those days.

I stared up at the old man in his box for a little too long, and so Lucy tugged my sleeve. "Don't think about him," she said, and then added, *very* quietly, "It is *you* I love." I asked her to marry me for the hundredth time, and she smiled and refused me for the hundredth time. "What *would* your parents make of me?" she asked, mocking me gently.

Later, in the still-darkening evening, Lucy and I sat side-by-side on a two-person cycle that looked like a horseless carriage. Laughing warily in this uneasy contraption, we pedaled up Riverside Drive to the tree-shrouded country roads that abutted the Boulevard above 100th Street. We lay in the grass by the River, and we watched the stars for an hour, our fingers entwined.

If only you could have seen New York City then, my 21st Century friends! Out West, once I'd left New York (sadly), I found myself sometimes nostalgic even for the walking races at Gilmore Garden, which Lucy and I attended regularly on Sunday afternoons. Don't laugh – all strata of New Yorkers used to pay to watch people walk very fast! It seemed exciting and novel at the time. So did renting a horse-drawn sleigh in Central Park on a snowy January day, at least when Lucy Billings was by my side: blond-haired, slim-waisted, wicked-minded, beguiling, and so temptingly innocent in appearance. Sometimes I would accompany Lucy to secret midnight meetings with a small shadowy group that she boastfully deemed subversive, and which seemed to rely to no little extent on her financial contributions. At these meetings, held in dark buildings in hidden side streets, Lucy would read from a notebook that she often kept with her – demanding rights for women, the right to "free love", rights for the Colored man. The overthrow, she suggested once, of the whole corrupt codfish aristocracy of the United States, to be replaced by something that she described in some detail and which (I thought) sounded nice.

Lucy was somewhere in the mid to late murk of her twenties, and she explained to me more than once that, as a twenty-one-year-old man who was "perhaps" (certainly) a bit younger than she, I was to "learn things" from her and to fall in love with her "madly, but only briefly." She was right about the "madly" part.

As I wrote those words in my journal, at the beginning of that perfect day that I wished would last forever, I could hardly expect that on July 13, 1863, which was the following Monday, Lucy would slip silently from my life, without even a goodbye.

After the havoc of that terrible Monday (which was also the day of the infamous New York Draft Riots, in case you haven't brushed up on your history), and after I'd stopped paying attention, she turned up in England, married to a man named Darryl Fawley. He was in his forties, with sagging, wan features, an unevenly balding pate, crooked, tea-stained teeth, tobacco-stained fingers, and a weak, lanky frame, an English aristocrat and mid-level embassy functionary who, even when he took the shocking step of turning outlaw, could not give up the comfortable trappings of his youth. Then, suddenly, the 1870s still dawning, Fawley and his wife disappeared thoroughly. His mysterious departure from England made the newspapers as far away as the States, though on my side of the Atlantic, pictures of his beautiful American wife dominated the coverage, based on interviews with American socialites who remembered her from years earlier when, at an apparently tender age, she had made her first appearance at society events. American readers were also treated to elegant illustrations of Lucy in her finery, depicted from her wedding portrait.

Her escape into infamy with her well-bred husband brought her notoriety, and the publication of those artists' renderings of Lucy – mostly wide-eyed, tenderly wrought, impossibly curvaceous, but, in my opinion, inappropriately gentle – made her, in the end, sort of a 19th century "sex symbol." That's how you might describe her, if you remembered her now, a century-and-a-half after the furor she caused in the civilized world. In your era, she would find her image on "t-shirts", and teenage boys would hang her poster on bedroom walls. Back then, in my century, she caused hysteria of a different sort. She sold newspapers, starred in dime novels and Sunday sermons, and inspired insipid theatrical presentations. Fawley, who had engineered the couple's disappearance from view, soon also disappeared from the newspaper, overshadowed by Lucy's "star appeal." Any mention of the uncomely Mr. Fawley detracted from the glamour of the mystery.

When Fawley and Lucy vanished, I was a drag rider bringing up the rear of a cattle drive fifteen hundred miles north across the Western plains, and I heard nothing of it. I was dirty and bathed in sweat, my clothes and my lungs coated in the dust kicked up through the blazing heat by the stragglers at the back of the herd.

Each day, I galloped through bullshit, by which I mean two things. First, my horse skidded so often on the excrement of our cattle that I sometimes thought it would be the end of me. But I also mean the myth that the West would allow a man like me to make of himself an easy success. I owned nothing but my clothes and my saddle – even my horse belonged to the ranch bosses – and on every trail, we left more than one colleague in a shallow grave. By the hour, I cursed the swing riders and the flank riders I could see through the dust, and the invisible point men who rode way up in front, and who didn't know my name but could determine my destiny.

Now, re-reading my journal, I note that, on the very day the English government made public Fawley's disappearance, I was pushing across the Powder River in Wyoming, trying my best to keep my cattle and myself from drowning. Of course, the trail boss couldn't deliver us the morning papers, and even if he somehow could have, I would not have spared even a glance. All I longed for as the long days passed was to eat, and then to sleep. Being exhausted and hungry helped me to forget. Even though Fawley had taken with him the former Lucy Billings, I remained (perhaps willfully) ignorant of their story. Like Darryl Fawley's disappearance into the wilds of China, my banishment to the Magic of the most desolate parts of what you readers would call "the Old West" (but which was at the time the New West) had cut me off decisively from the civilization I had once known.

Though Lucy married him to advance in the world, she could have loved Darryl Fawley the way he loved her. Really, she should have loved him. Perhaps the love of a beautiful and brilliant woman could have saved him. But Lucy could not quite manage to love Darryl Fawley, because throughout her entire life, Lucy would love only one man. And I was that man.

CHAPTER 1

My diary entry on July 17, 1874, begins:

"I was lost in a hail of bullets. Muttered, to myself, *Oh no – not again.*"

I don't pretend I'm the bravest man in the world. I'm afraid of plenty of things. I worry about my own capacity for greed and evil. I'm afraid of a woman's power to hurt me. I admit I'm frightened of waterfalls, and I don't imagine I could tell you where that phobia came from. But as the years have gone by, I've been surrounded by bullets so many times that they've slowly lost their power to terrify. Whether that's brave or just stupid, I'll let you decide.

After my behavior during the Draft Riots of 1863 (which I will continue to defend to my last breath), New York City, my hometown, cast down a big disapproving stare and spat me out. I joined the Union army, happy to spite my former friends back home. When the War ended, I had no place to go but West.

Later, after the widely scattered publication of my reputedly "heroic" actions in Little Mount, a small but flush mining town where I stopped to gamble away some of my cattle drive pay, I became a minor but noted Western icon to those Eastern readers who longed for rugged adventure and romance but couldn't brave the wilderness themselves. Like Lucy, I became the subject of dime novels and plays and breathless "eyewitness" newspaper accounts by city slicker reporters who'd hardly ever been as far as Brooklyn. Women fell in love with me – or, rather, with my fictional "adventures," and with the rather exaggerated likeness that was soon known far better and to many more people than my real face and body. I'm tall – six foot three – and strong enough to put up a good fight against most men, but through the 19th century's money machine of hype, rumor and lies, I became known as some sort of perfect ideal. In these adventure stories – none of them true – I killed Indians, I rescued women tied to train-tracks, I foiled bank heists, I dangled from cliffs, I fought duels atop speeding trains. I was America's brave new Western man, handsome and strong and invincible. I was Manifest Destiny, personified.

Well, the lie did the trick. New York, it appeared, was willing to forgive my past.

Theatrical producers called from Manhattan. A couple of plays, they said, had already hit the island starring New York actors impersonating me in my various adventures. A group of investors – including Drexel, Morgan & Company, a prestigious Wall Street firm I'd never heard of – was interested in bankrolling the real thing. Would I – *could* I – give up my Western life for a shot at the stage? they asked.

Could I ever! Of course, now I was a cowboy, and I was a shootist. I'd learned to fire a .45, and I knew to pay for my drinks in cow town honky tonks with bullets – "cowboy change," we called it. Though I hadn't chosen my new life, I was suitably proud of what I'd accomplished and the new skills I'd acquired. The legend that now followed me made me laugh, but it also turned my head, and I didn't mind being thought a hero, even though I wasn't. I had a new life. I was a new man.

But I also liked a long hot bath. I liked to shave every day.

I missed New York. I missed the things that Lucy and I used to do in New York, the fancy places we used to go.

I admit that I could also remember a saloon I frequented down on Pearl Street when money was tight, and images of the Randall's Island poorhouse were still fresh in my mind – and I could not ever quite forget an early childhood spent just barely surviving in the dark swamp south of City Hall that we called the Five Points – but my most prominent memories of New York, I realize now, were little more than dreams and fantasies, a tableau of what life might have become were Lucy and I the fashionable couple of leisure that we each had longed to be, back then. Back in my young adulthood, in the burgeoning 'sixties, when the Age really did seem Gilded.

When New York beckoned, I almost believed that I was returning not to a place, but to a moment in the past. I saw the brilliance of Lucy's wicked smile, and I felt her white-gloved hand in mine.

After a few letters and wires, my approval over a sketchy, plot-light script and a hefty initial payment to my bank in the little town where I was staying in Missouri, I got in touch with a woman named Emelina, a barmaid and prize-winning sharpshooter I'd met back in Blue Rock, Wyoming, and she agreed to come to New York and be in the show. I stocked my supporting cast with Sioux and Pawnee, cowboys and vaqueros who could ride and rope better than me, a staff of musicians to punctuate the excitement on stage, and a full contingent of horses, buffalo, Texas steers, and assorted donkeys and deer.

Emelina and I reunited in New Mexico, and we hopped on a lopsided coach, which keeled over twice, though there were no broken bones, and, indeed, no injuries worse than a couple of dusty bonnets and some cracked china plates. We took the coach as far as Promontory Point, Utah, where the Central Pacific and Union Pacific Railroads met, from which we set out East by train, staring out the window at hundreds of miles of track that stretched ahead and behind as though it went on forever.

"I always knew it was a good day, the day I met you," she said to me on the train. We sat face to face in a spacious compartment in a Pullman car. The train shook and rattled as it thundered down the track at less than thirty miles an hour, and black smoke belched from the open window into our room. "I knew you were different, the minute I met you," she insisted.

I asked her how she thought she could have known something like that, and for a moment she hesitated, deep in thought, as though a real answer were coming, but then she laughed and tried to change her mind.

"That's not true," she insisted. "I thought there was nothing special about you, but I liked you."

That I even set foot in Emelina's saloon must have meant to her that there was nothing even slightly remarkable about me, because no one special ever walked into her saloon. Failed prospectors, failed gambling men, gunmen, and the occasional sweaty cowboy looking to drink away the memory of his dusty life. On most nights, these were men Emelina had to warn off with her derringer – or that's what she insisted to me. When I stopped in her dive for a whiskey, I was no "hero." Little Mount was yet to come. I didn't know Magic back then, I couldn't roam through Time, couldn't see the future. I was no different from anyone else.

Emelina had blazing red hair, skin brown from the Western sun, and strong prominent cheekbones. Also strong arms and legs that felt good wrapped around a man. She radiated strength. I chose her for my show because I considered her the new Western g'hal, something the boys back East had never seen. I could invent a heroic myth for her, a whole new life – as a girl growing up in Kansas, I'd say, little Emelina saved her small town from bandits, fed her family by hunting for wild game and protected her widowed mother from wolves – and audiences would be able to look in her willful blue eyes and believe all the lies. Another reason I wired her with an offer of employment was that our few weeks together in her little room in the back of a Blue Rock boarding house had been much too brief, and I was lonely, and I missed her. I didn't think I loved her, but I wanted her by my side. Such a motive will be verboten for an employer of the 1980s, but back in the 1870s, lucky for me, it was almost charming.

As the train slogged and clanked along the track, the walls shook, and so did the floor beneath our feet, as though the entire contraption might any minute collapse and spill us all like a burst dam out into the merciless desert. I once rode a train that derailed. You can add train derailment to my list of fears.

Emelina had not always been such a strong woman. She'd gone West at the age of seventeen to marry a man whose letters seemed tender and warm, traveling with some other desperate young girls who'd sold themselves through the mail. At first she liked living in her new and snug sod house, its green grass-covered roof all that kept it from fading into the Kansas horizon. She said she preferred a hard life on the prairies to the hopeless life of poverty she'd known back East. She didn't mind taking orders from her husband to make such a challenging life work, and she could even abide the solitude. She bore her husband a couple of children. But then she left. Left her kids behind, too. I'd never understood that. Her husband swore to find her and bring her home, or kill her trying. She made it a long way, all the way to Blue Rock. As the train rattled and clattered down the track, I thought back on Emelina's story. There was something missing, some hole in there someplace. But I didn't know what it was. And I wasn't ready to ask her.

"Look at me," Emelina said. "Traveling in a Pullman car, on the Transcontinental Railroad." She took my hand and smiled at me, such a wide and hopeful smile, and I wished I loved her.

Three hours and a hundred miles outside of Promontory Point, the boiler blew.

* * *

After a few out-of-town shows and some complimentary local notices, our handlers booked us for an open-ended run into New York city's Great Roman Hippodrome, a gaudy and turriculated castle of a structure that filled up a few big blocks around Madison and 26th Street. Perfect for our show, the Hippodrome consisted of a wide open and prairie-like arena flanked by an elevated stage and encircled by rising tiers that could accommodate an audience of ten thousand. The building was new since my last visit to New York, and it would later go through a few quick name changes before its demolition and quick historical obscurity. But even if you don't remember its name, I'll never forget it.

I admit that I'm proud, even to this day, of the Western show I conceived, though it's recorded in no history books of the old West, has inspired no Broadway shows, no films, no TV programs. That's not because the spectacle wasn't exciting. The audience thrilled to scenes of Watt O'Hugh III battling an entire band of outlaws, single-handedly shooting them all dead, saving a stagecoach from ferocious bandits, riding on horseback across a lonely prairie town street and sweeping a little orphan girl (actually, a midget in drag) into my arms moments before a stampede thundered around the bend, and rescuing hysterical passengers from an exploding locomotive. In my show, buffalo pounded across the open plains; cowboys rode wild broncos and lassoed bulls; and natives roamed the land as though the white man had never set anchor off the coast.

Emelina was central to the show, of course, and she invariably made a striking impression right from her first appearance, riding out into the arena standing on a stallion, and though chastely garbed in an ankle length calfskin dress and topped by a cowboy hat, she was no less voluptuous and sexually captivating. The wind rippling through her long hair, she'd draw a sixteen-gauge, double barrel, breech-loading hammer-mode shotgun and blast a series of airborne glass balls as they plummeted to earth, shoot an apple off my head, and then, at the end of her act, and after a few more examples of impossible dexterity, she'd chase her stallion around the arena, leap onto its back, and gallop away waving her hat in the air, leaving the crowd coughing in a thick smelly cloud of gunpowder smoke.

The audiences during our brief run seemed ecstatic, and grew each day, but we courted controversy, mostly by accident. For example, one of the newspapers questioned my judgment in hiring Colored cowboys. And we also received quite a few letters puzzled by our treatment of the Indians, whom we portrayed in battle against each other or helping me save settlers from stage-coach bandits, but whom we did not depict going down in defeat by the white man's hand.

It would be easy enough to claim for myself an "enlightened" view of America's journey West, and of the chasm between the races, in the 19th century. I have the documentation; just take a look at the New York *World* from July 14, 1874, which called me an "apologist for Godless savages!" Therefore, if I so wished, I could today insist that back in the 19th century, I was far ahead of my time.

But, regarding Manifest Destiny, in the interests of full truth, I'll admit that I didn't really have anything against conquest. No one did back then – none of the conquerors, that is. At Randall's Island, the teachers made me read the Bible, after all. Though I was a man who liked and respected the Indians I'd met (as I've just explained, in spite of a particularly repellent "heroic" myth that dogged me all over the country, I've never been an Indian-killer) – and though, as you'll learn, I was a man who could not stand by and watch a mob hang an innocent child, whatever the child's race – I was also, in 1874, a man of my time in certain respects, and I'm not proud of it, but it's the truth, and there you have it.

In conclusion, to explain the "radical" message behind my production: First, some Colored cowboys knew how to rope and shoot, and I wanted them on my stage. It seemed natural to me. On a cattle run, no one had the luxury of even noticing the color of a man's skin. The public wanted the West, and that was the West. Second, I thought that white men with bullets defeating Indians with arrows wasn't particularly exciting or stirring. So I left that out of my Wild West Show.

On July 17, just a half hour into the show, and as I stood in the center of the arena preparing to battle a crooked prairie town packed with outlaws, I heard the sound of gunfire, felt bullets whoosh by my head like meteors shooting from the sky. I jumped off my horse, ran through the dust to the foot of the stage and scanned the theater's enormous and unfinished arch ceiling. A thin scaffold ran around the uppermost periphery of the theater, vanishing behind the tall curtain that ascended from the foot of the stage to the building's pinnacle, and a vast network of temporary wooden beams crisscrossed under the dome to serve as unsteady bridges for the army of artisans that might eventually complete the rococo ceiling. Somewhere up there, a killer waited in the shadows.

It may be self-glorifying bombast created by the distance of a half century, but I truly believe that I wasn't afraid for myself. As I've said, I'd been engulfed in bullets before, many times during the War, and also in Little Mount. Anyway, I'm only one man. But this time, I had my audience to think about, thousands of soft and laughing ruddy-pink faces attached to bodies that should have been ducking down and cowering under their chairs, and who, in spite of my most desperate entreaties, would not give up the delusion that all this was part of the show. Indeed, the more insistently I screamed at them to run for their lives, the louder grew their excitement, laughter and applause. Fat and content, their very arteries and veins lined with silver, gold and heavy cream sauce, my audience had forgotten the Revolution and what it meant to be either afraid or brave. Many of them needed to be struck down by a passing bullet just to remember what it felt like to be alive; but I would save them anyway.

I climbed onto the stage, and I leapt to a thin column that ran up the side of the building. I scaled the wall, and men and women slapped me on the back from the first tier, then the second and the third, and finally from the box balconies, their laughter ringing loudly in my ears. At the zenith of the column, the muscles in my arms aching from my climb, I pulled myself above the cornice, crouched and then leapt again and, almost drunk with my fearlessness, grabbed hold of a beam and scurried across it like a rat, the wood bouncing and creaking under my weight. The applause was now a distant hum. Again, descending bullets ruffled my hair and lodged in a balustrade a few yards below me, jarring an upper balcony and tickling its delighted occupants.

I looked in the direction of the bullets. The gunfire halted. He was reloading. Wobbling in the dark on shaky knees, I could see nothing. Then another shot cracked through the air, rising up from below like a rocket. That was Emelina, saving my life. I heard a sharp thud, and then I saw my assassin, a lone figure balanced precariously at the very edge of the domed ceiling just a few yards from me, camouflaged by a big ruffle of curtain. He wore a sack suit, a long coat with loosely fitting pantaloons and a red waistcoat, all dark, muddy colors that blended in with the shadows at the top of the theater. Blood drained from the killer's hairy face, his skin turned pale white, and sight left his eyes, his pupils growing large and dark like two black pools hovering in the air before me. He tried to raise his gun, as though killing me could somehow restore his life, but his muscles seemed to strain under its weight. The piece fell from his weakened fingers, spinning in the air on its long fall to the center of the arena. At last the killer also fell, backward, flipping up and over the curtain and dropping face-down into a tangled mess of ropes and pulleys which cushioned his fall and tied him up in a secure package, like a bug in a spider's web. As he twisted about lifelessly in mid-air, I stared at him, at the back of his greasy head, and I wished that I could see his face, to look into his lifeless eyes. I wondered why he'd wanted to kill me.

The audience roared its approval, ladies and gentlemen peering through their opera glasses, exhilarated by this realistic death. I stood, leaned against the wall, scanning the horizon. In spite of the cheers of the crowd, something was wrong, too calm. I questioned whether this were a lone gunman, or if someone else up here planned to carry on. I touched my gun, my fingers trembling.

Like a slow motion sequence in one of your motion pictures, something from the 1960s or 70s, some thirty or forty years after my death, something violent and directed by Sam Peckinpah or Sergio Leone – *especially* Sergio Leone, an Italian who really understood us! – I saw a puff of smoke and then heard a shot ring out. A bullet headed at me so slowly I thought I could dodge it. The bullet hovered before my eyes. Time seemed to have stopped entirely, my feet anchored to the spot as the bullet rose into the air and spun harmlessly up over my left shoulder and into the ceiling, cracking through wood and stone that fluttered in shards down onto my head. Another shot buffeted me on my left, and then one knocked me to the right, and I fell sideways, twisted about and reached for support, but my fingers swam uselessly in the empty air. I waited to fall, wondered what it would be like, how long it would take, how the wind would feel against my skin, and what I might see – might I see anything? – after my body crashed to the Hippodrome floor and lay crumpled and broken before the cheering and enchanted crowd. Somewhere in some dark part of my mind I saw my body flipping over and over like a rag doll helpless in a gale, cleansed in the dying sunlight that filtered in from the tiny western window.

This is the tough part. I've reviewed my journal, and searched my mind and my soul. Today, more than fifty years later, I don't know that I can explain to you what happened next, not really, and I don't know that I ever could have.

My journal reads, simply: "Didn't fall. Little fingers. Life saved."

I stared death in the face, waited for it. Though the laws of physics – Newton's theory of gravitation, to be precise – might mandate that I then die, I did not die.

I fell perpendicular to the Hippodrome wall, only so far before my downward momentum slowed and then stopped, and from out of the darkness, as I hovered above the crowd, an invisible hand reached out to me, a little hand with tiny little fingers.

My face alight with the warmth of a smile, I recognized the touch like an old friend, there in the small of my back, holding me aloft. Breathing more easily now, my heartbeat relaxing, I stared straight up into the vast domed ceiling, painted reddish-orange by the sunset. I gently rose to my feet, my balance restored by the little hand, one that was so weak in life, but so strong and powerful in death.

Thank you, I whispered.

I longed for a reply. But nothing. Silence. And then the touch left me.

I bounded behind the curtain into the fly loft, where the scenery hung for our drama, backdrops of rustic pioneer scenes, rickety Western towns, sweeping vistas and dusty plains. My right hand lifted as though it belonged to a different man, my fingers wrapped tightly around my .45. I turned to the left, and a black-suited figure rose above the gridiron, a dark shadow against a brightly painted silver boulder in an Arizona desert backdrop. My peacemaker discharged, and a gun flew out of his hand. Then I lurched to the right, and again, I aimed without thinking at a darkly dressed figure almost invisible against the elaborate, half-completed wood carvings that circled the edges of the theater, and I again shot blindly. Another gunman demobilized, his right arm jerking sharply behind him. I looked forward at another expanse of dangling scenery, and I shot at a man leveling a shotgun from the steps of a frontier post office, and I spun around, and I shot again – I didn't even know what I was shooting at – and then I shot just above me. Firearms flew out over the audience.

In less than a minute, six gunmen gunless. Events moved dreamlike around me and through me, as I hovered in the painted clouds, miles above solid ground; gaping; helpless.

Recovering from the shock of their defeat, the gunmen scrambled over beams and scampered under planks; one swung from a pipe batten and slid down a rope that dangled at the edge of the curtain, escaping across the arena and up through the aisle; another vanished into the dark shadows at the very top and furthest edge of the theater. To my left, I saw a flutter of movement, and as I turned, my gaze followed one figure who darted lithely along the length of the cornice. In an instant, I was on his tail and gaining ground, and a minute later had cornered him against a gigantic stone column that rose from the floor all the way to the ceiling. I shouted a couple of bombastic threats, my heart pounding up into my throat, and the gunman turned around, and he stretched out both hands behind him. His skin taut over a thin and bony face, which was white and young and almost pretty, like that of a girl, but his hair was streaked with gray. The killer's eyes were small and round, lips full and red as blood. The wind whistled through the eastern window, and the gunman's black robes fluttered around a long, wire-skinny frame.

"Who are you?" I said in a whisper that came out of my lungs as a scream, and then, with a tiny grunt, the figure dived with exceptional grace from the column, drifted in the air for a moment as his robes rose around him like wings, and then, plunging, seemed to evaporate on the long fall to the ground.

A beam above me creaked loudly. Then the cheers of the crowd drowned out every other sound.

The show must go on. It was time for Emelina's sharpshooter routine.

I hoped I hadn't upstaged her.

"How do you do that?" Emelina asked in her backstage dressing room, her eyes bright and cheeks rosy with excitement.

"I'm a good shot," I said, putting my .45 gently on her makeup table. "Thanks for saving my life up there, by the way." I pulled up a chair and sat, and Emelina leaned against the wall and slid down to the floor, tired and excited, tiny beads of gem-like sweat glowing prettily on her forehead.

"That was nothing," she said. "Listen, *I'm* a good shot. You do things that are impossible. In Little Mount, and today."

"Not impossible," I said.

She thought for a second.

"Are you a mathematician?" she asked. "I've heard of a mathematician named Leopold Kronecker who's calculated a way to shoot a dozen men dead with a single bullet."

I shook my head. I was no mathematician. If I were alive today, in your century, you would say of me, *He can't even balance a checkbook.*[*]

"Explain this talent to me," Emelina insisted. "I could use some of that in my act!"

Emelina had a right to understand what had happened in the Hippodrome rafters, but I couldn't explain it to her the way she wanted me to, because I didn't truly understand it myself. I knew that it couldn't be taught, that it wasn't science, or mathematics, or E=mc². It wasn't something I could replicate in the show to make money; it wasn't about money, it was about life and death. I tried to tell Emelina all this, at least to explain my feelings about these matters, but the words and clauses and sentences all came out crooked or not at all, and poor Emelina just sat and stared at me. I wasn't making sense, and I knew it, and I also knew that Emelina would keep asking me and asking me until I started to make sense.

I pulled my chair closer to her and stared into her eyes.

"Emelina," I said, and her face turned serious.

"What's the matter?"

"Look, there's something I should tell you, now."

I took her hands.

"Tell me," she said. "If there's something I should know."

I tried to tell her about the Draft Riots, and what I'd seen, and how those terrible days had changed me, but then I stopped.

I asked Emelina if she believed in ghosts.

No, she said. She didn't believe in ghosts.

I asked her if she believed in angels. Again, she said she did not. Didn't she believe in Heaven? I wondered aloud. She said that she used to believe in Heaven, that any teenage girl living in a sod house in Kansas has to believe in Heaven. But now, she told me, she didn't know. If angels and ghosts and God and Heaven and Hell existed, it had nothing to do with her. The people in that audience out there existed,

---

[*] As for Leopold Kronecker, I've checked him out, and I even met him once, as you will learn. To quote a late 20th century idiom, he's not the hot shit he thinks he is. His mid-19th century theorems pertaining to gunplay simply don't work and have since been mercifully forgotten. His theory of algebraic magnitudes – which, when Emelina was breathlessly citing his accomplishments, was yet to come – is, in my opinion, not triumph enough to justify an entire life of tedious dots and squiggles. I hope I don't sound bitter, but I don't like the man, his alleged achievements don't impress me, and the less said about the son-of-a-bitch the better.

and their dollars existed, and she always had to hope that her next meal existed. "And *you* exist, Darling," she said. "And I exist ... and so *we* exist." That's all she knew, she explained, and all that mattered to her.

"Then I don't even know where to begin," I said, staring down sadly at her.

"Begin at the beginning," she said. "Begin with the riots. You mutter about the riots almost daily, but you've never told me about them, and I've been afraid to ask."

I just shook my head. She asked me what I was worried about. Now I wished I'd kept my mouth shut, or told her I got lucky sometimes where guns were concerned. I had no choice but to explain everything. I said I feared that she'd think me crazy, and I sighed, and I know I sounded inconsolable.

But when I said that, about being crazy, all worry left Emelina's eyes, and she smiled easily. Leaning forward, she kissed me quickly and reassuringly on the mouth.

Then she nibbled my lower lip with her teeth.

I liked it when she did that. That thing with her teeth. Emelina was a good nibbler. She always knew just where to nibble, and exactly when. Not too hard, not too gentle. Back in the 19th century, to find a saloon girl who still *had* her teeth was epiphany enough – many cowboys and vaqueros were forced to tolerate, and some even came to enjoy, gummy women – but only that most rare saloon girl could use her teeth to work such miracles.

I found myself distracted. An image popped into my head. Emelina naked beneath me, in our Pullman car compartment, the train rumbling and clacking along the Transcontinental Railroad track. The engine blowing out with a tremendous, violent shudder.

I liked that a whole lot, the engine blowing out violently with Emelina naked beneath me.

In Emelina's dressing room, I remembered that moment, when the engine blew.

I forgot what I was going to say. I almost forgot where I was.

Emelina smiled into my eyes.

"I don't care if you're crazy," she whispered. "Darling. Be as crazy as you want."

She kissed me again. And all was lost. We tumbled together to the floor, fumbled our way out of our ridiculous cowboy outfits, and my dark, very dark story about ghosts and the Draft Riots was happily and thankfully forgotten in an ocean of kisses and passion.

Outside her dressing room, up in the Hippodrome rafters, a dead man's body twisted in the ropes. A drop of blood dripped from his chest, hovered in the air, and drifted away on the wind, breaking apart into nothing before hitting the ground.

CHAPTER 2

I was born in 1842, and that makes me, as I write these words, almost a hundred, and that's how old I look. It's not too pretty a sight in my opinion, and I'll leave the rest to your imagination. I can't give you any advice as to how to live to be this old. I chewed tobacco and smoked a pipe until 1890, when, along with the rest of America, I took up cigarettes. They were handy and convenient, they didn't dye my teeth brown, and I didn't have to worry about missing a spittoon with a lady present. Even now, I've got a cigarette in my left hand. It's almost done. When it's done, I'll start a new one. I've got another pack sitting right behind my notebook, next to a half-empty bottle of whiskey, another lifelong coffin nail that seems to have done me no harm. I can confirm that I never intended or expected to live this long.

It may occur to you that I've seen and done many miraculous things, and you may wonder why my life was filled with Magic, when yours is not. The cities have chased away much of the Magic, which used to roam free across the plains and hover in the trees, like an eagle. Though there is still a little bit of Magic on the continent, it is available only to one who can acknowledge rather than deny the most wonderful events in his own world. The kids around here all know my stories, and so do their parents, who haven't listened as carefully, having other things on their mind, like making money and getting food for their families, and frowning and growing older. They know my claims about heroic adventures, and the little details I claim concerning historic events. The kids believe every word, but their parents, having also heard my claims about roaming Time, tend to discount every word.

I didn't learn to roam Time until I escaped from Darryl Fawley's army in the Rocky Mountains late in 1874. I'll say this about roaming – it's hard to intellectualize, but once you get it, it's the easiest thing in the world. So even though as you read this journal I am dead, and I may have been dead for fifty years, or a hundred, don't be surprised if tomorrow you pass me in the street, and I'm young and relatively handsome, and then you see me twenty minutes later in a crowd on your television, and I'm a decade older with gray around the temple.

I understand you better than you know. There are other Roamers wandering among you. You can tell one of us by a certain distant gaze in his eyes, and a certain thinness in his outline when you stare too hard. He won't stop to say hello. When you shove by him on the sidewalk, you feel almost nothing at all, and when you turn around to look, a gentle wind strikes your face. And you turn away.

We can recognize each other at a glance.

We laugh together in your restaurants and your bars, and we watch the sunsets in your parks.

All but that most rare and skilled Roamer can have no effect on the future, or the past. If we try to change things we fail. We can have conversations with you, but only concerning matters of no importance. We leave no footprints. I can't explain it; it's just the way it works. I know the tragedies of the 20th century, and 21st. The 22nd century is still murky. I've been there, and it doesn't yet make much sense. But, still, I'm aware of a horrible thing that's destined to occur in 2150, celebrations of a new decade still fresh in the air. If I try to warn you about any of this in my narrative, the manuscript will be lost, in a fire or through carelessness or spitefully thrown away upon my death. So all I can do is hint, and grieve.

One Roamer I've known has the gift of molding the past, future and present to his whims, but he is a man with an utterly pure heart, something that, at least in the 1870s, I utterly lacked. I am not unaware, however, that my past and all our pasts are constantly changing beneath us, without our consent or knowledge.

I know that whoever first reads this journal may well laugh. Whoever you are, I ask you to keep these papers for five years, at which point they will begin to prove my claims. In a few decades, you can have no doubt. You will search for reasonable explanations, but you will not be able to find any, and in the end, after the evidence has piled up, you and your descendants will have to accept what I have written. The following brief and seemingly random remarks could mean nothing to an old man in 1936, but will mean everything to the community of man as your future unfolds.

1941 – Pearl Harbor. 1945 – Hiroshima and Nagasaki. 1963 – Oswald. 1968 – My Lai. 2001 – 9/11.

2030 – Rostag. 2064 – Utterbridge. 2150 – Migis.

I hope I've proved my point.

My boasts about my Wild West show may seem inflated or exaggerated. You've never heard of me, though you know, even now, Buffalo Bill Cody, and Annie Oakley, as though they were luminaries of your own age.

Though in my opinion I had the better show, more stirringly exciting and free as it was from the misconceptions of its age, my spectacle was short-lived. Our July 17 performance, which might have been the last night of my entire life, turned out instead to be merely the end of a very brief but, I still insist, *brilliant* theatrical career.

Stepping out of the theater, Emelina and I walked briskly across Fourth Avenue, both of us dressed for the evening, I tidy enough in a newly bought suit, and Emelina luminous in a long dark blue skirt with a puffed rear bustle, her brilliant red hair cascading over a short, stylishly cut and embroidered Zouave jacket. Heading to the cavernous dining room at the Café Brunswick, where Lucy used to treat me with her patron's money, I wondered how it would feel to pay for the evening myself. The idea was strangely invigorating.

But when we reached the other side of the Avenue, a horseman, who stood beside an empty carriage, called out my name.

"Mr. Morgan seeks your audience," he said, opening the door and urging us inside.

I don't know why Emelina and I didn't even question his command. Under the full moon, we stepped happily into the carriage, and the driver quickly shut the door. Maybe we were flattered. Deeming ourselves due hearty congratulations after our quick escape and another financially profitable performance, we thought the financier wanted to thank us personally for tripling his investment.

I knew nothing about him. He was not yet "J.P. Morgan," the invincible legend and myth. That would come some twenty years later. Still, he was a powerful fellow, with a close connection to President Grant, hundreds of tentacles wrapped around the major industries of the day – which, in addition to his minority ownership in my own Wild

West show, included his burgeoning interest in the railroads – and ostentatious displays of wealth that encompassed not only the imposing brownstone he'd recently acquired on the cushiest stretch of Madison Avenue, but also a rambling mansion in Highland Falls, where each summer he entertained the right sort of people and lit up the Hudson River with a private fireworks display.

While Emelina was, it would turn out, somewhat more steeped in House of Morgan lore, I knew only that he had a lot of money, and that, to Mr. Morgan, Emelina and I were not the type of animal ordinarily permitted to set foot in his beautiful home, except, perhaps, to empty the ash trays if our spectacle were to fail commercially. Yet, though I knew he would hold me in contempt, I admired him. Morgan had money; I, too, wanted money. So I admired him. I wanted to meet him, as though being in his presence might refashion me into a man such as he was and help me achieve greatness of a certain sort.

Well, in my long life, I met J. Pierpont Morgan more than once, and I've been led to understand that my existence even crossed his mind from time-to-time in the years in between. In fact, I may have played an occasional role of such importance in his life that, on his death-bed in 1913, he might have still recognized my name, had it been uttered in his presence. Yet as I write these words, I don't have a million dollars. I suppose I don't miss it.

Sometimes, now, I wonder what might have happened had Emelina and I run when the carriage driver approached us. I wonder how this story, and my life, might have turned out.

A lamplighter on Fourth Avenue poked open one side of a square gas lamp, turned on the jet and lit the flame. Behind him, the soft glow of gas lamps rose into the night and gently overwhelmed the stars. By the time we arrived at Morgan's mansion, at 219 Madison Avenue, the evening had darkened and the city bloomed like a tender yellow flower.

Morgan's mansion, like the houses surrounding it, was strong and solid and seemingly permanent. Elegantly dressed men in walking suits and women in bustles strolled arm-in-arm along the wide sidewalks. One couple pushed a baby buggy, giving their child a breath of fresh, early evening air, as four horses pulled an omnibus north up the Avenue. I thought it would last forever, and that New

York would always be a city of mansions. These people, this picture, seemed indestructible. But as you read this, even those wide sidewalks are gone.

We stepped down from the carriage and made our way up the front walk of a man who, in a few years, would make his mark indelibly on the race itself. Inside, as the butler guided us through the mansion's ornate front hallway, Emelina smiled and tried to speak as she imagined might Mr. Morgan's typical guest. She tried to walk as a lady would. But the closest to royalty that Emelina had come so far was a brief conversation with the wife of the richest man in the little Kansas prairie town where she'd given birth, and a few distant glimpses of the wife of the most powerful cattle trader in the Wyoming cow-town where she'd earned her keep the last five years, a woman who, for the sake of appearances, kept herself at great proximity from the profitable but seedy tavern over which Emelina presided most nights.

Unimpressed by Emelina's efforts, but strangely touched by them, I put my hand gently on her arm as we were ushered into J.P. Morgan's parlor, a large room of dark wood, which boasted two suits of armor, an exquisite crystal chandelier, finely hand-carved pieces of dark oak furniture, and a sweeping array of gold and silver-bound books lining the walls, interrupted by medieval tapestries. Over the fireplace was a striking painting of a young woman, very beautiful, but thin, sickly and fragile, whose eyes stared imploringly from the canvas.

Two men sat in plush chairs by the fireplace drinking port wine. When we entered the room, the taller one smiled confidently but remained still, while the shorter one hesitantly stood. He was almost completely bald, and his face was soft and unscarred, like an infant. His features were doughy and round. Though physically unimposing, he was magnificently dressed in a tailored suit. He had a hat in his lap, and as he stood, it fell to the ground. Bending over to pick up his hat, he knocked his head against the wooden side table with a sharp clunk.

"I am Mr. Filbank," he said, struggling to his feet. Gesturing to the taller man, he added, "This is Mr. Sneed." He sat, and he ran his fingers over the top of his head, wincing slightly.

Sneed, Filbank's opposite, had short blond hair, a ruddy face centered by a crooked, almost mangled nose. His fingers, clutching the edge of his armrest, were thick and calloused.

Sneed laughed, whether at me or at his ridiculous colleague, I couldn't tell.

"We," he said, "are government agents."

He said this as though it meant something. What kind of agent, he didn't say. What government – city, state, Federal, or even foreign – he also did not explain. I didn't bother asking. I didn't care. I didn't think he would have told me.

Then I recalled a possibly important detail of my recent life that I'd absent-mindedly left unresolved, and which, I thought, might be the reason I'd come under government scrutiny. There was, I explained in an awkward stammer, a dead man hanging from the ropes and pulleys at the very top of the Hippodrome ceiling. "I'd forgotten about him until now," I said with an involuntary and entirely inappropriate laugh. I tried to justify the man's mortality by describing how, with no excuse or warning, the anonymous assassin had opened fire in a crowded theater. I didn't want to take credit for killing the man, because Emelina really had performed a miraculous shot, but I didn't want to blame her, in case this were to lead to later repercussions. Staring into Sneed and Filbank's bored faces, I concluded that someone should probably be told about this little altercation and its unfortunate but entirely necessary finale. Who better, I reasoned aloud, than government agents? They could clean it up. Investigate. Issue a report. Exonerate me. Do whatever is done in a case like this.

Sneed waved these thoughts away with one hand. "Mr. Morgan has already taken care of that," he said. "It was part of the show. He was an actor. He is celebrating this very minute, drinking and whoring away his evening's pay at Harry Hill's dance hall. That's the story. No one knows different."

"Who was he?" I asked.

Filbank leaped to his feet, popping up suddenly like a gopher in one of those carnival games from the nineteen-fifties. That was none of my concern, he bleated at me, distressed and distracted, his voice squeaking like a rubber toy. Overexcited and trembling, he spilled some red wine on the sleeve of his beautiful dark blue jacket. I became convinced that Filbank's outrageous bumbling must be a terribly brilliant charade, part of a scheme so elaborate and ingenious that at first glance it appeared utterly idiotic, and that, between he and Sneed, Filbank had to be the true mastermind.

Sitting back down, Filbank stumbled slightly, and he loudly broke wind.

Still seated, Sneed said, "The assassin's identity doesn't matter. Forget about him. He is no one."

With a thud and a rumble, J. Pierpont Morgan himself suddenly burst into the room in a cloud of dense cigar smoke, a huge figure of a man with a thick strong neck, a bushy and meticulously choreographed walrus mustache and fat knuckles that, in my memory, dragged on the ground behind him. While a physically powerful man, he was also obviously dissipated, fat and sluggish, with a bulbous nose veiny-red and disfigured by eczema, acne rosacea, and gaping bloody pores a worm could have crawled through unnoticed. To me, he appeared at least fifty-nine years of age, and I would have been shocked to learn that at that time Pierpont Morgan had not yet passed the comparatively tender age of thirty-seven.

He seemed in a rush and appeared surprised to find us in his parlor. His face, afire, glowed with an unprovoked fierceness and anger.

"What is the meaning of this!" he demanded. He repeatedly tapped one gigantic foot against the hard wood floor, waiting for an answer.

Emelina and I, and Sneed and Filbank as well, were speechless.

Sputtering, Morgan briefly left, and we could barely make out a hushed conversation in the next room.

The great man returned.

"I am very late," he said brusquely, "but I thank you for coming."

He paused a moment, looking at Emelina, who was, here in the dim light of this millionaire's sitting room, a pleasingly stylish presence. Morgan's exploratory gaze began at her face and then rolled down to the floor. He seemed to approve of my taste, as a faint smile appeared in his eyes. His teeth stiffly clenched his Cuban cigar.

"Thank you ever so for your invitation, Mr. Morgan," Emelina said, in an exaggerated, affectedly elegant and completely unconvincing tone of voice. When it came to society fakers, I guess no one surpassed Lucy. I wasn't happy comparing Emelina unfavorably to Lucy, and I forced the thought from my head.

Whatever spell she might have begun to cast over Pierpont was immediately broken when he heard her speak. With a look of disappointment, he turned from Emelina to me.

"I have an important task for you, Mr. O'Hugh," he said. "It's not in the realm of the theater, of course, which I have discovered is not your main forte." He explained in a hurried and pained voice that he'd paid for a spectacle depicting heroic white men battling savages, that he had neither the time for progressive ideas nor any intention of putting New York audiences at mortal peril by bankrolling "a man who, I've learned too late, has long been a pariah on the East coast."

Emelina and I stood by the window, unable to speak. Hoof beats clattered by on the Fifth Avenue cobblestones.

"Needless to say, I thank you in advance for your services," he said. "Mr. Sneed and Mr. Filbank will explain everything." Without smiling, he carefully placed his hat onto his big head and draped a long black summer topcoat around himself.

His stare for a moment lit on the painting over the fireplace.

He looked back at me.

More gently, and with a distinct fragility, he said: "I do appreciate anything that you might be able to do to help me. You will be generously rewarded. It's a matter of great importance."

He didn't wait for a reply. As suddenly and as noisily as he had appeared, he was gone in the night. Crushing our lives had taken all of twenty-five seconds. Yet there was something in him that inspired both Emelina and me to pity.

The parlor door shut behind us. We were left alone with Sneed, Filbank, a room full of cigar smoke, and the distant clamor of household staff.

Filbank smiled uncomfortably.

"J. Pierpont Morgan," he said, realizing that no proper introductions had been made.

"Yeah," I muttered. I'd made the connection. "A big fat rich guy running around J.P. Morgan's mansion like he owns the place is probably J.P. Morgan. Thanks."

"We have to leave," Filbank added with another unspoken apology. "He doesn't want us to spend too much time here. Mr. Morgan doesn't allow show people in his house." With a glance at Emelina: "You understand."

Emelina shrugged, her face dark. She was angry and embarrassed and confused, and unable to hide it.

We retreated to a Faro bank on an elegant side street a few blocks away, one of the relatively rare first-class gambling halls in Manhattan. The house itself looked as any of the other palatial brownstone mansions on the street but for the blinds that were tightly closed and the silent carriages that patiently clustered nearby. Inside, the house seemed furnished for slightly perverted royalty, with thick velvet carpets on the floors and beautifully rendered yet completely lascivious nudes framed on the wall. Colored servants ran about with trays loaded with caviar and other delicacies, and elegantly dressed men drinking champagne stood over the roulette and faro tables, laughing and cursing and occasionally cheering with raised fists.

In a quiet, plush back room, we could hear the celebrations shaking the rest of the house.

"Why have you brought us here?" Emelina asked. "Gambling is illegal in New York."

"Important point," Sneed said. He leaned casually against the wall, a painting of a magnificent naked woman leering at him over his right shoulder. "What's important isn't the law, *per se,* but getting results. Do you understand what I mean?"

Emelina and I said nothing.

"And," Sneed continued, as a servant entered with a pheasant on a silver tray, "this den of sin has the third best food in the city, after Delmonico's and Café Brunswick, which I believe was your destination for the evening, so at least we owe you a good meal." His tone was patronizing, and I ignored the delicious aroma that was quickly filling the room. Emelina shook her head, and I said nothing.

Sneed shrugged. "It's your decision. It's not drugged, if that's your worry."

The two government agents quickly and happily filled their plates, leaving behind the ravaged skeleton of a bird. Sneed opened a bottle of Merlot with an enticing pop.

Filbank, mouth full of poultry, began to speak.

"Have you heard of Allen Jerome?" he asked. "Financier, who vanished at the end of the 'sixties?"

I indicated ignorance, and Emelina showed no response.

Sneed smiled.

"Mr. Jerome," he said, "was a rival financier. Brilliant, Harvard-educated mathematician, but childish and infantile, prone to petty tantrums. Until the age of thirty, when he terminated his role in the New York business world, a woman had never been observed on his arm, or rumored in his bed. In the mid-'sixties, he turned gold speculator. He got in just before the start of the bull market, and he saw his initial investment explode. His investors came from all over the map. They included President Grant's brother-in-law. Drexel, Morgan & Company had a chunk. On September 24, 1869, the Treasury Secretary announced sales of federal gold that would deflate the price and inevitably destroy the fortunes of bankers all over Wall Street. Just the day before, Jerome had somehow figured out that it would be wise for him to cash in."

"Mysterious," Emelina said.

"Not very," Sneed admitted. "But the next chapter *is* something of a mystery, because rather than take his rightful place as a hero of Wall Street and accept the acclaim that would have followed, Jerome simply absconded with the money. His share was sizable, and given his talents and connections, he could have easily earned far more in just a few years than the relative trifle he chose to steal from his investors.

"Subsequent rumors," he went on, "pinned Jerome down in Latin America, living in a mansion, with bodyguards, government protection and several beautiful courtesans. The whole enchilada."

I had never before heard that expression: *the whole enchilada.* Though nonsensical, the phrase would become quite popular in the middle of the 20th century, some decades after my death. To this day, I remain convinced that Mr. Sneed invented it.

"What does this have to do with Watt?" Emelina said; the juxtaposition of *What* and *Watt* made Sneed laugh.

"This has everything to do with Mr. O'Hugh," Filbank said. "It's said that Jerome has moved North from Latin America, and that he's living as a fugitive on the American frontier with a sizable army of outlaws. Why? I can't tell you. But an even more puzzling development is that he's alleged to be allied with one Darryl Fawley." After a pregnant pause: "Have you heard of Darryl Fawley, Mr. O'Hugh?"

I shook my head.

"He's married to a woman named Lucy Billings. Ring any bells?"

With some effort, I shrugged, but I said nothing, because I knew Emelina would hear the shock and anguish in my voice.

"Who's Lucy Billings?" Emelina asked me.

I shook my head, then, holding my voice steady, I quickly said, "No one." Then I added: "Not anymore."

Sneed laughed heartily, and Filbank tried to join him, but his laughter at my misfortune was joyless. The homely Mr. Filbank, it seemed, could empathize with my plight.

The more I thought about it, as the two men sat chortling, the more I realized that Lucy might well enjoy being in cahoots with Allen Jerome, a man who'd rather steal from a group of robber barons than allow them to give up their money voluntarily. Lucy Billings, my self-styled subversive, might have found great appeal in a man who'd choose to make himself a fugitive from the law rather than participate in a system that sought to keep some men permanently in Five Points' tenements and others lodged on estates in Highland Falls.

"We had a mole planted in a gang sympathetic to Jerome," Sneed continued. "The mole was recently discovered and killed, but not before wiring us of a planned prison-break in Wyoming."

Filbank leaned forward. "We intend to plant you in that prison," he explained excitedly. "The whole place will be leveled, the whole prison population freed, to join Jerome and Fawley."

"We've designed a cover story for you," Sneed went on. "*Hero of the Wild West implicated in passion crime.* It will hit the papers tomorrow. A warrant's being issued by the U.S. Attorney in Wyoming as we speak. By tomorrow, if you're still on the street, every rag-picker and his wife will be after you for the bounty."

He smiled, proud of his plan.

Their story finished, both Sneed and Filbank sat back simultaneously. Filbank crossed his legs nervously, and Sneed took a calm, leisurely puff on his cigar.

"J.P. Morgan arranged all this?" I asked.

Sneed nodded.

"Look. Allen Jerome stole from him. He wants his money back."

Sneed sounded uncertain for the first time, and something seemed unlikely in this explanation, but I wasn't sure what. Emelina figured it out.

"It's not about the money," she declared quietly. "You don't know the first thing about him, even though you work for him. He doesn't care about money."

Sneed laughed. "That's the very first time I've ever heard that particular theory." He laughed again. "I think our Pierpont cares *only* about money."

What else was there for him? the government man wondered aloud. Morgan was ugly, uncomfortable in his own ravaged skin, unhealthy. He treated his wife with a famously distant respectfulness.

The man couldn't even play *tennis* anymore on the courts he'd carefully built on his estate. What *could* he possibly care about, other than his money?

"Morgan personally shuts down a successful Hippodrome production, losing his ten percent interest, with the recession a year old," Emelina said. "Morgan calls in a favor with the government to frame an innocent man. All on a probably impossible quest to get back a small percentage of a cache of gold he and many other investors lost in the 'sixties? That's irrational. A man who behaves like that as a matter of habit with his finances cannot amass a fortune, and he certainly can't hold it in a bad economy. I learned better than that from running a whiskey house."

"He wants to show," Filbank offered lamely, "that no one can steal from him. As a deterrent to others. He also wants his revenge."

I interrupted: "But I thought you said he wanted – "

"And, as gravy," Filbank went on, "he wants his money back."

Emelina shook her head, and her blue eyes glowed with passion. When she spoke again, her voice was tender and sympathetic.

"This isn't about the gold," she said. "This is about love."

Sneed was looking through Emelina, at the wall behind her, a puzzled smile on his lips. Filbank rapped his fingers impatiently on the platter that, minutes earlier, had held a large, gloriously delicate pheasant. Emelina knew something that they did not; it was a matter of the heart, and so they didn't care, and they didn't ask.

"What do you have to say to our proposition?" Filbank asked kindly.

"Bearing in mind," Sneed added with a sneer, "that you have no choice."

Good cop, bad cop. Back then the strategy was novel.

"Why do you want me?" I asked. "I'm not anonymous. I'll have a hard time convincing them that I'm anything *other* than a mole planted by the government. Why have you chosen me?"

Sneed took a sip of his Merlot, held it in his mouth for a moment while swirling his glass about, the lamplight casting an eerie glow through the red liquid. From his smug and self-congratulatory expression, I figured that Sneed was attempting some sort of dramatic effect, something he might have seen at the theater.

Filbank, impatient, leaned forward.

"We think," he said, "that you are the best man for the job. We've studied your exploits." He settled back into his chair, left his statement ringing ambiguously in the stuffy room.

My "exploits," as Filbank put it, were up to that evening no more than legend. Not a single persuasive witness had come forward to verify any of it. Mostly old prospectors and drunken failures who raved about me to equally drunken newspapermen, whose accounts in the end bore very little resemblance to the truth. I did not believe that my government was stupid enough to assign me a task of any importance based on pure myth.

As I stared Filbank in the eye and witnessed the small, confirming smile on Sneed's face, two theories occurred to me, and I remain convinced, all these years later, that one of them must be the truth. It's possible that the five assassins who fired on me that night were sent not by my enemies of ten years earlier, but rather by Drexel, Morgan's henchmen – or, that is to say, by the U.S. government – scientifically testing the newspaper accounts of my alleged invincibility. My second theory is that the government knew the New York gangs planned to disrupt my show but did nothing to stop it. Either way, once the performance was over, they had powerful evidence that, were all choice and hope taken from me, I would be the man to bring Morgan's thieves to justice. Or to achieve whatever hidden goal the great man had in mind.

I heard Emelina, calling my name. I turned to her, but her lips were almost still, quivering just slightly, like a skilled ventriloquist throwing her voice.

I'll get a room at the White Squall Inn, I heard her say, through a vibration that seemed to come from deep within me. *If you can get away, meet me there, and we'll escape together.*

Emelina's eyes said that she was talking to me – talking without speaking – and that I should just listen.

If they get you, I'll be waiting for you in Wyoming, after the prison break.

Emelina gave me a little nod, and a very small, very sad half-smile.

I hadn't realized, before that moment, that I was going to make a break for it. I'd pretty much assumed that I'd go quietly. But I couldn't deny Emelina's deep, romantic faith in me.

Pounding inside my head, Emelina's voice felt more urgent, more desperate, and more tender than I'd ever heard it: *I won't lose you again, Darling – run for the hills. Keep yourself alive for me...*

CHAPTER 3

I pulled Filbank to his feet, punched him once hard on his nose, which exploded against his face like a balloon. He flew backwards, up and over his plush chair, and then he crashed against the opposite wall, rattling the management's fine collection of valuable first editions. Filbank lay crumpled in the corner, motionless, looking less like a man than a stylish suit casually discarded in a wrinkled pile during a moment of passion.

Sneed stood and tossed off his jacket. He loosened his tie, and his eyes shrank to tiny slits, his lips thin and bloodless.

I took a quick jab at Sneed, who repelled my attack with a strong left arm. Seeing an opening, I cut from my left with all my force and struck him square on the jaw, but his skull barely trembled. I retreated, the joints in my fist throbbing. I spun about, and kicked him hard on the right side of the head, but my boot just bounced uselessly away, and I briefly lost my footing.

Sneed smiled.

I could feel Emelina's impatience, urging me to escape, and so I fought to restrain my passion and my pride. I bolted from the room, careening through a houseful of startled servants and drunken gamblers. A hat rack easily shattered the window pane in the front parlor, and I slithered through the opening, landing on my side on the soft grassy front yard. I suffered a deep gash on the left side of my face, and on my right arm, but I didn't feel it until much later. I hopped to my feet.

On the street, a driver stood waiting in front of his coach, and two beautiful black steeds stood sleeping in the gaslight. He was a small man, with an unsuccessful, wiry little mustache. I smiled at him, shaking glass shards from my jacket.

"I'm stealing a horse," I said.

Which is what I did, and soon I was galloping across the cobblestones on Fifth Avenue. I had to make my way south and then east, to Houston Street, just off Mulberry, but I suspected that my trip would not be without complications, and I waited expectantly for the men that I believed would soon come in pursuit. I planned to speed south down Broadway, almost to the foot of the island, and then veer left when I saw the White Squall's red and blue lanterns beckoning from a side street.

My hat blew off in the wind and fluttered behind me up Fifth Avenue. I thought of Emelina, sitting on the edge of a bed in one of those seedy rooms, in that just-better than crummy part of town. The Inn was, I suppose, better than the cut-rate, basement brothels behind City Hall, but a universe below the respectable, shuttered mansions on Fifth Avenue that lingered on, even then, anonymously. I laughed bitterly. The Squall. I pretended to wonder how she knew the place.

Two mounted policemen turned onto Fifth Avenue from the south, and so I cut right, across a side street made up of dark, imposing mansions shrouded in towering oaks. I held on desperately; my horse now seemed to enjoy himself. He was free again, a wild colt running through the mountain grass on strong young legs, while I was one step away from a prison sentence. We turned just shy of Ninth Avenue, galloped under the shadow of the El as the train clattered deafeningly up the track. Out-of-breath, I glanced quickly behind me to see half a dozen pursuers, uniformed policemen and determined looking fellows in plain-clothes – probably Morgan henchmen – joined now ominously and from out of nowhere by a pack of panting dogs, all forging straight ahead through the ocean of pedestrians and carriages that meandered slowly about the train station.

I kicked ruthlessly, my horse screamed and, lifting itself on its hind legs, seemed to explode into the night like a rocket.

Did I think there was any chance I might escape? I don't know; probably not. I couldn't tell you where I thought I would go, either, if I were to escape. Emelina and I might wander the West again, always looking for the posse over our shoulders. Not a happy life, though I ran for it as though it meant riches and bliss. Emelina was waiting for me, in a little room, in a dark corner of Manhattan, and I knew she'd have a smile for me. This is what I saw as I cut back across another side street to Broadway, which, this far north, was dusty and undistinguished, the wide avenue empty and dark and more than a bustling metropolis resembled a small and dying mining town that I once knew. I galloped past the marble works on my right and, on my left, a small shuttered building with a sign out front that said "New Washington Market."

As I headed south, the avenue grew busier and more confusing, but I galloped on, urging my horse faster and faster. Emelina in that little room was the only thought in my head, and the only sight in my eyes. I almost didn't notice the well-dressed street-walkers heading towards the Fifth Avenue Hotel, who dodged and shrieked as I passed. I hit Union Square, and all of Broadway in its famous glory spread out before me like a rainbow, the grand buildings of marble, granite, red and brown brick, cast iron and green limestone; the beauty and wealth on display in the blazing windows of the great stores, jewels, toys, paintings, gold, the brightly lit omnibuses and carriages, the glare of the lamp-lit hotels, the massive throngs, who dived for cover in the brilliant artificial light of night when the police whistles grew nearer, the happily drunken crowds stumbling out of Wallack's Theater, or the imperial, turreted show-place run by Mr. Booth just a block to the east. None of this glory was any more than a great wall, blocking my path to freedom. This was not my home. I was blind to its charms. It hated me, this starless city.

What I wanted was Emelina; to be alone with Emelina on a moonlit night, a thousand or two thousand miles west of here, the dust in our throats and on our clothes, whiskey in our bellies, anonymous and cold and happy. I had once lost a woman, swallowed up by the world, and I did not want Emelina to see another sunrise, or ten, or twenty, or decades of sunrises, without me.

It was for this that we ran, my horse and I, and ran some more.

From Bowery, I cut through to Chatham Street, the clamor more distant now, the barking dogs and screaming coppers a faraway din. As I passed the dark and locked German and Jewish junk shops that lined the street, I optimistically plotted my escape. I could hide in my old neighborhood, ditch my horse, take refuge in the shadows, and in a couple hours creep uptown, where Emelina would be waiting.

I descended like Dante behind City Hall, into the Five Points, the saddest neighborhood in New York, where I'd grown like a fungus on the underside of a log.

I glanced behind me, and from this vantage point, as the stench of my old home sank into my lungs, I could see the marble castles of the financial district, like a cruel fantasy hovering in the airy clouds above the misery of the beggar's city. Sidewalks crumbled away, and my horse stumbled in the marshy mud that oozed up through the broken pavement. Garbage lined the narrow and crooked streets, rising from the gutters almost alive. I turned onto Baxter Street, passed by brothels and basement rum shops, decaying one-story shanties and tall, overcrowded brick tenements, babies screaming from the depths. As though I were racing through a medieval labyrinth, each turn blocked the view of only a moment before.

My horse stopped, and I almost flipped forward into the street. Up above, at the top of a small hill on the horizon, just barely visible through the soot and the fog, three men sat on horseback, in silhouette against the gray sky. I couldn't see their faces, but I knew who they were. They moved slowly toward me, hoof beats a muffled clump on the swampy street. I pulled left on the rein, turning quickly, but I was greeted by the same sight on the opposite horizon, three more men, three more horses, dogs marching silently beside them on the street.

I stopped, sweating in the rancid night, my horse breathing heavily between my legs.

I wished I had a gun, so thoroughly a part of me was the ethos of the West. I thought I'd have a chance of shooting my way out of this, or at least perishing dramatically, the subject of legends and tall tales and a terribly hummable folk ditty that school children might still sing a hundred years later.

The cops drew silently closer, smug in the calm and quietly fearless way they approached. I could see curious eyes glowing in the darkness of the highest tenement windows.

Dumb, gut instinct took over; I kicked, the horse trotted off into a side alley that ended in a brick wall. I stood up, gave the horse a mental farewell, and I hopped onto the top of a one story shanty, then onto a two story shanty, then scurried up the side of a tenement building, climbing from window ledge to window ledge. As I reached the roof I was covered with urban grime, a familiar but long absent sensation. I began to run, leaping from rooftop to rooftop, now above Cherry Street, now flying over Gotham Court, a dark figure in the night sky. I could hear laughter and amazed cursing from upper tenement windows. More troubling, though, was the cursing and shouting that followed me. I glanced back over my left shoulder, and I could see a growing crowd, and still more rising up from all sides.

Cops and detectives and probably some thrill-seekers climbed onto the roofs to my left and to my right.

From a three-story building I scaled a five-story structure that abutted Pitt Street. I'd meant to turn and jump across a side alley to a smaller three story tenement, but two fierce men climbed up onto the building from that direction, their guns drawn. So instead, I took a running leap and pushed off the edge of the building, out over the narrow intersection, aiming for a building one story down. A crowd of kids on Pitt Street, far below me, stared into the sky with awe on their smudged little faces.

I hit the edge of the roof, which crumbled under the impact. My ankle snapped as I slid down the wall; I grabbed hold of the eaves with my left hand. Gravel and stone cascaded down on me, and pain shot up my leg. Below me, Morgan's dogs leapt into the air, barking and snarling. I grasped a window molding and swung up onto the roof, my left ankle making another terrible painful crunch beneath me. I hobbled to the other edge of the building, peered out over another alleyway. It was too far, and I knew that I could not make it. My ankle throbbed, and I clenched my teeth in pain. I turned around, my heels at the edge of the roof, and I put up my hands.

I had surrendered. I'd mashed my ankle, I couldn't walk, and I certainly could no longer leap from building to building. I was unarmed, and outmanned. I had no razor-sharp canine teeth. I had lost. I was ready to go quietly and to do whatever Pierpont Morgan required of me – to steal back his money, settle old grudges or even get deeply involved in dark forces I couldn't control or understand. I thought I had a right to be treated with the dignity owed a noble warrior.

One cop moved a few steps forward, and he wore on his face the condescending smirk of authority I recognized from my days as an unwashed waif. When he spoke to me, it was from a distance of several yards, and with the sort of contempt the police had often hurled at the little nameless boy I had once been, loud angry words filled with hatred and scorn and profanity.

He pulled out a gun.

"Wait a second," I said. "You're not supposed to kill me. This is not a 'dead or alive' thing." To the silence of the posse, I screamed, "Ask Morgan! Ask John Pierpont Morgan! He wants me alive!"

The cop laughed, his straggly, overgrown mustache quivering, and his pale-eyed partner standing a few paces behind him also laughed, and then the faceless crowd behind them on the neighboring rooftops, and then even the snarling dogs at their side seemed to break into laughter.

"If you kill me, boys," I shouted, "then there's no reward! Did no one tell you?"

The gun dangled from the cop's fingers; sweat dripped down his forehead and into his eyes, glowing on his skin like oily diamonds.

He raised the gun. And then he fired. I felt a sharp pain in my side, and then, with another shot, a sharper pain near my heart.

The night grew darker; my legs buckled beneath me.

I fell.

CHAPTER 4

I could not be upset with Emelina for the yawning gaps in her life story that, up until now, she had kept from me. Never did I feel even a trace of disappointment. Things were just different in the 19th century. It wasn't the world that you know. Most of us didn't have the luxury of being respectable, not if we wanted to survive. As a very young woman, maybe even a girl, Emelina'd had a "past," of a certain sort. That was that.

I was familiar with the White Squall Inn, but not as a customer, or as a worker. As a young boy, only ten, or maybe only six, or maybe younger, I became acquainted with the owner of the place, a slim woman in her mid-forties who, so help me, seemed gentle and kind. She regularly gave me a bit of food or a coin or two, if I'd go around the back way early in the morning, well before the place grew busy. So I turned up there frequently. Not every day, because I didn't want to become a nuisance, but as often as I thought I could, and not just for the food, but also for the kind words the owner could provide me. Her name was Mrs. Welch. I don't know her first name, and I don't know whether she were really married. I imagined sometimes that she were my own mother. I didn't really believe back then that I'd ever had a mother or a father. I still don't believe it, not in my heart. My earliest memories are of the street, scrounging around the east side markets just uptown from the sewer where I made my home, avoiding the cops as I darted in and out of a crowd, my practiced little hands snatching an apple or two from a table. It's as though God himself somehow willed me into being one day as a little boy without a past, living by his wits on Worth Street in the dirtiest possible life. (If there were a God.) At night, crammed into one of the dark tunnels in the back of the Old Brewery, a huge and hugely dilapidated tenement building filled with squatters and assorted thieves, or maybe, on warmer nights, lying on a stoop with the midnight moon glowing over me, sometimes shivering a little, I often imagined a different universe as I drifted off to sleep, a fantasy world in which I lived in a brightly decorated child's room in the White Squall Inn, and that Mrs. Welch tucked me in each night, smiling at me maternally, maybe singing to me. In retrospect, I can now imagine that a slightly seedy gentleman who'd visit a cut-rate brothel also liked being greeted by Mrs. Welch, beaming as she swept down the stairway on the thread-bare red carpet that lined the front parlor, making him feel as unashamed of his carnal desperation as she had once made me unashamed of being a filthy little beggar.

My early childhood was pretty low, I guess, since my fondest dream was to live in a broken-down whorehouse with a madam for a mother.

That chapter in my life came to a close one evening when, still a boy, I was caught lifting a handbag, and after a night at the police precinct, a horse drawn prison van carted me, a group of vagrants, hardened thieves and even a murderer to the city prison, commonly known as the "Tombs." The Tombs were a massive granite hall that occupied an entire square, framed by Centre, Elm, Leonard and Franklin streets, standing just over the Old Collect Pond that at one time supplied New York with its drinking water, and occupying the Eastern edge of the Five Points. The van entered through a dark portal, and immediately a damp chill hit all of us. We passed under the stone bridge that connected the two main prisons, and I shuddered. The "Bridge of Sighs," we called it, by which convicts passed from their cells to the scaffold.

I was familiar with the prison as a native of the Five Points. On execution days, the buildings adjoining the Tombs, from which a view of the courtyard could be had, would be dark with spectators, and I'd personally witnessed a hanging on more than one occasion from the roof of the Old Brewery. That was as close as I'd ever hoped to get to the Tombs, but these crowded, dank cells, occupied mostly by the worst city murderers, also doubled as a homeless shelter for vagrant children and as holding pens for petty little thieves.

So there I was. In the prison pen, I could barely move. I tried to sleep standing. I tried not to breathe.

I didn't think that my situation had improved when, two days later, I was hauled before the Commissioners of Charity and questioned harshly by a very tall and thin man with a long mustache and angry looking green teeth. I remained mostly silent; maybe I cried. I'd stolen food. I was hungry. But I denied everything. I took the oath and lied until my eyes near bled.

That afternoon, a policeman accompanied me and about thirty other children to the edge of 27th Street, at the East River, where he escorted us onto a steamer to Randall's Island. The other children, both boys and girls, were either thieves like me, or no worse than mere peddlers. Some were the offspring of rag pickers – families who scrounged through garbage for items to sell to junk shops – who could no longer afford to raise a family and had sadly sent their children away.

As you might imagine, my memories of all of this are vague. I recall that the policeman on the boat was kindly, and that he comforted me and the other children. Standing at the front of the boat in his long black frock coat, the water rising up around him, he told us that we were going to homes for orphans and that we would be taught a trade and cared for. I think that we didn't trust him, not completely; to us, the police were not our protectors. They existed only to stand between New York's poor children and a decent meal. I do remember that when we arrived on Randall's Island, I was taken to a spare room, where a woman who reminded me of Mrs. Welch – something in her eyes, or in her watchful smile – sat me down in a little desk-chair. She had gray hair that she wore in a bun, but her face was unlined. Her first question startled me.

"Now then, little one," she said. "What is your name?"

No one had ever asked me that before, and without a pause, I said, "I have no name."

She shook her head, and she laughed a little bit.

"Don't be afraid," she said. "Just tell me. You *must* have a name."

I had always considered myself a boy without a name. In my opinion, this was not good or bad. It just *was.* Before that precise moment, it had never occurred to me that a name was something that I should possess. But if this nice lady believed it – and, while hardened by the street, I was exceptionally susceptible to a generous smile and a patient voice, especially in a woman who might be someone's mother – then it must be true.

I didn't know where a name was supposed to come from. But I was afraid that, if I denied it again, I might make this woman angry, and I saw her as an ally, or at least a kind person who wanted to help me, and so at that moment I chose as my title "Watt O'Hugh the Third." I didn't think much about my choice, but I believe even today that it was the best possible name, invented, as it was, merely to assert my utter anonymity.

To explain:

"Watt" came from *What?*

"Hugh" – as in *Who?*

And "the Third." Well, I'd heard it one time, attached to a most impressive gentleman, and I just thought it sounded good. I didn't know exactly what it meant, except that it told the world that there were others like me. Which there were. Many, many forgotten children just like me.

And that's how I got my name.

So it was as the third of the Watt O'Hughs that I set about my first transformation, in a neighborhood of tidy brick buildings, in a little cell that was locked and bolted each night. I was no longer free to roam through the darkness until sunrise. I was just one of a jungle of children on a green island, I was now so small and clean and well-fed, and the stench of my past life was more noticeable in its current absence than it had been when it had clung stubbornly to my skin and the rags that had once hung loosely from my skinny body. We were the formerly idle poor, suddenly industrious. Eight hours of labor each day – supposedly learning a trade, but I think mostly earning money for the Island – and four hours of school each night. I learned to read and write; not very well at first. I started scribbling in my journal. I grew excited by books, and I yearned to become an author. Events got in the way of that goal, but I did keep a journal, and have decided, late in life, to return to my childhood dream – hence, this narrative which you hold in your hands – although I know that I will never live to see my work earn acclaim or derision, or whatever its fate may be.

Throughout my childhood education, Manhattan sat just across the river, waiting for me, and for all of us. When I graduated, Randall's Island puked me out like a piece of chicken bone lodged in its windpipe – on the Island I learned about *simile,* too – and I returned home, a young man, eager and clean shaven, with some sort of senseless gilded optimism. I bought a suit – just one, for Sunday church, which I thought I should attend – and I also bought one nice hat. I got a job (not a very good one). I sacked out at a somewhat classier tenement, a little uptown of the Five Points, just a few blocks north of City Hall, where I lived by myself in a dark but legal apartment, with a tiny kitchen, and even a sitting room.

I was grown and, for that particular place and time, I was sanitary and hygienic. I was a new man. As you may now understand, I've never had a right to judge Emelina's past. We both had reasons to forget, and to lie. We were just lucky that the West was out there for us.

The taxi would take Emelina only so far as Bleecker Street, a tree-shrouded block lined with once-stately mansions that now served as boarding houses to show-folk, prostitutes, homosexuals, and, notably, hot-blooded upper-crust ladies who wished a discreet room in which to bed their gigolos. From there, my beautiful and fashionably dressed sharp-shooter trudged the remaining yards to the White Squall Inn, feeling neither fear nor trepidation, but only a weariness and a sad sort of fatalism that somehow her life had brought her back to this very corner of the world.

When she entered the front parlor of her former residence, whatever communication passed between Emelina and Mrs. Welch occurred without words. The madam was older, but still herself. She retained the gentle and inviting manner that could make sin and adultery seem as appropriate as a Sunday morning spent in church, and which had made her, over the years, a solidly anchored New York institution. Emelina brushed by Mrs. Welch in the narrow corridor, past three teenage girls in pantalettes, and, ignoring the dance music ringing at the end of the hallway, wearily trudged up the creaking stairs.

On the second floor, and three doors to the left, Emelina entered a room painted a gaudy red and blue. After pulling the curtains, she tossed her hat on the bed, then her jacket, and at last struggled out of her dress and underclothes. Naked, she slumped to the floor, leaning against the cold wall, and she shut her eyes. She kneaded the warm air with both hands, humming softly to herself. Gray winds streaked across the back of her eyelids, and visions rose before her, the faces and gnarled bodies of demons and spirits and the ghosts of wizards and murderers whose names she didn't know.

Emelina hurried further into the darkness until she came upon a lonely prairie under the stars, where a sad boy sat listlessly against a sod house, his father, inside, dead by his own hand. The boy's tears dripped into the dusty wind, his father's bad whiskey burning his throat.

Then Emelina flew away from the little boy, and she began a new search, looking for me, for Watt O'Hugh, for the third Watt O'Hugh, who, she knew, had learned to use twelve of his twenty-one essences. She watched again glimpses of my past, witnessed sweat-drenched crowds screaming through the streets, and paused to observe my scorching love for Lucy Billings, which burned Emelina's cornea like the glare of the sun. When she searched my future, my destiny, she found nothing at all. I was wet clay, and anything could be made of me. She hunted for my present, but Emelina saw only darkness, and she worried for me, and she despaired of hope, and a tear came to her eye.

Before she fell into a deep sleep on the worn whorehouse rug, an unheralded image appeared to Emelina: John Pierpont, a younger, clean-shaven man, vigorous and sharp and almost-handsome, cradling in his arms the emaciated body of a young woman, wracked and broken by constant coughing; tiny flecks of blood stained her lips. The young Morgan's face was innocent and open and lacked the pompous hostility that so tarred his older counterpart. The strong sun of Southern France shined through broad eastern windows. Pierpont wept, tears flowing like rain on the girl's yellowing skin.

This image broke apart and scattered into the air, and Emelina fell into a deep and exhausted sleep.

CHAPTER 5

I am quite sure that you do not expect to read a first-person memoir in which the narrator summarily and unheroically expires at the conclusion of Chapter 3, so I'll eliminate the suspense, such as it is, and admit up-front that I survived my adventure with J.P. Morgan's henchmen, although not without some pain and suffering. Up on the rooftops, a bullet quite distinctly pierced my left shoulder, then one grazed my forehead, then two shots cut through my left leg at once, spinning me about like one of those Olympic ice skaters. As I plunged, I waited for little fingers to break my fall, and waited some more, and did not give up hope until I felt my body crumple on wet, swampy cobblestones, and, wondering what had become of my ghosts, I guessed that my last sight as a mortal would be the tenement city's starless night sky. And so when I was next greeted not by Heaven or Hell or oblivion but instead a vague, feverish unconsciousness, a damp and enveloping chill that wrapped me like an old blanket and terrible smells of body odor, mildew, human waste, and something that smelled like death, I believed for more than a moment that it had all been a dream. And by "all," I mean nearly my entire life as I have so far described it to you: escaping my destitute childhood, meeting and falling in love with Lucy Billings, fighting the Civil War, starting a new life out West and performing before cheering crowds. Cloaked in this cold, and surrounded by these smells, I could assume only that I was back in the one place I would ever really call home and believe it: a squatters nest in the belly of some abandoned tenement in the Five Points. Maybe the 'Sixties as I recalled them had never happened. That wouldn't have been so bad, I figured, after all. No Draft Riots. No Lucy. No longing for Lucy, no mourning the riot's little victims. My heart unbroken.

I was certainly nothing more than a full-grown, two-bit hoodlum in the Five Points, which was all Destiny had ever intended for me, in spite of the delusions of escape and heroism that, apparently, came to me in the night. My head pounded. Maybe too much drink at one of the cheaper and less reputable Bowery beer gardens. My stomach churned – probably from a ten-cent bowl of soup at a restaurant on the docks.

Those explanations satisfied me for a while, but then, when I tried to open my eyes, sunlight along with frosty mountain air poured in through a tiny window far above me, and my skull screamed. I tried to stagger upright against cold stone walls, but my ruined legs refused to move.

I heard a voice, so soft and kind and smooth that it might have been the voice of God, if there were a God. This wasn't the voice of God, but just a man, a man with a voice so soft and kind and smooth, and commanding at the same time, that if there were a God, He'd have pilfered it long ago.

"You're a wreck, brother," he said gently. "Take this slowly. You've got all the time in the world."

"Help me up," I gasped. My throat was sore and parched, and my words came out of my mouth in a dull croak.

He grabbed me under the arms, and he hoisted me up to the window, which was sealed with steel bars. I clenched the bars in my fists, and I gazed out the window, across an icy and forbidding river that met gray grassy plains freezing into snow-capped mountains in the far northwest. The frosty wind slapped me in the face, and I realized for the first time that this was reality.

I was really here in this cell, the pain in my legs was real, the bruises all over my body were real, and the man who now supported me like a steel pillar was my only friend.

With a painful shudder that crunched through my broken body, I recognized my surroundings. I had seen it all before ... those mountains, that river.

Welcome to Wyoming Territorial Prison. 'For evil-doers of all classes and kinds.'

I'd been as familiar as I'd ever wanted to get with this prison from my days as a cowhand passing through Laramie in the summers. It was the looming stone acropolis that sat darkly on the horizon beyond the busy train tracks and the river. Filled with evil-doers, to which I could now add my own name.

After that I spent some time – I'm not sure how long – just drifting in and out of delirium. Sometimes I would awaken in something like my right mind and see my cellmate pacing about. Sometimes I would awaken, even in the middle of the night, to find myself alone, and I would wonder where he had gone. But I would quickly fall back into sleep, where feverish dreams would haunt me. In the most frequent, Emelina came to me, standing at the door to my cell, dressed as she had been on that last New York evening in blue and red finery for dining at the Café Brunswick, her thin white arms reaching out to me through the bars. In these dreams, beautiful Emelina urged me to stay strong, her painted red lips sobbed promises into the icy Wyoming wind, the words breaking apart and falling like bits of hail into the deathly currents of the Laramie River. I would awake in my empty cell, sweat like ice all over my body, calling her name.

Still, I was glad to see her.

At one point, I suppose I grew so ill that someone in the prison administration determined that I should be removed from my cell and carted straight away to the prison's makeshift infirmary. A prison guard arrived, loaded me clumsily and painfully into a wheelbarrow, and the two of us bounced off down the hallway, the wagon's squeaking wheels moaning through the prison. Out of the cell for the first time, I looked around me, at the twisting stone stairs that connected the three stories of human cages, at the small, crowded cells, and the men staring out through the bars at me. As we squealed by, and thunked down the stairs, I looked only briefly at each prisoner we passed. They were of all shapes and sizes, mostly strong and rugged young trouble-makers locked up in a new young world along with the occasional hardened old convict, but what I noticed most as they spun by in a blur were the things that I didn't see on their faces, which were empty of anger, hatred, sorrow and hopelessness and instead filled with an almost religious elation, the sort of quiet joy that, when I was a kid, I used to see in the eyes of the devoutest of nuns. (That is, before I robbed them, sacrilegious and hungry rapscallion that I was.) It was calm and, to my mind, anyway, totally misguided, oblivious optimism.

I wondered what had come over these prisoners.

Back in my cell, maybe days, maybe weeks later, the fever having broken. Drinking water out of a tin cup, trying to straighten my back against the cold stone wall. Now my eyes focused on my company. He looked to be in his early twenties, a strong and vigorous man with a knowing laugh in his blue eyes. He did not look, to my mind, like a guy broken by a brutal penal system, and I wondered why. Already, I did not get him. But I had no one else.

"Explain this to me," I muttered. "I'm awaiting trial, right?"

He just stared.

I muttered. "That must be it. I'm innocent, though."

I tried to catch the man's eye. I tried out my story.

"Listen to this," I said. "I was framed."

I smiled nervously, nodding, trying to convince him, as I thought that I would one day convince a jury.

"You know who framed me?" I asked. "J.P. Morgan himself." I nodded again. "J.P. Morgan. And the United States government. Secret agents of the United States government."

I wondered if I was the first crazy accused murderer to come up with this excuse.

The man held out a hand.

"I'm Billy Golden. We've been sharing this cell for some time, but this is the first you've been sane enough to talk to. Careful shaking my hand. You broke a couple of fingers there."

He pointed to a mangled middle finger on my right hand.

"That one didn't heal right," he said.

I placed my hand gently in his.

"Watt O'Hugh," I said.

"The Third," Billy said. "Famed Western hero turned passion killer. We all know you here." A self-conscious, disingenuous smile came to his face. "You're a legend. I'm no one. I'm just a mule thief."

Now I'd heard everything. Not only didn't I get him, I didn't think I could believe a word this guy said. With his refined manners, his perfect grammar and his subtly ironic tone, he reminded me of the youthful, well-educated Church volunteers who, during the summers of my youth, occasionally showed a fleeting interest in filling my stomach, before turning to other fancies, returning to school, working on Wall Street, courtship, cheating on their wives. I wondered what Billy's story was, and who he thought he was fooling. Why would this guy need a mule so badly, anyway?

"Yes sir, I'll soon be forgotten. But the world will never forget the strange life of Watt O'Hugh the Third and his violent fall from grace. I think there's already a sad and bloody little folk song roaming the prairies about you. Author unknown, of course.

"Passion killers," he added, "make for the best folk songs."

"I'm not guilty. J. P. Morgan. Secret agents. I told you."

"You're a little late with your cover story, brother. In case you don't recall, your trial came and went. The Third took the stand and confessed everything."

Billy's voice echoed in the bare cell.

"I admitted murder?" I asked.

My words came out of my mouth in a cloud of mist.

He nodded.

"You're one of the bad guys, now, Mr. Watt O'Hugh the Third."

"One of the bad guys ...."

"It's official."

I smiled ruefully.

"It's a lie," I said.

"I know it," Billy said agreeably. "I didn't steal that mule, either. We were just good friends, you know."

"I've been framed."

"So have we all. No one cares anymore. You're a convicted murderer, and that *makes* you a murderer, whether you did it or not. Your guilt or innocence doesn't matter anymore."

He kept quiet, and I just thought about this, trying to let it sink in.

"We've designed a cover story for you," Sneed had told me. *"Hero of the Wild West implicated in passion crime."*

I had not thought that anyone would believe it, or even imagine it.

I'd killed men, and I had been reputed, since tales of my legend had spread, to have killed many more. I am rumored to have killed bandits and outlaws who, in reality, had long since retired and set down roots on the prairies as respectable and legitimate homesteaders. I was *supposed* to be a killer, of course. A killer of hundreds. With ambitions of many more, all men who deserved to die. That was part of my "mystique." No one had ever found anything wrong in this until now.

The cell I shared with Billy had two hammocks, which I was not inclined to navigate, on account of my mangled legs.

So I slept on the floor, but, that night, I did not sleep well.

It became clear to me, as I trembled on the cold stone floor, that Billy did not spend his night locked up. I wondered how he managed to come and go so freely. I wondered who he really was.

When I woke in the morning, Billy was resting in the hammock, like a 1950s hardware store owner relaxing on a July weekend.

Now I stared at him, and, though I recognized the same man, the same concerned eyes, I was surprised at my estimate of him on the night before. Billy was clearly far older than I had originally thought. He was a vigorous but ageing man, near fifty as well as I could calculate. His hair was almost completely gone but for a couple of surviving clumps of growth just above his ears.

"You look different," I whispered.

"Could be someone's grampa, right?" he asked. Then, with a weariness and resignation that was obviously feigned: "That's what one night too many in this place will buy you, brother."

That morning, once I got up the energy, I crawled up the wall, my useless legs hanging limply beneath me, and I managed to pull myself up to the window, to stare dully out at the icy Laramie river, at a train as it chugged into the nearby town, hobos streaming from box-cars. I saw some of the men in their stripes, their legs and arms chained one to another, marching off to work in town; others, hammers in hand, slumped over to the quarry, trudging through light brown ice and slush.

From my window, I observed a few things that I think are worth noting. First, in spite of a manner that he might have cultivated at Harvard, Billy was clearly a respected leader of the prisoners, perhaps the top dog, and he frequently called out orders to the others, which every prisoner obeyed without hesitation or resentment. Second, while most of the prisoners kept a distance, he appeared to be the confidante of a bald-headed Chinese man, who was bone thin, but strong and formidable. The other prisoners paid them both deference, in their words, and in their body language.

When he returned for lock-up, Billy told me that the Chinese prisoner was named Tang. "*Madame* Tang," he said with amusement, for this Chinaman wasn't a man at all, just a very mannish woman – for her era, anyway – with muscles and attitude built from years working the railroads disguised convincingly as the stronger sex. She did it to support her children when she could see no other way, he told me, but how she got to America from Kaifeng, in an era when immigration was closed to Chinese women was, he said, another story.

She was desperate, and she first found one way to survive, and then she found another. Risked her life every day and many times to give the robber barons their transcontinental railroads. She dangled a hundred feet over Canyon Diablo from a half-built, teetering wooden bridge; as one of five men in hanging wicker baskets planting explosives in sheer rockface to build a trestle in a Rocky Mountain peak, she lost her left foot when her dynamite detonated before she'd cleared the cliff wall.

Some time later, arrested as a man, she was thrown into the pen before anyone found out the truth. Now, though she was the sole current resident of the women's quarters at the other end of the prison, the warden worked her just the same during the day because of the extra money she could bring in. The other prisoners left her alone, a woman in their midst, Billy said, because they were "afraid of her." This, with a glint in his eye; he liked her, and he was proud of her. What was she in for? I asked him, and Billy said, "Murder – Like you. A murderer." Then, quickly: "That's not what frightens the other prisoners, Watt." He paused. "She scares people. That's all."

I could think of nothing to say to this, and so I kept quiet. After a little while, he said to me, "You know you've been left here to rot, Third, don't you? Are you willing to take your punishment like a microbe in the body politic? Or do you want to break out?"

Here it was. I grabbed my chance.

"I'm breaking out," I said, as certainly as I could. "I owe the government nothing."

Billy let out an almost invisible sigh of relief.

"In that case, I suggest you treat Madame Tang with all the respect she's earned," he said. "You'll meet her soon. You'll see. You'll be scared, too."

At two in the morning, my cell door creaked slowly open. I awoke and skidded back two feet on my palms, looking unsuccessfully for cover, or some sort of weapon. Two striped figures stood in the doorway, their hands on the bars. Billy spoke softly, calming me. They moved into the moonlight that swept across the cell like an ocean wave. The other prisoner was Tang, stony and formidable.

They knelt down beside me on the floor of the cell. Billy was young again, younger than I'd ever seen him, with a full head of hair and strength even in the way he moved across the cell. If he could manage such a recovery, he could do anything. And as for Tang, I had never seen a woman like her. I had never seen a Chinese woman before – that was also true. So I attributed her difference to race. To the reader of the 21st century, she would not be so unusual. She'd lived the life of a man, the most rigorous and brutal man's life imaginable, and so she was muscled and slender, and strong and so fearsome. I think, even in her prison stripes, even grasping a sledgehammer and busting up rock, she could stare out of the pages of one of your fashion magazines – one of the edgier, racier ones – and inspire the envy of women by the hundreds of thousands, and the lust of men in equal numbers. But in the 19th century, men feared her, and women turned away. She didn't care; I believe she didn't care what anyone thought.

"How'd you both get in here?" I asked.

Billy said, like a bad comedian, "Through the door."

I asked how they managed to move through the prison at will. Billy said, "Sometimes we turn into mice and squeeze between the bars and then scurry down the corridors under the guards' feet," and Tang said, "Sometimes we turn invisible and fly through the air on imaginary magic wings," and then Billy said, "But usually we turn into chocolate pudding and drip through the drain into the penitentiary's sewers," and Tang concluded gravely, "Yeah, that's what we usually do. That's the plan that works the best. It's easy once you know how."

I gave up.

Billy changed the subject. He said he knew I'd seen the Laramie doctor who popped by the infirmary on Wednesdays, but Tang knew a few things that had never made it into the medical books. Would I mind if she took a look at my legs?

I weakly nodded assent.

Tang rolled up my pants legs, clucking with no little astonishment at what she saw. She poked and prodded me, only briefly.

She motioned to Billy. "Sit him up straight."

Billy grabbed my arms and pulled me upright so that I could look at the twisted mess that my legs had become. Tang gestured up and down both legs, pointing from time to time at a twisted muscle, or a cracked bone, poking me in spots that had gone completely numb, explaining dully in detailed medical terms every disaster that had struck my pitiful body. I didn't know what she was saying, but I knew it wasn't good. I felt mothered by her – an uncomfortable feeling that brings on a certain yearning in an orphan boy, even one who's gone to the trouble of growing up. I wondered now what kind of parent she'd been. The strict kind, I figured. I wondered how old she was; I didn't know. Maybe old enough to be my own mother. But maybe young enough to be my daughter.

"Let him down," Tang told Billy.

He gently lowered me to the cold cell floor.

Then, not even looking into my eyes, she made her diagnosis.

"You know that you will never walk again," she said.

The words, so quiet, made barely a stir in the angry silence of the penitentiary but echoed a thousand times in my head.

Now she looked up.

"Did you know that, O'Hugh?" she asked.

Billy just grimaced, and I stayed silent.

"Did anyone bother to tell you that?" Tang asked, more insistently.

I summoned the strength to speak, and I tried to hold my voice steady. Did a pretty good job, I thought, given the circumstances. No one had told me this, I admitted. No one had bothered to let me know I was a torso with no legs attached.

"What do you think?" she asked Billy. "Is he worth saving?"

He shrugged, and then he turned to me, and fixed me with a penetrating stare, which, in its severity, seemed capable of exploring my mind, my motives and my character.

"Watt here is no fan of the government," he said at last to Tang, his gaze incessant. "He doesn't really know what's happened to him. Either that or he's the best actor in the world." Then, with a smile and a wink for my benefit: "I read his out of town notices. If you ask the Philadelphia critics, he's not the best actor in the world."

Tang began speaking Chinese to Billy, and to my surprise, he replied in kind. After an exchange that was brief, urgent and serious, they both fell into silent thought.

At last, Tang nodded to Billy, and he nodded back, before turning to me.

"Watt," he said. "We all know why you're here. J. P. Morgan wants to get his hands on Allen Jerome, and in that mission he and various arms of the United States government have enlisted your help."

I tried to object, and my stuttered explanation gradually degenerated into a torrent of unconvincing half-lies, after which, sweating and nervous, I fell silent. My words, which still echoed through the empty cells, taunted me.

"Why did Morgan plant you in the pen?" Tang asked.

Billy, a hand resting on Tang's shoulder, addressed me more urgently.

"You told me this morning that you don't owe the government anything, and I hope that you really believe that. Morgan is not your friend. The United States government is not your friend."

Outside, in the wind and hail, the ice in the river crashed and shattered on its banks; a late-night train to Laramie squealed into town, its brakes desperately clinging to the icy tracks – sounds to which I'd grown so accustomed over the last few days.

"We know why you're here," Billy said, "but we're willing to trust you. Tang can cure you. No doctor can cure you. If you join us, Tang and I will give you a second chance. President Grant at best may be kind enough to leave you to live as a cripple on the floor of this cold cell for the rest of your life if he doesn't see fit to hang you for your faithful service to his corrupt administration."

I tried to put the politics to one side. I'm no radical, or revolutionary. I've never voted, I don't know an anarchist from Schuyler Colfax, and I don't give a damn. I admit that, as a man in my twenties, I wholeheartedly favored Lucy's subversive politics – her "Party of Free Love" – but no more than any other young man in good health would have done, and for reasons that had absolutely nothing to do with political protest.

So when Billy Golden – the best educated, most articulate and suspiciously crafty convicted mule thief I'd ever met, by the way – rapped to me about the common man, about Mammy and Pappy out on the plains fighting the great grasshopper plague of '74, I almost stood up on my mangled legs to hurl myself at the metal bars.

On the other hand, when he started talking about Watt O'Hugh swinging from the end of a hangman's rope, I had to admit he made a lot of sense.

"What do I do?" I asked.

Billy smiled.

"Allen Jerome presents himself as a revolutionary who can help the common man of the continent," he said, "but he's just one more populist nobleman with ulterior motives. You will work for us now –

Madame Tang and me. The boys in this Pen ... we believe in their ultimate goal, but we know that Allen Jerome won't bring it, and that his movement must be destroyed before things get even worse."

Tang still seemed wary towards me, even as she loosely summarized their plans to break out of the prison and roam the West as a sort of an independent militia, devoted to nothing more than the "Cause" of the homesteader, the pauper, the suffering freedman and, not least, she added, with a mischievous glint in her eye, the orphans of the Five Points. Even in letting me into their gang, in requesting my pledge of undying allegiance to their Cause, whatever it was exactly, their offer was laced with unsubtle threats. If I were lying, Billy told me, he would find out. If I even thought about double-crossing the Cause, he would know, instantly. Or, anyway, Tang would know instantly, Billy told me, nodding in the scowling woman's direction. I'd been pretty smart and crafty so far in my life, Billy admitted, but he and Tang were not your average Western outlaws.

"You realize this, don't you, Third?" he asked me, and I said I did. "You can't hide things from us," Billy added, and I agreeably promised not to try.

"Who do I work for again?" I asked.

"For us," Billy said. "You pretend to work for Allen Jerome, you blend in with the boys from the Pen and win their trust, but really you work for us. And Watt – you are our soldier till the day you die."

"And what if you two have a spat?" I asked. "Then who do I work for?"

"Billy," Tang said without hesitation. "If Billy and I have a fight, you work for Billy Golden."

I held out one crippled hand, and the deal was sealed.

Was I still a mole, infiltrating Jerome's gang, observing and reporting back his sinister machinations?; was I hoping to save Lucy from Fawley's army of darkness?; did I believe, suddenly, in the justice of Billy's mission?; or was I just trying to save my own skin?

I didn't know the answer to any of these questions.

Tang asked me to shut my eyes, and in the ensuing darkness I felt a cool breeze spread through my body, and then I felt muscles untangle, bones snap together, nerve endings, swimming lost through shadows, reconnect. I don't know how long the entire process took. I also don't know what it sounded like, but at the time, I thought this process of reconstruction must be making a terrible racket, enough to wake the warden in his private quarters, to catch the attention of the guards in their towers.

When I opened my eyes, it was hours later. My body reborn; Tang and Billy gone. The morning sun lit the cell like a palace in Heaven.

* * *

The Laramie doctor examined me one more time, and he proclaimed me fully and remarkably recovered. I saw him scratch his prematurely bald head with some wonder as he looked me over, but then almost literally shake awake his puzzlement. He was a busy man with a full itinerary back in town. He was an upwardly mobile professional, and the government didn't pay him enough to expect him to ponder miracles.

"These things happen," he said with a small smile, "I suppose."

CHAPTER 6

I could probably write a book just about the prison and the men I knew who were housed there, and if I have the time, maybe I will, but this is not that book, and if you were not looking for a lengthy and dry catalog describing in voluminous detail the inner social workings of the Wyoming Territorial Prison, then maybe you're glad of that, too.

If you're lucky enough to live in the late 20th or 21st century, and if you want to learn more about the penitentiary that I once called home, the whole thing's been turned into a museum, Wild West amusement park and dinner theater.

If you pop by, please give my regards to my old cell. It was number 17.

For now, I'll just mention that there were more than thirty of us at the pen in 1874, civil war veterans mostly, nearly all cowboys laid off in the hungry wintertime who'd been looking for a little easy money that in the end turned out not to be so easy. They were men like those I'd known during my few years on the cattle trails, and, though they were amused by my fall from legend, for the most part they didn't seem to mind me so much, which came as a relief to me, since I could have taken any two of them but not any three.

I was in the stone quarry half a mile north of the penitentiary building for ten hours four days a week, hammering out flagstone and limestone for construction of Laramie's new school and hospital (the city council paid the pen eighty-two cents an hour for my services), and waist-deep in the river every Friday afternoon, fishing out ice for the Union Pacific Railroad Company, which paid by the ton. Some of the more artistically inclined prisoners were employed on the premises making furniture. The pen was a relatively profitable factory for the warden, after all. At night I would return to my cell, grateful for the rest but apprehensive about the violence to come.

Simply because you're readers of the post-modern age, you might be wondering about a certain other matter, so I'll answer this touchy question as quickly and simply as I can: No. I've heard what goes on in prisons of your era, and I can state that inmates of the 19th century had other things to think about. Such as, for instance, escaping! Prisons and jails in my time were about as strong as a house of cards – even barbed wire, in 1874, was something out of Jules Verne – and so my not-unrealistically-optimistic colleagues in the Wyoming pen saved their appetites for the toothless strumpets who they knew would lustily greet them their first post-breakout night in town, while their aggression they conserved in abundance for the robberies and petty crimes that their continued existence would undoubtedly require. I had plenty of worries, but getting raped at knifepoint was far from my mind.

I was working one afternoon in the quarry, breaking out rocks, my back aching and my sweat freezing to my skin, when one young cowboy said, "I couldn't hardly take this, if it wasn't for Sidonia," and another said, "Now's I see Sidonia in my dreams, I go to sleep happy," and the others – every single man in the quarry but me – murmured assent.

At the edge of the hole, Tang had stopped pounding rock, and she stared over the mass of straining bodies, a small look of satisfaction on her face. The prisoners were like thriving but helpless little babies, and she was their resourceful mum.

"Anyone's'll tell ya' ..." a grizzled old miner said to me, confidentially, walking back to the pen, the sun low in the sky. "Ask anyone, he'll say as how I vanished every day for a week. Walking to make bricks, poof and I was gone. Then poof and I was back." The old man had killed his cousin's husband in a vicious argument about the civil war that had gotten out of hand.

It had been an accident, as the old coot repeated again and again. The dead man had simply fallen at an unfortunate angle after the old miner had given him a well-deserved but hardly fatal knock in the chops. He became a fugitive from justice, his wife forgot his name, and he'd led the bounty hunters and the Pinkertons on a merry chase across a few territories and a couple of states before being led out of a boarding house on his hands and knees all the way out in California. Since then, he was a ruined man. At least, until Sidonia beckoned him in his dreams, a golden city in a valley in the mountains.

"So where'd you go," I asked him, "when you vanished?"

Around a bend and into another world, he said, a world where his joints still worked, where his head didn't throb day-in and day-out, a world where the weather was always temperate yet the air was nevertheless skeeterless, where a beautiful young woman with deep blue eyes and foggy black hair waited for him on the front porch of a white columned stone house at the top of an elevated cobblestone path that abutted green pastures dotted with olive trees. Lovers strolled the fields with bottles of red wine, serenaded by musicians in tails playing violins. The woman welcomed him into her bed-chamber, disrobed for him, loved him and asked him to love her back, didn't charge a penny and promised to wait for him in front of the white stone house every day as the sun set into the distant sea.

"I caught a glimpse of myself in a hallway mirror," he said to me, drool gathered in pools in his gums. "I was a handsome young man."

He had not discovered merely a fountain of youth – the ugly old miner had at twenty been an ugly young vagrant, teeth already gone, skin gray and sallow. To revert to his own life as a youth would have meant merely forestalling the inevitable and re-living decades of pain better left forgotten. No, he told me, the man that he became each day for a week put his true self to shame, and gave him hope, at last, that Destiny had something more in store for him.

He'd stopped to admire himself in the full-length mirror, the broad shoulders, the deep blue eyes, and the winning warmth in his smile. There in the hallway, in the empty house, he'd cast off his clothes and stood triumphant in front of the mirror, memorizing, as quickly as he could, every inch of this magnificent new body.

She crept up behind, this woman from his new life, wrapped her arms around him from behind, told him he was handsome, very handsome, and asked if he agreed.

He readily agreed.

"Marry me," she said. "In Sidonia."

You can tell a Sidonian town when you reach it, he told me. The Sidonians left a trail of Magic in their wake. If you come to a place in which the townsfolk no longer dream nightmares and, in day, their beloved dead again walk the Earth – "deadlings", they were called, these recent returnees – in which barren fields suddenly burst with vegetables and enemies embrace and become friends, tears melt away into smiles ... if I were to come upon such a town, the old man said with assurance, then the Sidonians had been there, tossing peace and happiness through the countryside like powdered sugar. Peace and happiness, and more than a smattering of deadlings, wandering dazed through the countryside.

"They're the future," he said, staring up into the sunny sky, religious bliss lighting his face. "Remember my words, O'Hugh."

OK, I know what you will say now. *Ahah!* I hear you cry. *Zombies! I knew it! Or, maybe, vampires!* I wish I could tell you that the deadlings were zombies or vampires, because I understand that both vampires and zombies will also become quite popular in the 20th century and the 21st century. Why, if I could just promise that there would be vampires or zombies in my book, I could have lunch in the ABC commissary with Carlton Cuse tomorrow. If I wanted my *Memoirs* to sell a million copies, and if I didn't care so much about the Truth, I would shout back at you, *Yes, my friends! Zombies! You love zombies, so let me give you some zombies; and you know what, there were vampires in that crowd: beauteous, randy vampires!* Unfortunately, no. They were neither zombies nor vampires. But, as I have told you, I will die on January 1, 1937, and it is now early 1936 (as I write this, it is February 21, 1936, and oh how I wish that it were a leap year, and I could have that one, long, beautiful extra day of life). That I am a dead man means that I have nothing to lose or gain, and that I can afford to tell you the unvarnished truth. They had not molded in the grave, they had risen from the consciousness of those who remembered them, as fresh as the best day they were alive. They didn't eat flesh or drink blood, or anything like that. The unvarnished truth is that these men and women who rose from the dead in the service of the Sidonian cause weren't zombies and they weren't vampires.[*] They were just people who used to be alive, then weren't, then were again, sporadically. But it made them erratic, and, as I later learned, they can kill a body. So deadlings always make me nervous.

Lying in the hammock, one night, I whispered to Billy, "Where is Sidonia? *What* is Sidonia?"

He didn't speak for a while.

---

[*] I know something about this: Zombies don't exist. (I don't count living men who are given an herb that mimics death, and who then rise up from their coffins. The effect is startling, but those guys never really "died", and so they aren't zombies.) Vampires, on the other hand, are as real as the Grand Canyon, and there is nothing romantic about them. They want to live forever, and they're a rotten bunch. You've probably been bitten by one and don't even know it. I found out a bit about them in 1911, which I will relate in a later volume, if I manage to tell the tale before I succumb.

"You'll see," he finally said. "Soon enough." Then, after another long pause: "Some people say it's the coming Utopia. Some say it's Heaven on Earth. Maybe not."

The wind skimmed over the river, whistling.

"Ready to break out, Third?" Billy asked me, very quietly. "Are you ready to be a free man?"

CHAPTER 7

One frigidly cold early evening, the prisoners began tapping their noses, one to another, as they headed back to their cells, and I knew what was coming. At lock-up, Billy was on the hammock across the room, but when I awoke at midnight to the sound of the sparse contingent of guards filing through the corridors, shouting and cursing, Billy was gone.

Here's how you can tell that this story I'm relating to you is one hundred percent true: if I'd made it all up, I'd have enthusiastically given myself a more active and dramatic role in the prison breakout. But in reality, events rolled right over me, and I just tried to keep up. John Wayne would have been in the thick of it, but he was just a figment of your collective imagination, and I am – or, rather, I *was* – a real living breathing man.

Someone fired gunshots over on the prison's western wing, and a man fell to earth from the furthest tower, his heavy coat aflame, lighting up the cloudy, starless night. In a fog of mist and dust lit by torches, a small army of bandits appeared motionless on the opposite bank of the Laramie with more than twenty extra horses behind them. A prisoner I only barely recognized ran from cell to cell, a peacemaker in his left hand, a set of keys in his right. He was trembling with fear and tension, but, when he appeared at my door, there was a crazy kind of exhilaration in his eyes. I followed other prisoners through the corridors, leaping over bullet-riddled bodies – guards and prisoners both, and, twisted impossibly into the steel bars of a cell on the first level, the warden himself – up a rickety metal ladder on the third level, through a hole burnt in the prison ceiling. I joined the other prisoners who wobbled unsteadily on the roof of the pen, sliding down ropes and bed sheets, then plunging as one man into the excruciatingly frosty midnight waters.

Tang was the first to get across, riding the warden's horse. Billy was nowhere to be seen. Around me, I saw convicts sink beneath the ice-slicked surface and never reappear. I wondered how many of us would make it; I wondered how many would die shivering on the opposite bank.

The water of the Laramie freezing on our prison stripes, we rode screaming through the void, galloping over brittle ebony grasslands, the penitentiary a looming medieval fortress watching us like a black god in the night sky.

We galloped over the train tracks, past railroad shops, mills for manufacturing tracks and iron spikes, shuttered soup shacks and the locomotive round house, where a few escapees abandoned their horses and vanished into idle boxcars, certain, I thought, to be man-sized blocks of ice by the time they reached Nebraska. We continued, racing through the sleeping town, past Overbay's Dry Goods, Fisher's Druggist, Johnson's Shebang, and the local saloon, which, in a hand-painted sign beside the front door, proudly offered faro games each evening. There was no one behind us, no one ahead and no stunned witnesses lining the dusty city streets, so we continued on easily for twelve miles into the darkness, the wind howling in our frozen ears – free men.

We hit the mountains like satellites into orbit, vanishing into the trees, kicking just a few more miles out of our pitiable, exhausted horses, stopping only when we reached an abandoned, heavily overgrown logging camp high in the peaks. The camp was decrepit, two long rows of abandoned wooden shacks fallen into disrepair. Each of us grabbed shelter from the cold, sitting hunched beneath frozen and rotting wooden beams. I looked around for Emelina, who had promised (in her thoughts) to meet me here.

Shortly after our arrival, a squat former pick-pocket, who'd made the rank of corporal in the Sidonian army, handed out new uniforms to each of us, rugged cowboy gear for the ride ahead, dapper go-to-meeting clothes to help us each blend in as gentlemen, or at least dandies, when we arrived in a new town. The same to Tang, a man as far as any of us were concerned. As always, the other fugitives spoke in hushed and eager tones about the great village of Sidonia; these men, some of whom left behind fingers, or arms, or feet in the last War, speculated impatiently on the great social revolution that would soon sweep America right out from under its witless ruling classes.

I was all for that, but I didn't think Darryl Fawley was the one to lead us, I didn't have another great war in me so soon after the last one, and I didn't think the underclasses of America were up for it either, economic depression or not. I slipped away from camp and stomped through the crunch of the hardened snow to a cliff's edge, and from there I looked down on a landscape of white-tipped pines sliced into bits by the ice-filled river, and beyond that the dark stone walls of the penitentiary, a black scar burned into the frozen mountain peaks in the far distant west.

CHAPTER 8

Those escaped convicts all had one common destination, Darryl Fawley's village of Sidonia in Montana, and so I suppose now is as good a time as any to explain how Darryl Fawley and my beloved Lucy went from a quiet if stagnant existence in rainy old England to the outlaw life. Indeed, I have sometimes found it difficult to imagine Darryl Fawley on his journey of discovery, as he told it, in the most remote Chinese countryside, or struggling through the fog in the mountains of Guilin. I find this exercise disorienting not just because of who he was, but because later, when I came to know Fawley somewhat, when I finally managed to infiltrate his army out in the American territories, the man himself had re-written his Chinese expedition into something like a fairytale. There was some truth to it, undoubtedly, because whatever he had found in the mountains had changed his life, had caused him to take his wife and flee everything that he had known before.

As he told it, Fawley hired a guide, a translator, and a strong black horse, and they followed a rumor across the Chinese plains and into the distant mountains. He covered his fine English clothes with Chinese robes, as though the villagers, farmers and innkeepers they would pass on the most remote steps of their journey might somehow overlook his round eyes and the ghostly pale, grayish pallor of his face.

I try to picture him struggling over the rugged, knife-like Chinese mountains, a quiet model of decorum who was all the while inwardly raging at enemies real and perceived. I can't imagine he truly believed his journey would prove a success, yet he trudged onward, clinging to some long-ago legend as his last hope. I sometimes wonder what he would have done had he found himself again a failure, a sad and insignificant figure sitting in the shadows on the outer edge of a Chinese scroll. I wonder if he could have killed himself, or if he would have slunk back home in defeat.

Fawley and his party rested for the night at a tiny and ramshackle inn located in a little village three mountains from the final destination. In their spartan bedroom, sitting on the floor in her pajamas, Lucy pressed him again for answers, but Fawley again demurred. "No Western woman has ever seen this part of China," he said. He urged his wife to breathe in the beauty of the country, to feel its power and magic on her skin.

Lucy didn't argue. She now liked Fawley more than she had when she'd met him, and more than she had when watching him in his element at Embassy functions, and back in England in the controlled and stifling world of society. There was something almost heroic in his eyes. Something reassuring, steady.

He kissed her pretty lips, and his exhausted wife fell quickly asleep.

Hours before dawn, a buzzing, constant but low, woke Fawley. He lay awake, his wife beside him. Fawley listened to her as she cooed and whispered and rustled about in the bed-clothes, fast asleep but far from restful.

Fawley's eyes were wide open. Though drained by the day's ride though the mountains and the vertigo that still afflicted him, his curiosity and childish almost-fear of the unknown noise so close to his windowless room kept him awake.

At last he crept out of bed, tossed on his robes. He struck a match, and his lantern lit up the room with a sudden whoosh. He shielded his sleeping wife from the flame, then, quickly, so as not to disturb her, he padded barefoot out into the chilly, dry mountain night.

Outside, the glow of the night sky blinded his eyes. Distant peaks and the lush, quilt-like farming valley far below were lit up by the same blazing electricity that rendered the heavens a scattering, flickering white. Yet the lightning that cut through the occasional cloud overhead did not thunder and crack, but instead murmured quietly, like a swarm of distant bees.

Fawley darkened his lantern, and he set it to one side. He stood in the middle of the narrow road, his eyes wide open to the glaring sky. The farthest mountain summit began to darken, and gradually a shadow wandered across the sky, heading toward the little village where Fawley had settled for the night.

Fawley didn't know how long it took for the cloud to reach him. It was as though he had come unstuck in time, standing in the tiny lane, the minute hand on his watch glued to the spot, as the cloud spread gradually across the blazing night. The cloud upon reaching him opened up, pouring a chilling mountain rain down on Fawley, drenching him in his robe, which clung to his skin. The water tingled on his skin and in his eyes.

The rest of the town, the mountain slope beyond and the valley below remained dry. A puddle grew beneath Fawley. He held up his hands to the black cloud, and he fell to his knees in the mud. This, he knew, was the end of his journey.

Thunder crackled, lightning pounded the ground around him, and the earth cracked beneath him. Wind blew up from deep below, and for a moment or an hour, Fawley floated evenly on a pocket of air, gradually descending into that hole in the world. He felt as though something were still holding him, guiding him, and, as he would later tell the story, he wasn't afraid. He fell further, and through black and bony tree branches that twisted and wrestled in the wind, Fawley glimpsed an army of clay-red soldiers on the march in a dark hilly landscape. He heard music pounding in his ears, the sounds of a Chinese harp and lute fusing seamlessly with the strains of a medieval orchestra, harpsichord, satyr pipe, dulcimer and bagpipes, and then he was at sea, one small man alone and lost in a typhoon on a black boiling ocean, sinking, his lungs filling with salty white foam. And his world went black.

He awoke in an Englishman's vision of Heaven, in a soft and enveloping bed, beneath impossibly white sheets in an impossibly white room. He wondered for a moment if he *were* in Heaven. He got up from bed, his limbs strong and agile – the chronic pain in his back gone, the click in his knee healed; gone, too, the persistent threat of flatulence, a painful and humiliating presence in his life up to that moment. His lungs clear, again, the way they'd felt when he was a child. Lucy sat naked by the window of the big bedroom, looking through the golden-tinted windows at the heavenly green of the pastures that spread out before her to distant, silver-capped oceans. Fawley touched her bare shoulder, and gently she reached up and covered his hand with hers. Fawley found himself laughing, his body filled with contentment for the first time in decades.

He and Lucy rose on soft breezes and floated through the wall up into the sky, above a dark, lush forest. They turned, looking back, and saw a vast, multi-storied building of ivory and marble held up by heavy columns, and a thousand fleshy, white-robed figures sang out to them from tree-covered terraces. The castle was surrounded by gardens of blooming lupines and lavateras that changed color as the wind shifted.

Fawley, suspended miles above this vision, took Lucy's hand. A prize was being offered him, a wonderful prize, and all he need give in return was blind devotion to a cause, the ultimate goal of which he didn't even know, and couldn't guess. And didn't care.

The ocean briefly glowed blood-red. The journey would not be without dangers and pain, sacrifice and tragedy.

The blood quickly washed away, and silver fizz returned to cap the waves of a sea that rippled a dark and velvety blue.

Fawley smiled, then, in the glorious glare of this mythic mansion, and he nodded.

Lucy woke smiling. They could hear activity outside, but the little windowless room was still dark.

"I had a strange dream," she said, in the soft chill of the morning. Kneeling beside her, Fawley smiled back.

"Good-strange," he asked, "or bad-strange?"

"Strange-wonderful," she whispered. "So strange-wonderful, I wish I'd never woken." She yawned a delicate yawn, and she stretched out her long, beautiful body, and, eyes still shut, she smiled at her memory.

This story became religion – the creation myth, if you will – to those strange men and women who dwelled in one narrow and green Montana valley, which a 19th century adventurer might reach only by traversing a seemingly endless row of mountain ranges. Here lay the flush little town known as Sidonia, which was then, as now, hidden in myth and legend. In the center of the little town, one sunny but chilly day in 1875, a small boy no older than five ran joyously up Main Street, paved and smooth, chasing a crowd of Sidonians past the three-story apartment buildings of polished stone and the exotic, fully stocked shops that lined the tree-shrouded thoroughfare. The boy's heavy boots clomped by elaborate side streets that, he knew, led to other luxuriously furnished homes and treasures yet discovered by no one. Today, he was alone. His mother, dead, back in those terrible, barely remembered days before his father had moved to Sidonia. The boy's father, also absent today, was engaged in important military maneuvers as one of the armed sentries who sat on the mountain peaks above the golden city, vigorously watching the isolated landscape for U.S. cavalry come to destroy the Sidonians' perfect lives.

This was the town's most sacred day, commemorating the birthday of Darryl Fawley's mother, Sidonie, who had died young and, to Fawley's mind, beautiful. Fawley had modeled Sidonia in her image, every corner celebrating an uneventful life remarkable only for the fact that, decades after it ended, it was remembered at all. Her picture adorned the local administrative building, the local saloon and the local playhouse, which was christened the "Sidonie Theatre."

The excitement pounding through the sprawling village that day was a result of a proclamation made by their leader: Fawley had promised to resurrect Sidonie herself for a fleeting, deadling appearance at this year's Sidonia Day Parade. Of the well-wishers, the formerly destitute – gold miners, rag pickers, tenant farmers, drunken cowboys, ageing streetwalkers – made up the bulk (like the little boy's father and mother, who had sold all their belongings just to feed their growing child), but the Sidonian citizenry also included its share of the "cream" of American society, the idle, frightened children of old wealth families, and even the occasional lonely Wall Street titan who'd found that his money could, in the end, buy very little that was genuinely worth acquiring. They mixed freely on Main Street.

Trumpets and bugles blared from behind the Fawley Palace; the little boy leapt into the air again and again, catching each time a brief glimpse of the festivities on the Palace's greens, where Darryl Fawley stood and, behind him, the shadowy Allen Jerome. Fawley was the more gregarious and, in the boy's opinion at least, the more beloved of the two. Even now, on this solemn occasion, he stood about telling amusing anecdotes and doing his best to charm his subjects. These stories were lost in the wind before they reached the boy's ears, but he could nevertheless feel the good will that moved through the crowd. Allen Jerome, who stood silently with a thinly disguised scowl on his gaunt face, was lanky and ragged, his features unthreatening and unremarkable in spite of the gloomy disposition he sought to communicate, and, in both manner and appearance, he made a startling contrast to the cordial Fawley. He was not an ugly man, not exactly. He was forty years old, with a slight loss of his light brown hair at the very top of his forehead, piercing blue eyes, and a rare laugh, when he was not sunk in self-defeating rumination and the endless strategizing that had burdened him since his childhood. To the boy and the little friends he had made in Sidonia's public school, the bonds that connected these two were as inscrutable as the force that brought to them the marvels of Sidonia and the debt that it would one day exact.

The opening ceremony complete, the little boy could at last spot the pageant heading his way. Several minutes later, the deadling Sidonie's horse-drawn carriage appeared before him, the red and gold curtains parted, just briefly, and the deadling Sidonie herself peered out. For years afterwards, the boy would recall with utter certainty that he had made passing eye contact with the shadowy matriarch, who waved one ring-covered hand solemnly at the adoring throng, then at once vanished back into the carriage and the darkness of the underworld.

I visited Sidonia some time later, under heavy disguise, and in deep fear of discovery. Beyond the town's agreeable thoroughfares lay beautiful green pasture and lush farmland, all of it rigorously exploited. But the sweat of the area ranchers and craftsmen could not explain the elaborate nature of Sidonia's many pleasures. It's hard even to describe a place that, by any reckoning, was so impossible. Maybe the passage of time has blown it all out of proportion in my head. Certainly, when you read my recollection, you will not believe it. Knowing this, I will still try my best to give you a thorough and truthful tour.

My memory is of a town equal parts past and fantasy, an impression corroborated by acquaintances who visited the village in its early days. It was impossible to have hauled over the Wyoming and Montana ranges the supplies needed to construct Sidonia in this particularly isolated valley. And it was equally impossible to keep the remote town supplied. Yet here it was. The most rustic neighborhoods in Sidonia reminded me of nothing I had seen in the 19th century; it more resembled the nostalgic "frontier towns" that arose in the late 20th century, clean and scrubbed Western amusement parks rebuilt from the discarded garbage of ghost towns for the enjoyment of round little chocolate-coated children and their pasty, squishy-in-the-middle parents, Polaroid cameras in tow. The more lavish arondissements, to give my readers yet another example that they might recognize, reminded me in spirit of the Atlantic City of the late 20th century, in which grand thoroughfares were lined by vast, majestic structures bursting with opulence yet inhabited not by princes but by the slightly bedraggled, slightly befuddled, vast unwashed American multitudes, trudging over red carpets in their dirty sneakers.

Sidonia itself grew more labyrinthine by the day, or perhaps by the moment, based on nothing more than the individual whim of each increasingly pampered Sidonian. Any trinket, any fondly remembered memento of childhood could be found in a local shop. Any production would eventually perform beneath the Sidonie Theatre's velvet curtains. Any food, from any country, could be sampled under the crystal chandeliers of a local bistro, usually found on a side street upon which the surprised Sidonian had never before stumbled, and would never find again. In spite of the fact that pilgrims chasing a myth arrived daily, and in further spite of the fact that no construction crews were ever spotted sweaty in the hot mid-day sun, there was never a shortage of housing. On the flip side, homes, shops and entertainments that ceased to charm or amuse simply ceased to exist, although wrecking crews were similarly never spotted sweaty in the hot mid-day sun.

The Sidonians remained ever loyal, to Fawley, to Sidonie, even to the elusive Allen Jerome, in spite of the fact that their new kings, or spiritual leaders, had never pretended to explain to them the philosophy behind their largesse. The town, like a living breathing God, and Fawley and Jerome, in their roles as Sidonia's chief priest and minister, provided the grateful residents with all they might require; what church, what government, had ever provided them more than the empty promise of some far future Paradise, if that?

There was a place in Sidonia for anyone willing and able to give himself over entirely to the great Cause, whatever it was. Even, I might add, for citizens who might be deemed utterly useless in any functioning society as previously practiced. For example, if you took a left off the main drag, then the second right, the third left, followed a narrow alley for a quarter of a mile and then curved left again, you'd come to a vast, bullet-proof building where, on most days, you'd find that cursed idiot, the fat and whimpering Leopold Kronecker, sitting at his shooting range, testing each new mathematical theorem, trying, with his little X's and Y's, to perfect the art of mass murder. With each new day of failure, that damnable Kronecker's cussing grew louder and more desperate, while his self-promotion grew more shameless. (His overrated theory of algebraic magnitudes was still yet-to-come.)

At the very end of Main Street, carved into the side of a mountain that glinted a blinding gold in the noonday sun, sat the palace where resided Darryl Fawley and, in a distant, western wing, Allen Jerome. The palace, as was apparent to any observer, grew or contracted by the day, depending on the momentary larks of its revered, honored and deeply feared occupants.

Darryl Fawley walked through the grand entrance of the palace, passing masterpieces of every previous era and some yet to come. He was still shaken from seeing his mother; his whole body trembled slightly, he wobbled as he walked, his face ashen.

His unsmiling colleague met him in the foyer, a young woman beside him. Dressed in a yellow spring dress, she was thin and pretty and no older than her very early twenties, with light brown hair tied in a loose bun, fair white skin and sad eyes that seemed eager to sparkle. Confused and disoriented, she held onto Jerome's arm as though for support, and without any particular affection.

"This is a new arrival," Jerome said to Fawley. "Miss Amelia Sturges. 'Mimi,' for short."

"My friends do call me Mimi," the young woman agreed.

Fawley bowed graciously, introduced himself and lightly kissed the young woman's hand.

Fawley guided them out of the foyer and into the first corridor.

"Today," Fawley said, "we have a garden in the southern wing."

They continued to walk through the silent shadows of the palace. Torches burned on the walls, and their footsteps clattered noisily through the mountain chambers.

Fawley could not take his eyes from Mimi Sturges, the glow of youthful, misguided optimism on her fine, fragile face, the smell of new life pumping through her body.

Finally, he could resist no longer.

Fawley turned to the young woman, and he whispered gently: "Are you deceased, Miss Sturges?"

She looked momentarily sad.

"I believe I am, Mr. Fawley," she said softly, as though just now realizing the terrible truth.

They continued a few paces in silence.

"Try to think," Jerome said.

She took a deep breath.

"I remember very little. Just images. I remember warm sun."

She paused, groping for the courage to continue.

"I remember wilting," she blurted out in an embarrassed stammer, "like a Swiss mountain flower in the Mediterranean sun."

Blushing, she smiled humbly and averted her eyes.

"That's very silly and melodramatic," she said. "I'm sorry. It sounded better in my head."

"Not at all," Fawley said. "Maybe you were a poet in life. At any rate, a girl with strong passions."

"Is this Heaven?" she asked.

"Oh, I don't know," Fawley said absently. "Maybe." He held out his arm, guiding them to the right.

"We've reached the Garden. I think you'll both be pleased."

They turned, the corridor widened, and an explosive burst of sunlight struck them like a locomotive. Mimi gasped, and Jerome smiled slightly at the watercolor impossibility that spread out before him. Like a child's finger painting, colors merged into one another, sweeping into the endless horizon. Untamed hollyhock escaped from the center of the garden and grew wild along the outer edges, twisting through wisteria and chrysanthemum beds, wrapped about wild tulips from the African continent that grew amidst wild splashes and dabs of color, which, on closer inspection, revealed themselves to be gladioluses, geraniums strawflowers, crape myrtles and on and on, and even some flowers that Fawley had invented just for today's display, big, knobby and gaudy flowers too grotesque for God Himself to have created. Fawley beamed with pride.

The glass dome showered them in sunlight, and Mimi blinking as one who has just come out of a long and deep sleep – as, indeed she had – ran into the garden, bathing in the rays of light, her arms up above her.

Surveying the garden, Jerome slapped Fawley cordially on the side. "Good work, Mr. Fawley. Very good work."

Fawley searched Jerome's face for scorn, but he could find none, and so he smiled affably.

"You've outdone yourself on many fronts today," Jerome muttered. "I must not forget to mention that Mommy looked beautiful today. Much more beautiful in person."

"Thank you, Allen."

"I believe the citizens were pleased by the pageantry," Jerome went on. "A bit of this and that, some oompah, an explosion or two, and it's cleaning bills for everyone."

Jerome sat down in a stone chair beside a bush sculpted to resemble a stone fountain, crossed his legs, cocked his bowler to one side, leaned back and watched the young woman, as though she were a performer in a theatrical production.

"Don't think I don't know who this deadling is," Fawley whispered, "even if she herself is oblivious. You are transparent, Allen Jerome. Why is she here?"

Jerome studied Mimi intently, as she walked sweetly though the garden, touching each plant in confusion, getting used to life again.

"I wanted to understand," his colleague replied. "For what sort of woman would the Great Man risk his fortune, and the fortune of the world? I needed to see this."

He cradled his chin in his hands.

"She is remarkable," he said, "for her unremarkableness. One plus one equals four, for our friend Mr. Morgan."

"Why can't we let him in?" Fawley asked. "Wouldn't he benefit us?"

Jerome shook his head.

"Sidonia will not allow him in," he explained. He shrugged slightly, and without regret. "It's not up to me." Sidonian agents were currently penetrating every region of America, looking for strong individuals willing to devote their whole souls to some larger ideal in exchange for a Utopian future for themselves and the world. "Morgan has come here more than once, you know, trying to buy a salvation that would preserve his ruling role in American society. The city would not let him in. Sidonia knows. It expelled him like a mush of rotten chyme from a fat man's duodenum."

Fawley nodded at this, although he was, as usual, unnerved by Jerome's pungent simile.

"Like Mrs. Fawley," Jerome said, passionlessly, as though he were noting an interesting parallel, and nothing more. He left his observation hanging in the air. Darryl Fawley did not need to be reminded of his wife's precarious health, or that the city of Sidonia did not and could not take to its heart the sort of independent thinker that Lucy Billings Fawley would always be, regardless of her circumstances. Her most heart-felt oaths of fealty could not fool Sidonia. With every new day that passed, Lucy grew weaker. Every day, her eyesight dimmed. By the time Queen Sidonie made her remarkable ghostly appearance at her birthday festivities, the city walls had become nothing more than pale shadows to Lucy.

Fawley said nothing, but his eyes mourned.

Jerome and Fawley had discussed Lucy's fate many times before, and with increasing frequency. Fawley claimed to love her, and Jerome wondered what his ultimate choice would turn out to be. Jerome had no doubt what he would choose; but then again, he was different from other men. The blue-blooded young women to whom he had believed his New York eminence had entitled him had turned quickly away from him. In South America, he'd surrounded himself with well-paid female companions who demanded ever higher raises, sometimes on a monthly basis, before ultimately, in each case, giving him their notice. There was something that they all saw there; something even Allen Jerome didn't understand. Yet, clearly, there were some things that even money, power, and an endless reserve of Magic could not buy a man.

"It's ironic," Jerome mused. "You thought she would love you for Sidonia. Instead, she tried to love Sidonia for you. And failed."

Jerome clucked, as though this were merely an interesting observation.

"Don't torture me," Fawley said.

Jerome kept his eyes fixed on the garden, where their beautiful deadling guest still played. Mimi took one little flower in one little hand, and she sweetly bent to smell, being terribly careful not to dislodge the bloom, or even to bend a stem ever so slightly.

Jerome's expression, as he watched this, wavered between curiosity and near-disgust.

"It's terribly peculiar," he said, baffled. "I am a man who has never been in love, evidently."

He smiled sadly. Fawley said nothing, but in his silence, he seemed to agree.

"You know," he went on, steadily, "I studied mathematics at Harvard. I have a Ph.D. in mathematics."

Mimi, in her yellow dress, spun about lightly in the cool Spring air, her hem spinning slightly, and her hair catching the sunlight.

"I thought I had loved." He picked up a glass of shambro that rested nearby on a small, polished marble table. His gaze still on Mimi, he continued musing. "My princess was the most brilliant mind on the East coast. She was small, squat, mannish, but in her hands, the laws of quadratic reciprocity took flight to the Heavens." He smiled with the memory. "Our sentimental ties, I thought, were like a Mobius strip, leading one to another with a certain undeniable, linear associative logic. Naturally, there was no logical reason not to love her. So I loved her, as might be expected of me; irrevocably, I thought; passionately, surely."

The simple Mimi, enraptured with the feeling of life, of the spring in her limbs and the sound of her voice, had begun to sing a lilting, tuneful song and to dance a stumbling little waltz.

Fawley remained silent, standing just behind Jerome.

"On an unsteady wooden bridge outside of Cambridge, one cold night," Jerome went on, "in the midst of a romantic midnight stroll, she lost her footing, and over she went. I was dressed in my best courtship suit, there was ice in the river, a frigid chill was in the air, and I detest swimming even under the best of circumstances." Unspoken, to his silent colleague: *I wonder what you would have done, Fawley, old chum.* "Of course, as a mathematician, I mourned the lost knowledge, the proofs that would go unproved. Needless to say. D'you get my point?"

"No."

"I worked beside him for years, Fawley. I believed that Morgan, though my enemy, was my kindred spirit. He could crush the lives of thousands, millions, if the numbers did not add up. But now I have learned that he would risk everything – his own fortune, the economic stability of the United States of America, and perhaps also of the entire world – to see this dim, sorry, pretty girl again, just one more time." With a cruel laugh, still studying Mimi: "To feel the touch of her bare skin against his for the first time, for the only time. This is a man who can have as many beautiful naked girls in his bed each night as he can handle, at once or in combinations of which I've never dreamed – and, to make matters worse, by all reliable reports, he does, the fat eczemous whale! Yet for this, for *her,*" he said, gesturing wildly in Mimi's direction, "a woman who couldn't learn the first thing about monopolies or international currency trading, Mr. J. Pierpont Morgan would sell the moon. For a love that has come about for no logical reason, a love that defies the laws of mathematics." In a low hiss: "You silly, fragile, pretty little girl."

Suddenly, Jerome jerked his body about, grabbed ahold of Fawley's veiny red nose and twisted.

"He is a numbers man by circumstance, not by inclination!" Jerome shouted.

He let go of Fawley's nose, which flopped like a grounded walrus onto his bony greenish-grey mustache, and Jerome gently slapped the Englishman's ruddy cheeks, loudly shouting, "And it makes me hate the fat bastard even more! I hate you, you soft-hearted, love-struck buffoon – John goddamn Pierpont Morgan!" and his voice exploded across the daffodils and petunias, up over the sunflowers and into the Bitterroot Mountains, his words shooting like rockets down the endless stone corridors of the Sidonia Palace.

At mention of this name – a name so imposing as it echoed through the twisting and completely fictional maze of this golden mountain castle that it seemed to have been years earlier predestined to drag its possessor to greatness, regardless of the lucky individual's particular merit – at first staccato stammer of this loaded appellation, all joy vanished from the eyes of the lovely and vacant phantom counting the flower petals beside a distant waterfall on the far horizon in Wednesday's Sidonia Gardens. The color drained from her cheeks, the memory of a brief and painful life filled her body and mind, and she stood, ghostly white in the blinding sunshine.

She was Mrs. John Pierpont Morgan, she suddenly announced, gathering up the folds of her dress and bounding through expansive green and purple fields to a scowling Jerome, who stood from his chair and stamped out of the garden, shambro in hand. Pierpont, she continued, quickly drawing to his side, had been her loving husband, caring tenderly for her in the sunshine of the Cote d'Azur when she had expired. She remembered everything now, the sickness that drained her body, Pierpont's love, so bottomless that he would marry a woman doomed to die within the year, and in all likelihood much, much sooner. She could not stop talking, as memories flooded her mind. She told Jerome about the ocean voyage to a warmer land, about how Pierpont sat at her bedside throughout the night, holding her hand, fighting against sleep. She remembered – how could she remember this? she wondered – Pierpont's face, the way his face had looked just at the moment when life slipped from her body and she spun out of control, a dizzying whirl about the room and through the blue waters and green valleys of a foreign land, and then nothing, darkness, and the distant wail of her husband's anguished sobs.

Jerome, uncomfortable, tried to pull away, but the gaunt young woman dug her fingernails into his camelhair jacket and refused to let go.

"Is he here?" she asked desperately, clinging to Jerome's side as he stalked off down the hallway, heading to his quarters. "Is he here in Heaven with me? May I see him?"

"He's a busy man," Jerome grumbled, dragging Mimi's limp body with him. "You know Mr. Morgan better than I. Always a project, and that never stops, not even in Heaven. Railroads, and all that. Working on the Jesus Christ - Holy Ghost express. We'll try to find a free appointment on his calendar."

He yanked his arm away with such force that the startled Mimi stumbled into the opposite wall. In shock, her strength ebbing, she sank to the floor, and her quiet, desperate sobs filled the air. Jerome strode briskly down the hallway, heading toward the distant patch of sunlight that marked the courtyard, which led to his wing of the palace. He heard the sobs subside, and before turning into the outer atrium – a well-kept plaza festooned with fountains and sculptures by prodigiously gifted medieval artists who never existed – he stole a glance behind him. Her shadow against the marble wall had disappeared, and, supine, sprawled across the floor, she resembled more a wisp of mist than a young woman. Her breathing labored, cleaving again to the world through force of will, she held out one long, transparent hand in his direction, begging his mercy.

In a few minutes, she would be gone, to some other world, to a glorious afterlife ... or perhaps nowhere, perhaps snuffed out in some dark oblivion. Allen Jerome turned, stomped through the corridor that led to the courtyard, and the warm sun struck his face. The love-ravaged wails of young, yellowing Amelia Sturges Morgan rang through the palace. With a deep sense of loneliness and longing, the mathematician forced his golden key into the golden lock on his sparkling diamond door, pushed his way through the portal and sat down, alone, on a velvet and silk couch stuffed with dodo feathers.

CHAPTER 9

In J.P. Morgan's mansion, the great man jerked into consciousness, as though awaked by his late wife's desperate pleas, a thousand miles to the East. Frances Louisa Tracy Morgan – Fanny to her friends – lay beside him, snoring like an old cow, big-boned and obstinate even in sleep. He felt that Mimi was near at hand, here in the room. Watching him, a little sadly, with a touch of disapproval. With this thought in his head, naturally, he could not sleep. *"Mimi,"* he whispered, a melancholy little summons drowned out by his most recent wife's racket.

He heaved himself out of bed, staggered into a day suit, stumbled heavily down the long staircase and rapped impatiently with his walking stick on his carriage driver's bedroom door. Hearing no response, he loudly opened the door himself. His driver lay horizontal across the floor, a bottle of scotch - house scotch! - in his hand. He breathed heavily, his lips flat against the wooden floor, his silver hair glowing like the moon in the light that seeped in from the hallway.

The room smelled of drunkenness.

"I won't tell on you, old man," Morgan whispered.

He went to the stable. He would drive himself.

Morgan in the driver's seat of the carriage clattered over the quiet, pre-dawn streets until he reached a tree-lined enclave in Greenwich Village, clambered down from his perch and tossed pebbles at a familiar window on the third floor of the fourth house on the left. At length the light came on, a face appeared at the window, and then a few moments later a lithe figure beckoned hurriedly from the front door.

In the dark wooden stairway: "What brings you here, at three in the morning?" She laughed, and Morgan looked her over, his twenty-three-year-old paramour, her dimpled, almost innocent face, her curly red hair. In a low, unsteady whisper, he attempted a joke: "I read the notices of Saturday's performance," he said. "I wanted to pay my respects to the new toast of New York."

"Your toast considers respects fully paid," she said, and she kissed him in the darkness.

The railroad king's mistress was a woman named Georgina de Louvre, or at least that's what she claimed, and in 1875 she was briefly a hit in the musical theater, but not so successful that she felt she could turn away from a man like Morgan, which was her problem, I suppose, and why she was ultimately doomed to failure. I met her some years later, after her affair with the big bear had waned, but not her strange enthusiasm for life. She told me stories about him, things that I probably didn't want to know, but which serve me well now in understanding him. For a very obvious reason he fell for an actress, a good actress, and a beautiful young woman with a pure white face – a girl who could be another girl.

And so it was that one dark night in 1875, finding himself unable to rest, John Pierpont Morgan hoisted himself from a bed chamber in which he saw ghosts and bounced along over cobblestone streets atop a wobbling, speeding carriage, all to bark orders at poor Georgina – to put her hair in a bun, to smile more subtly, not so deeply, to cast a timorous glance downward when she laughed, to speak more gently and to feel shyly attracted to him, but almost afraid to show it, like a young woman in love for the first time with a young man. He told her what she should feel in her heart, how her mind should work, the things that must interest her and the things that must not, and when the portrait and the performance were both complete, the most powerful man in the world settled comfortably and restfully into her arms in her little flat on the third floor of a rickety old wood-framed Greenwich Village house.

When Georgina told me this story, some years after its occurrence, I said that it reminded me of a motion picture called *Vertigo* that I'd seen on a trip to the 1950s, and which starred Jimmy Stewart. Although his politics were egregious, Jimmy Stewart at his best could be a good, obsessive actor, I pointed out to her, so I had some idea of what J.P. Morgan at his angst-ridden zenith might have been like. Georgina sort of laughed at this. Not knowing what the

1950s were, or motion pictures, or Jimmy Stewart, she thought I was making an obscure joke and not a very good one, but she was a polite girl who liked to please, and so she sort of laughed.

Georgina lay naked on the big bed. Morgan buttoned his pants, straightened his jacket, and examined his now-wrinkled suit in the mirror over the dresser. He looked like a gigantic ham stuffed into a beautifully tailored potato sack, and he knew it.

Georgina propped herself up on two elbows. Long dancer's legs stretched out along the length of the bed.

He cleared his throat, too loudly.

He squinted at himself in the mirror.

"Would you love me if I were not rich and powerful?" he asked.

"Of course," she replied. She was kidding. "Who says I love you, anyway?"

"Point taken."

He sat down at the edge of the bed.

"Scotch, please," he said.

"Yes sir."

She got up, poured him a glass, placed it in his hand, and wrapped her arms around him from behind. He took a big gulp, shuddered, and then he sighed.

"When Mimi died," he said, "we were in the Villa St. Georges, in Nice. At the top of a beautiful stone-walled street, with a view of the Alps. You should find a rich man to take you there, someday, Georgina. Not me, for obvious reasons."

Georgina smiled just a little.

"The Paris doctors said she had tuberculosis, prescribed turpentine pellets, cod liver oil, donkey's milk, and warm weather."

She knew that Morgan was beginning one of his rambling monologues, something Georgina expected from him by now, and, for that matter, from any man married to a woman who did not care for her husband.

"We traveled first to the Hotel de la Regence in Algiers," he said stonily, "but the consumption galloped through her body like a wild horse, from her left lung to her right. We went to the Riviera. She liked it there, as much as she could enjoy anything in those terrible precious days, I suppose."

Georgina took his hand, which was dry and hard.

"On the day of her death, we'd been married four months and ten days."

Morgan's eyes were glassy and brittle, like two muddy, frozen puddles.

"At our wedding, she wore a veil, so that the guests could not see how thin and pale she had become. She'd almost refused to marry me, on account of her illness, but I was convinced that my love could cure her. If not my love, then perhaps my money, which could buy her Paris doctors. The doctors recommended we not consummate our marriage until Mimi recovered; she never recovered. Hence, a marriage devoid of love-making, but not devoid of love."

His voice never cracked – he just spoke and spoke, his inflections blank and dull but somehow full of pain that could be felt in the room.

"On February 17, 1862, I saw her breathe her last breath. I begged her say one more word to me; just to hear her voice again, I would have given my entire fortune. I would still render myself penniless, just to see her again, even for just a moment. Maybe I will at that." He smiled slightly. "Then I will be a pauper. I will have no one. Not you, not Fanny. Not," he added, with near disgust, "the cheers of millions."

Georgina pulled him closer, pressed her face against his swollen, vein-tracked cheeks.

"Some people," she whispered, "think that you're a mean old bastard. Without any heart at all."

Morgan visibly shrank, his gigantic girth deflating, as air from a child's balloon.

"Some people," he grumbled, "say they can bring the dead back to life. Just for a while. For a hug, a kiss. A long-delayed honeymoon night. That's all. Some people make that claim. That's all."

Here he was, so weak and hopeless and without power. How did Jerome see his old boss now? Morgan might reasonably have wondered. As the mightiest man on Earth, the way the press, Wall Street's financial institutions and, increasingly, the average apple-seller on the street, viewed Morgan and his growing and tentacle-like influence? Morgan knew the answer; he was human, he had proved unable, with all his millions, to save the woman he loved more than anything on Earth; and he, too, would die. In Jerome's eyes, the stalwart Morgan had seen nothing more than pity that bordered on contempt. How did Jerome and Fawley and the Red Eyebrows do the things they did? It was something that he, Morgan, would never understand, and that all his money could not buy. He would never possess what his former protégé had found.

After a while, Georgina slipped from his arms. She was asleep.

The great man was alone in the dark.

CHAPTER 10

My night in the mountain mining camp passed without incident, and one hour before dawn, an emissary arrived from Sidonia, a burly but soft-spoken man named Monroe, who trotted into the ramshackle village on a big black horse. We lined up to greet him, but when I introduced myself, concern crossed his face.

"The great frontier hero?" he asked.

"The stories are greatly exaggerated," I said humbly, "many of them, of course, flattering, but completely untrue, while others have some basis in fact but were incorrectly reported by the newspapers with respect to certain details. And, furthermore, sir, as you may have heard, I've recently fallen from my professed 'greatness.'"

I heard myself talking too much, but I felt powerless to halt, and I kept going, like a toboggan down an icy hill. "Though, I should add, that the charge leveled against me, to the extent that I understand it, is completely – "

Holding up one mammoth hand, Monroe interrupted me impatiently.

"Shut up, Mr. O'Hugh."

He turned to his men.

"I don't trust him, I won't have him riding with us, and I won't allow him into Sidonia. Who will kill him?"

About two-dozen men, eager to prove themselves loyal to the Cause, stepped forward immediately, speaking quickly and urgently in unison.

Suddenly, Billy Golden, whom I had not seen since the night before the breakout, stepped from the crowd of rebels as though he had been there all along.

"I'll take him," Billy suddenly said, forcefully drowning out the din.

"You're his friend," said one young bandit.

Tang took a step forward. She lifted an enormous hog-leg pistol, against which she seemed to shrink into the cold dirt. The other fugitives moved away from her, nervous and a little frightened.

"I will kill him," she said. "I have no friends."

This, said with more than a hint of pride. The other fugitives, though bearing Tang no ill will, murmured in assent: none of them was her friend.

Monroe nodded to her.

"Take him away. I don't want to watch this. I don't want his blood staining our camp."

"Yes sir."

"Remember where you left the body," he added.

Tang turned to me, and her face was stony, but there was a smile somewhere in her head, in some nerve ending or synapse, and I heard her voice inside me, speaking to me as Emelina had once done in a sumptuous, wealthy and illegal gambling den just a few steps down the street from J.P. Morgan's mansion.

Don't worry, O'Hugh, she said to me. *Don't worry.*

Pushing our way through the closely packed spruce and fir, we marched over a small hill sandwiched between sheer granite cliffs, then over another hill, the clamor of the mining camp growing more remote. Tang was always a few feet behind me, but still I could somehow feel her pistol aimed at me, tickling my back. After twenty minutes or so, we advanced to a dead-end, a frozen clearing in the mountain wall surrounded on three sides by cliff. I turned around, my hands above my head. Behind Tang, a slight, crouched figure scrambled out of the brush almost without a sound, fluidly raised a shotgun and smacked the barrel against the back of Tang's head, shouted "Hands in the air!" and lifted her chin to the sun.

It was Emelina – my rescuer, my fearless hero. She'd followed me to Wyoming, hunched in the dark and watched the prison burn, finally tracking the band of outlaws through the mountains ahead of any lawmen or Laramie vigilantes. I wondered how I could have ever doubted her. Emelina's horse shuffled nervously behind her, ready to gallop on her command.

Emelina held her shotgun tightly against the stubble on the back of Tang's snow-white scalp. Tang raised both arms, her pistol dangling from her fingers.

"I won't harm him," she whispered into the cold wind.

Tang turned, her hands still above her head, until she was facing Emelina. A look of some significance passed between them, and then Emelina lowered her shotgun. She turned to me, and she walked a few paces in my direction. Tang didn't mean me any harm, she told me. Tang wouldn't hurt either of us.

"Keep your gun up!" I hollered at Emelina.

Emelina remained motionless, her shotgun idly aimed at the tangled root of a nearby tree that grew parallel to the jagged cliff wall.

"Watt," she implored, as though my distrust were unreasonable.

"Tang's gang wants to see my dead body," I said. "She can't return to them without my hide. Will she abandon her holy quest so readily? Are we three to run off together? Will we live as fugitives in the woods, with a little cabin, a brood of hopping outlaw children...?"

At these words, Tang in one swift motion lifted her gun and pulled the trigger. My forehead split in two, and I wondered, not for the first time, if this were what it felt like to die a terrible death. I staggered backward, skull aflame, and Tang's angry shriek echoed through the trees.

We all sat together beside the dead body, his head bloody and empty.

"Don't make jokes about a woman's children," Tang said.

She didn't look at me; her gaze was fixed to one dead hand, which was limp and bluish and burning a fist-shaped dent in the thawing ice.

"Explain this again," I said, my throat dry.

"Everyone is born with twenty-one essences," Emelina said. "You, remarkably, have learned to use twelve of yours without any instruction or tutoring. This" – pointing to the body lying face down in the ice – "is one you don't use, don't need, and won't miss."

"This is one," Tang said, "that could have wound up hurting you."

"Is it like killing?" I asked. "Is removing an essence like you're killing a person?"

Emelina thought about this for a moment, then turned quizzically to Tang, who grimaced.

"It is," Tang said, with just a hint of remorse. "A little bit."

The body, all six foot three of him, lay flat on his stomach in the mud, his blood flowing steadily into the dark red snow.

"Poor fellow," I said gently. Then, to Tang: "Maybe it was a bad idea to shoot me in the face. You have to deliver them a body, to prove my death."

She shook her head.

"I shot off his forehead," she said. "Face is recognizable."

I cringed, and Emelina rested her hand on my forearm.

"Tang knows what she's doing."

Tang nodded. This was, she told me, a good way to fake a death. In fact, the only infallible method. She recommended that I ask Billy, if I were to see him again. "He faked his death six times. Three times to get rid of bad essence, like taking out a tooth that aches. Twice to save his life. Once just for fun, just to read the obituaries." Billy, she told me, regretted that last one. Too many old ladies cried at his coffin. He felt sorry for them. He wouldn't try anything like that again.

"This kind of Magic," Tang said, "isn't meant for fun."

A map spread out on the rocks, Tang directed us to an efficient escape route through the west and then the southwest, pushing us into the Utah and then Arizona territories, vast, deserted areas, she believed, where the Sidonian influence for the time being was little felt, and where an outlaw could settle down for a time in anonymity. She tossed me a small cloth bag, tied at the top. "Here's money," she said. Then she remarked, rather carelessly it seemed to me, that she, Billy and the rest of the gang were heading hundreds of miles to the northeast, deep into Montana, a state she advised us to avoid entirely. I wondered aloud if her location were something she really wanted me and Emelina to know, and why she should deign to help us at all, now that Monroe had officially branded me an enemy of the coming revolution. Tang shrugged at this, and the tone of her reply was as impassive as ever.

"Do you think I am being nice?" she asked me. "You swore allegiance to Billy Golden and his Cause. We need you alive and healthy and waiting for the day that Billy calls on you to serve. I don't know why, but Billy thinks you are important. We have a deal, Watt O'Hugh."

CHAPTER 11

The two of us on Emelina's patient black horse, we crept nervously through the mountains, until, sufficiently east of Laramie that we no longer imagined the law sniffing our tracks, we descended to the Medicine Bow range, bought another horse from a ranching village, then galloped along the rolling grasslands, following the Oregon trail almost to the border of Utah territory. Every few minutes, I scanned the horizon in all directions, looking for small bouncing specks against the open sky, which might signal that a riding party had picked up on our escape route.

Maybe a washed up Western "hero" who'd done more good than alleged harm wasn't enough to warrant a bounty worth anyone's time. Emelina and I stayed ready to cut north again into the mountains, but, except for some lonely homesteaders' hovels standing forlorn in a sea of empty plains, we'd hardly have known that this was the Wyoming of the 19th century, and not some far earlier era. I was relieved that Emelina and I seemed to be safe; but I was a man who had recently danced on the roof beams of the New York Hippodrome to the cheers of multitudes, and I did not relish fading gently and anonymously into the grey skies of the frontier.

Under a small cluster of trees beside the bank of a trickling stream, we set camp for the night. By the light of the fire, huddled over our dusty map, we charted the course of the months ahead, a trek across Utah territory's brutal and endless desert basins and its green river valleys, followed by a nervous search for potential enemies from atop the lonely mesas that looked down on Arizona territory's empty plains. We would never dare travel by rail, lest a traveler spot my "Wanted" poster at his local train station. The more we planned, the further away our goal seemed.

Emelina put the map to one side.

"As I see it, we have a few options," she announced, her cheeks rosy from the glow and the heat of the fire. "Plan One: We can follow

Tang's directions, pick up a few unbranded strays, and settle down inconspicuously on the prairie."

I nodded. I saw some appeal in this scenario. Not a lot. I wasn't a real outlaw, I pointed out, and so I had no alliances with the underground. Were I to be recognized, I'd have a hard time developing trust, and the leaders of any bandit enclave might consider it to their economic and security interests to turn me over to the law. A lengthy or permanent sojourn south of the border, where Tang's money might really buy a fresh start, might be the most sensible plan.

"Or you could hide out," she suggested, "and I could travel back East as a liaison to Morgan. He seemed to like me. Right, Watt?"

Till you opened your mouth, I thought. But I kept quiet. Emelina must have left her clairvoyance switched on, because her face flushed with momentary anger.

"I could argue," she went on, brushing hurt feelings aside, "that you've done all you can. That you don't expect payment for your exploits, but that you've been shot off a building, slithered down prison walls, half-froze in a mountain river and took a bullet in the head, and that out of gratitude for a noble effort or penance for the injustice of it all, he might see the charges dropped."

I thought this sounded fine, but it's easier to railroad a guy into prison on trumped-up charges than un-railroad him. Too tough to explain. To Morgan, probably not worth the trouble or the considerable risk. He'd be more likely to use Emelina as bait to catch me than to set me free.

"It's remote," I said.

She said she knew, and she insisted that she was honestly ready to consider settling on the range with me, or even passing time in Bolivia. But she wouldn't wind up there as a victim of circumstance.

"Rough times squeezed me to the Kansas prairies and a life that yielded nothing but a hate-filled union and a couple of boys I probably wouldn't even recognize anymore."

She leaned closer to me. The firewood popped and hissed, loudly. "You understand, Watt?" she asked.

I was, she told me, still stewing over that infamous date: July 13, 1863. Now it was more than eleven years ago, but it burned in my mind as though it were yesterday.

"In July of 1863," Emelina asked me harshly, "did Lucy Billings desert you?"

The fire was burning out, just glowing embers now, but I hardly noticed.

"Riots were sweeping the streets," I said.

"But Lucy Billings," Emelina said, not letting up. "Did Lucy Billings leave you because she just didn't give a damn anymore?"

New Yorkers with no sympathy for President Lincoln protested the draft, I explained to her, set buildings aflame, chased the wealthy out of the city to huddle in fear behind the locked doors of their vast summer retreats. Except for the taverns, which did bustling business keeping the enraged rabble enraged, and some terrified and endangered Colored New Yorkers with no place else to go, the entire borough closed down and moved out.

"I spent July 13 facing down the mob," I added, "trying to save innocent lives. Without much success, I might add."

"Without *any* success, Watt, which is what *I* might add," Emelina pointed out. "It was an impossible goal, and you knew it."

"I saved a couple of them," I said, and I saw in my memory the faces of the ones I had saved. Then the faces of the ones I had lost, as the crowd carried me away.

I asked her what else she thought I could have done.

"Another man could have run and hid. But not you. It was your moment of pure, hopeless, crazy greatness, your moment of history, and you rose to it. How could I have turned you away after that?"

I asked how she knew about my past and about those terrible days. She sighed.

"How do I know anything?" she asked. "I just know, Watt. I've known about you from the beginning."

"Do you know about my ghosts?" I asked. "Do you know everything?"

Emelina smiled sadly, and she reached up and placed one hand tenderly on the side of my face.

"I know about your ghosts," she admitted. She knew, she said, about those unpredictable wraiths I'd carried with me from Little Mount to the Great Roman Hippodrome, who'd protected me from the bandits that night in Blue Rock – "Don't think I didn't notice!" she laughed – but, like the innocently callous children that they were, deserted me on the tenement rooftops.

"Who would you be, Watt O'Hugh" she asked, "without your little ghosts?"

Emelina didn't believe in my ghosts. She didn't believe in ghosts at all, or God, or Heaven, or meaning or purpose. She thought it made me feel brave to believe that my ghosts were there protecting me, like a child's guardian angels, which was why, she surmised, I so completely believed.

But in Emelina's view, even with apparitions swirling about me, unseen, perhaps twenty-four hours a day, I was still haunted most of all by the ghost of Lucy Billings, in her long-faded 1863 incarnation. I'd survived the riots, and when the smoke cleared, the last fire was put out, the rioters returned to their homes to sober up and prepare to fight the Confederacy, I'd found myself unexpectedly alone. Lucy Billings had left Manhattan, had left her furnished flat at the Fifth Avenue Hotel, had deserted her benefactors and her various devoted lovers, one and all; not least, Lucy Billings, without a tip of her ostrich-plumed hat to my heroism, had forsaken the one man who'd sworn always to love her more than any of the others could.

"Why did she do that?" Emelina asked. Surely, Lucy would not have fled, even given the disasters of the moment, had she truly loved the young Watt. Without so much as a letter of farewell? In spite of all the circumstantial evidence of her casual betrayal, the older, embittered Watt still needed more proof.

"The flame's burning out," I said.

"We'll toss more kindling on when we get back," Emelina assured me. "The whole journey will take a second. Less than a second. No time at all."

We sat together in the faint warmth of the dying fire, holding hands, the evening wind growing colder.

"Watt, you can't change anything. You must realize that. Where we're going, you can observe, but you can't change history. Do you understand?"

"What is this," I asked. "A séance?"

I'd heard of séances.

She shook her head.

"Close your eyes," she said. "Soon you will be back in July 1863. Soon you will be walking the Manhattan streets as they were before the War."

"I don't believe you," I said. "How is this possible?"

"Understanding it doesn't help," she said. "Not any more than understanding Newton's law of gravitation helped you keep your balance when you cycled down Riverside Drive with Lucy. If you've done this once, doing it again is easy. Just hold my hand."

I held her hand, and everything was very quiet.

"Try to listen to me – to my heart, to the sound of my auricles and ventricles, follow the electricity flowing across synapses to my cerebrum.

"Listen," she told me, "to the things you don't ordinarily hear."

I didn't know exactly what she meant – those long scientific body words were alien to me at the time – but I caught her meaning, mostly.

"Follow me," Emelina said, "down the rabbit hole."

I followed.

CHAPTER 12

Do different decades smell different? Does the tickle of a breeze or the heat of the sun in the 1860s feel different from the wind and the sun in the 1870s? I'd never wondered before, but when Emelina deposited me on Twenty-third Street between Broadway and Fifth Avenue on a sunny July day eleven years in the past, I felt as might a man of the late 20th century watching a rerun of *The Honeymooners* – even the air itself did not look the same, people did not move the same way. Everything was different. The past itself does not seem real when we visit it.

There I was, in my best going-to-meeting suit, standing before the Fifth Avenue Hotel, a bouquet of flowers on my arm. Built of gleaming white marble, six stories high and held aloft by rows of small columns fronting various fashionable stores, the Hotel had served as Lucy's tony home for a brief fourteen months, but on that fateful day, all those years ago, she already seemed an integral part of its mystique.

Feeling younger and unburdened by the traumas of the decade, I stepped across the front porch and into the spacious reception hall, with its frescoes and marble tiles, past the reading room and the elegant bar, which was already, at this hour, jammed with the oblivious and doomed gentlemen of the moment, many shortly to be ruined by the terrible gold crisis of 1869, though I felt for them no pity or sympathy, nor any urge to warn them of the coming tempest.

I swiftly strode past the Hotel's luxurious highlights, reached the front door of Lucy's flat, hesitated just a moment to get my story straight, and knocked.

It did not take much to explain, after all, my unexpected intrusion into her life at that moment. I had seen her just a few evenings earlier. I was a regular character in her ongoing melodrama. When she came to the door, her face lit up upon seeing me. I held out my flowers. She beamed more deeply. Golden hair danced about at her shoulders. Our eyes locked. My mind reeled. My world whirled. I fell for her, more deeply than before. I was lost.

Standing in the doorway, Lucy was dressed for her afternoon's lecture – a planned piece of political theater that she'd been rehearsing and re-writing for the last few weeks, ever since a splinter group of the Knickerbocker Ladies Cotillion had taken up the suffragist cause and had invited Lucy, a well-known high society free-thinker, to elucidate her thoughts on the right to vote. Though properly attired, she had not yet pinned her hair into a chignon; her locks hung freely, and she looked every bit the savage that she was.

"You tired?" she said to me.

"Tired?"

"Old. You've aged ten years in a day." She held a finger up to my face. "Around the eyes," she said, playfully massaging my new bags and wrinkles.

"The first New York draft notices are published tonight in the evening post," I said. "Just worried, I suppose."

"You've come to the right place," she said. "If you're drafted, I'll pay your way out."

She'd use money earned from sleeping with a wealthy geriatric murderer to bribe some other poor Five Points sap to get killed in my place. Perfectly legal, but questionable from the standpoint of social justice, which I might have thought my subversive Lucy would have realized. Now, anger rising, I remembered the sorts of arguments that Lucy and I used to have, passionate screaming matches about anything and everything that from time to time interrupted the delirium, yet had the beneficial effect of making our blissful interludes all the more happy for their absence. I restrained my righteous indignation, reminding myself that, after all, I'd fought the war, seen my share, and all that was over and done with.

"Consider yourself an Astor, my boy," she added reassuringly. "Astors never die, you know."

With a laugh, she bounced through her doorway, and I caught a glimpse of the lavish trappings inside her home, the fine furniture and expensive oil paintings expected of a cultivated lady of society, as indeed she was. I longed for that flat, for my nights in that flat. I longed for Lucy in that flat. I longed for Lucy. Even as she stood before me, young and vibrant and alive, I missed her terribly, this young woman, who naively thought she could protect me from the coming War, from death, from everything bad that Fate had in store.

A thought then occurred to me, as I'm sure it has to you, so I might as well address this delicate issue squarely and then move on quickly without dwelling at unnecessary length on prurient matters. Trans-time love-making, you ask – can it happen? As I've said, with the rarest possible exception, the only things a Roamer can affect are those that make no difference in the long run anyway, so the only kind of relations that could occur between a man and woman of different eras would be the empty and meaningless sort. For Lucy, even given her long list of lovers, it could never be that way.

We two stood in the hallway, Lucy's door just slightly ajar, and memories flooded my mind. I put a hand on her shoulder to draw her to me, and as the old fire lit up in her eyes, I felt my presence in this decade grow shaky, as though one inch closer and I would be cut free and shot back through the vortex. So I withdrew.

"Hungry?" I asked.

"Famished," she laughed.

"Take me to lunch," I said.

She shut her door behind her.

The Hotel was equipped with the first elevator in America – an "elevator," we called it back then, a novelty encased in quotation marks – but we avoided the ride and instead swept up the massive white marble stairway to the spacious hall on the second level, and into an enormous dining room with broad windows looking out over the bustle of Madison Square, the carriages clambering up the avenue and the throngs flowing along the broad sidewalks. The restaurant was already filled nearly to capacity with hundreds of lunch-goers.

Lucy, to the maitre-de: "You know Tomas, my brother."

The tuxedoed gentleman bowed to me slightly. "Good to see you again, sir."

Some of the items on the menu cost nearly five dollars, but I averted my eyes from the price. Lucy was quoting to me some of the most pleasing bits of propaganda from the text of her afternoon lecture, some of it fiery, some of it ironic and witty, all of it designed to tickle and please like-minded ladies. Without an omen of the portentous afternoon in store, Lucy began to plan for the evening's celebration, for a coming weekend in which she would entertain me in the surrounding countryside, and for the many weeks of summer to come.

Moved quite immensely by this itinerary of wonderful forthcoming events that I alone knew were fated never to occur, I said something charming and sincere, yet something so "of the moment" that, were I to scribble my words here for public consumption, I would render them maudlin and lachrymose and strip them of all poetry.

In response, Lucy smiled her most generous and eloquent smile, and she reached out and touched my hand.

"Why don't I skip this afternoon's presentation?" she asked. "Why don't I skip the rest of my life, Watt O'Hugh the Third? Why don't I change course? I have enough money to settle upstate, even if I marry a poor boy."

Of all the lousy timing! I'd spent the better part of my youth proposing to Miss Lucy Billings, offers she'd turned away so pleasantly and with such good humor that I'd never really minded. But why now, on this day of all days, did she choose to accept?

The string quartet quavered and wobbled out of tune, the bodies of the musicians twisting and turning like thin reedy trees in the wind.

Any desire to leave me heart-broken had occurred to Lucy Billings only much later in the day, likely after her much-anticipated lecture had degenerated into a free-for-all. If only the 1863 version of Watt O'Hugh – the one who wandered the city streets somewhere beyond the border that separated rich from poor - if only *he* had chosen this afternoon to appear at Lucy's door with an armload of flowers and a heartful of poetry.

The chatter of the crowd seated at the tables around us began to echo, as though I were separated from the other customers by a long, empty and dark tunnel.

I thought bitterly of my lost decade, the years I could have spent in Lucy's arms, had I only seized the moment.

Now my view of Lucy grew dim; I was watching her from underwater.

Her smile faded.

"You look odd, Watt," she said. Quizzically: "You look smoky. *Inconsequential.*" She laughed. "I don't even know what I mean by that."

I knew what was happening. In a moment, unless I took control of the past, Lucy would be sitting alone at the table, or back at her apartment, all memory of my visit erased from her mind. I summoned all the control I possessed and took a deep breath.

"Go to the meeting," I said, my voice weak. "You'd hate yourself if you didn't go to the meeting. We'll talk tonight."

She looked down at her food, fidgeted carelessly with her fork.

"You don't sound very happy," she complained.

Because I know what's coming, I wanted to tell her. *Because I know how this afternoon will end.* I wanted to shout this at her, to caution her, but I didn't do so, because I knew that the second I tried, the moment I opened my mouth with a warning in my heart, I would vanish from her reality, and I would never see her again; each instant was worth a ton of gold to me, and so I stayed quiet.

"I'm very happy for you," I said. "I'm very proud of you." Then, with more than a little effort: "I'll marry you in a minute, Lucy, Darling, if you mean it. All right? We'll make our plans tonight."

After we parted (with a kiss that nearly shot me back to the post-Reconstruction era), I made my way through the hazy, smoke-filled Hotel air, past porters lugging heavy trunks brimming with ladies' summer wardrobes, the office bell ringing and clanging non-stop. At length I reached the meeting hall, vast and elegant yet utilitarian at the same time. I sat in the back, the only man in the room. A few puzzled ladies looked my way, but most ignored me. Perhaps many could not even see me, this demon from an ugly future.

The chairwoman, plump, fiftyish and filled with decorum and light good humor, introduced Lucy as some sort of original thinker, cloaking her veiled words in euphemisms that I don't believe even she understood herself.

Then Lucy rose.

Her speech was both more riveting and more dreadful than I had once imagined from hearing the gossip afterwards and reading the newspaper accounts of the riot that would erupt during Lucy's lecture. She began by offering blank platitudes designed to accommodate the well-dressed throng before her, pat applause lines that fell within the framework her colleagues had uncompromisingly constructed. But only about two minutes into her presentation, her eyes fell upon the crowd, and I could see her discomfort begin as she looked out at the aristocratic and refined masks her erstwhile allies wore on their much-kissed kissers, applauding Lucy's prosaic speech with their spotlessly white gloves. Her face lost its docility, and her rebellion began in earnest.

I held my breath, as though the events of the afternoon were not pre-ordained. (To give you an example that you might understand, when you watch *Gone with the Wind* for the tenth time, maybe you still yearn for Rhett Butler to stay with Scarlett (and maybe someplace in your heart, you almost believe it can happen), or when you watch the Zapruder film, you hope against hope that this time through, the bullets will somehow miss, or perhaps hit only that rotten, two-faced Texas governor. Which is the feeling that came over me as Lucy pondered whether to confront the frauds and moralists before her – a fervent wish that, this time around, things would go differently.)

I could see the gears turning inside Lucy's head; her face hardening as she consciously rejected the bromides she saw now in her pages of notes, she turned away from the lectern and gazed angrily into the fat, pale faces bobbing before her like so many porpoises in a stormy sea. Suddenly, for the very first time, she was unwilling to overlook their lies, their bigotry, their sexual insincerity and their racial hatred. At the worst possible moment, she no longer wanted to be a part of their gold-plated world.

"Hypocrites," she cursed them, then outlined in graphic detail the daily life as she observed it of one of New York's ruling class trollops, an upper-class lady who meets a lower class companion (or the boyfriend of her sister, or daughter, perhaps!) in the elegant yet seedy uptown restaurants in the early afternoons, then squires him off to a downtown apartment kept, with her husband's idle acquiescence, for rendezvous of this sort. "You do not feel you are breaking anyone's trust, since you married the man who shares your chamber only after your first lover – a man to your liking, but not up to your social standing – made you with child at the age of seventeen, *yet again,* and your father refused to pay *for yet another* visit to Madame Restelle" – the wealthy abortionist to Manhattan's ruling classes, whose mansion on Fifth Avenue and 58th Street represented a sprawling, extravagant and taunting rebuke to the licentious rich and their indiscriminate children – "and insisted that something be done, and done quickly, leaving you with a passionless, almost neutered marriage and a child who resembles and daily reminds you of the man who, in the distant mists of memory, still makes your heart pound, still makes you fall to the bed in a swoon." She berated the urbane cotillion ladies for hiding – as though such things were shameful! – carnal desires more passionate, important and indeed urgent than the irrelevant right to choose a corrupt Tammany Hall fat-cat to take bribes for Boss Tweed as local city council representative, and she condemned them angrily for channeling the desire for the freedom they truly needed into this utterly pointless exercise. Did they fear, truly fear, as their propaganda stated, that if the federal Constitution were not amended to grant the women of New York the right to vote, freedmen from the soon-to-be defeated South would storm the cities, ooze up Fifth Avenue like a river of molasses, rip each rich lady from her effete husband's sickly arms and ride her into the night like a white bareback horse?

"Instead, I suggest," she said, her voice rising, "that you secretly desire this. You read your pamphlets by candle-light after your husband, fat and exhausted in his marble palace bedroom after a morning crushing the poor of the city and an afternoon spent whoring, has fallen instantly asleep. You read this again and again, you imagine these men arriving from the land of swamps and bogs and sweat and muscle. Your eyes scan the purplish paragraphs over and over in your back parlor when the lights are low, and the blood rushes from your head and you no longer think as a woman of society, a woman with a tea-cup in her hand and a finger sandwich in her mouth."

She pounded her fist on the lectern, seeking to silence the gasps that now rumbled throughout the meeting room.

"Why must you continue to punish the world for your shame? Must an earthquake swallow you whole, must Jesus himself walk on water in your very own bathtub, before you will admit who you are and demand to take pleasure where you find it?"

This dirty and blasphemous talk was bad enough, but when she called on one of the hotel's Colored cleaning women to enter the segregated meeting hall and demand her own rights in a firm but quiet voice, the assembled ladies had heard more than they were prepared to tolerate. One bejeweled woman with a hand-painted poster board stood up and stormed the stage, waving her sign vigorously and flattening other outraged suffragists in the process. As the mob charged like a herd of elephants gone mad, fear came into Lucy's eyes for the first time.

From behind, I felt Emelina touch my shoulder.

"There's nothing we can do," she whispered.

The chairwoman of the meeting reached the dais and leapt to Lucy's side, petticoat and bloomers fluttering as she flipped and flew like P.T. Barnum's most graceful acrobat-contortionist, grabbed hold of Lucy's chignon and pulled until the bun had come loose; fingers and fists tugged at long beautiful blond curls, Lucy's neck snapped to and fro like a piece of rubber, left and right, back and forth, and then other suffragists jumped in, grasping and pulling and dragging, and in a few cases, kicking and punching, until all of them were rolling about on the stage in a great screeching purple and blue ball of silk and velvet and lace.

Outside on the street, in an unrelated catastrophe, New York was about to descend into riots and burst into flames; already the screams of bystanders and miscreants wailed faintly in the far distance. Inside this hotel meeting hall, hands and knees pummeled the woman I loved; somewhere out there on the city streets, in a few hours, my younger self would fecklessly try to save the city's little children from the lynch mob's noose. Yet even with all this knowledge, and with all this urgency in my heart, there was nothing that I could do about any of it. The suffragists ran screaming around me, and, as my desire to save Lucy grew stronger, they ran straight through me. Emelina and I hurried out of the meeting hall into a hotel promenade now flooded with gaslight, where together we slipped from the moment. Our hands clenched tightly together, we slid through the darkness that separated me from my past, and we landed with a very gentle thump in Wyoming's dusty mountain snow.

It took me a few minutes just to get my breath back, to blink the fire and soot out of my eyes, and to erase from my mind the conviction that, as blackness closed in, I had heard, once again, the children screaming when the mob pulled them from my arms.

"That was quite an afternoon," Emelina said gently. "Quite a performance."

Shaken, I agreed. "Lucy was never one to do as she should." She was too disobedient even to engage in a bit of organized civil disobedience! I described her to Emelina, her self-education, her impossible temper, her fierce intelligence and a moral code that seemed to have wandered lost through a mirror from another world. My voice was filled now with more affection than usual, discovering, as I just had, that although Lucy had been forced to flee New York, she had done so with her mind filled with genuine love for Watt O'Hugh the Third. I realized, too late, that I was describing Lucy as though she were still mine, as, in fact, I deep-down believed she always would be, no matter how many miles, years, or gentlemen-callers separated us. "I guess she thought she'd get respectable in London," I explained. "Settle down to a regular, comfortable life. That sort of thing eludes her."

"You love her still," Emelina said. "You will always love her. Now you know that she loves you, as well."

I said that I was sorry in a dozen different ways, muttering and explaining and even trying a little prevarication in the cold midnight air; I almost said I'd marry her anyway. Why *not* marry her anyway? Lucy made me giddy, entranced, crazy and worse, but she didn't make me happy. I was happy with Emelina; now, decades and decades later, I can say that I think I was never as happy, before or since, as I was riding that rickety train with Emelina, a new future, we thought, opening up in front of us. Yeah, and that engine blowing. I'll never forget the way that train engine blew, the look on Emelina's face and I guess probably the look on mine, too, and thinking that this is what my life would be like from now on.

I didn't ask Emelina to marry me, though. I touched the side of her smooth face with one calloused hand.

"I must be out of my mind," I said.

"You must be," she agreed readily and sadly. "You must be crazy, Watt O'Hugh."

I just looked into her eyes, drinking them in, a thirsty man embarking on a long journey with one last sip of water.

She spoke to me again in my mind, her lips not moving.

You can join us, I heard her gentle voice whisper. *Don't you see, Watt, my Darling, what I can offer you if you will turn your back on the past, and Lucy Billings and terrible memories? Join us. Become like me. Never get old. Never die. Or, at least, not for a very very long time.*

With these words, and without warning, Emelina and I spiraled up above the mountain peaks like fireworks into the speckled night sky. Were we really flying, was my physical body violating all those laws of physics that no one had ever bothered to teach me on Randall's Island, or were our minds, beautifully intertwined, soaring loop-de-loops through some waking dream? Again, I don't know. All I can tell you is what I saw, felt and heard that night, and what I saw were the brown tips of dry and brittle trees and our little smoldering campfire far below us, a glowing pinprick amidst hundreds of grey miles of dusty, grassy plains; what I felt was the night wind blowing through my hair as we glided into the sky; and what I heard was Emelina's voice, pure as spring water, sweetly reciting blasphemy as though it were a psalm. *I cannot be saved because I do not believe. You cannot be saved because there is no one to save you. Saint Peter cannot await your arrival at the pearly gates, because there are no pearly gates. There is no God. There is no Jesus, not anymore. All that exists is what you see: the parched Wyoming plains and our dried out stream, and the mountains on the far horizon. You have a few more years of life, or a few thousand. Or more.*

Depending on what I chose. I turned to her, and she was floating in the stars, a beautiful constellation holding out her hand to me. Had I reached up to touch her, who knows how high we would have flown?

There were others like her – legions, or a small, exclusive club? I didn't know. Tang was like her, and yet they'd never met before that evening by the cliff wall. I wondered who they were, what they were, but only slightly. A coven of witches was the simplest explanation, so that's what I figured.

Maybe *you'd* guess they were from outer space. Or members in an international Internet cult. Or you'd suggest I was just hearing voices.

These are 21st century obsessions. Back then, in my time, we didn't think too hard about aliens walking among us, or about international conspiracies, or even about people with voices in their heads. How could we? We were too worried about the *witches,* for God's sake!

As for the life she offered me, I can't say whether I really believed her at the exact moment that such a proposition escaped from her mind. All I knew was how much I would miss her, and miss her more, as the days turned into weeks, and weeks into years, and years into a life stretched beyond breaking. I believe her now, decades and decades later. But I suppose the young Watt O'Hugh reasoned that everything in life has a price; even if she told the truth, a gift that miraculous could not come for free. And I could never meet her conditions. I would never forget Lucy. I would never leave her behind.

"When I'm an old man ..." I said haltingly, after I'd turned away, obliquely refusing her gift, and after we'd suddenly reappeared beside our little fire, by our little stream. "If I'm an old man, I mean, and if I live through all this, come see me, Emelina. Knock on my door and come in, young and beautiful, and laugh at a silly old superstitious man."

She smiled, but she stayed silent.

"Please, Emelina?"

"It would destroy you," she said. "I don't think it would make you happy to see me again, if I were young, and you were old. Knowing the life – the *lives* – that you had refused. I think you would hate to see me again."

"I'd like it," I insisted. "I mean it."

I did mean it, too.

Emelina made no promises. I still think about her every day. Maybe the choice she made was evil. Maybe there's no such thing. Now, so close as I am to Eternity, I don't care anymore. All I know is that I miss her. In the world's cities, I have seen her smile out of the corner of my eye at numerous street corners. I turn, and she's gone.

Did I *never* see her again? I will leave you in some suspense on that question. But I can tell you that she's not here with me now, and that at night, even here on my ranch, when the night is the darkest, and the wind howls outside, and the house creaks lightly, as though a young woman were scurrying on tiptoes across the floorboards, and shadows pass before the moon – even now, every night, I wait for the door to fly open, and for Emelina – surely more beautiful than I remember – to walk slowly and gently into my room, to stare into my eyes and, accepting the invitation I offered her all those years ago, to laugh at the silly, superstitious and deeply regretful old man I've become.

CHAPTER 13

When Darryl Fawley entered his wife's domain, he came upon a beautiful, dying woman lying in a once-magnificent bed chamber that now seemed to be clinging to its existence as precariously as was the young woman. The velvet walls were tattered, and satin sheets wrapped about Lucy Billings Fawley's frail, exquisite body were moth-eaten and frayed.

When Lucy heard him enter the room, she looked up and opened wide her blind eyes. Fawley walked under an intricately carved stone portal past roses that bloomed, as ever, a deeper red than existed outside Sidonia. As he approached, his fingers idly touched the priceless and beautiful treasures that his wife could no longer see, and he sat down at her bedside. He gently took one feeble hand in his.

"Darryl," she whispered, and he hushed her, but she kept speaking, wearily begging his indulgence. She had tried her best, she insisted to him; couldn't he remember, years ago, that she had accompanied him on the arduous and dangerous trek to the inner reaches of Cathay in search of the secret of the Red Eyebrows, that she had joined him in his dreams, they had held hands in the clouds, above a make-believe castle surrounded by gardens of blooming lupines and lavateras that changed color in the wind? She begged him to remember that she had been there at the rhapsody's birth, and that she had loyally followed her husband to reality's edge.

He tenderly caressed the pale skin on her hand. There was nothing that could be done to help it, not anymore, he told her. With tears in his eyes, he asked whether she realized that she would have to abandon the palace, and that otherwise she would die. She nodded sadly.

"Let's leave Sidonia," she said. "Let's leave it to others. Surely Jerome will send you a stipend to reward you for your foresight."

They could live out their lives at the English seaside, she told him as forcefully as she could. She tried to describe this other life, the sound of the waves, and tea on frosty mornings. She tried to make it sound very quiet and comfy and English, her voice subtly, politely sexy and inviting – as bluntly sexual as she thought English marital protocol would allow.

"Rescue me, Darling," she implored him.

Fawley was quiet, his mind racing in the stillness of the room. Could it be, he must have wondered, that anything in this world really meant more to him than the heavenly Lucy Billings, whose heart he had fought so hard to win? Perhaps even then, with Lucy at her weakest, drained of her life and fire by the unknowable force that resided in this imaginary city, he knew – as I, hundreds of miles from her bedside, also knew so clearly – that now Lucy could never love him, no matter how hard she might have tried, and would, true to her promises, continue to try, to the end of her days. Perhaps that was why he turned from her in her most desperate moment.

Fawley stood from the bed, his back to his wife, and he stared out the window at the childish and mythical landscape he had designed for her amusement when she first fell ill. Outside, Satyrs and unicorns still frolicked in fields of clover, but less happily than before. Fawley wondered if they knew why the spring had gone out of their step, why the scent of lilacs had left the air.

"I cannot leave here, Lucy," he said. "I'm sorry."

"I have tried my best, Darryl," she said. "Will you give me my freedom?"

She couldn't see him shake his head, but she heard his answer in his silence.

"There is a little town in Nebraska, called Weedville," he said, "which is loyal to Sidonia. You will convalesce there until you are well enough to return."

"I will never be allowed back in," Lucy said. "You know that. Set me free. Let me return to New York. Let me have a new life."

"All your needs," he said softly, "will be attended to in Weedville."

He didn't move a muscle. In the distance, a faerie fell suddenly from flight and fluttered about in confusion on a patch of parched, gray grass.

"I will be imprisoned," Lucy said calmly. "You are imprisoning me."

"I will always love you," Fawley said.

"I," said Lucy, "would have been loyal to you for the rest of my life."

With a hurried abruptness, and without another word, he made his way out of the majestic bed chamber, pushing from his mind the single image that had occupied his thoughts for the last several years, that of Darryl and Lucy Fawley seated atop adjoining thrones to usher in a new era of peace and happiness. He blocked out, as well, his starry-eyed dreams of earlier years, of leading a simple yet happy life with Lucy's arms about him, loving him with all her heart, a scenario he knew his overwhelming ambitions and deep lustful hatred had now made utterly impossible.

As he left, Lucy said not a word, wept no tears. He did not look back, but if he had, he knew, he would have seen the old rebellion shining in her sightless eyes.

CHAPTER 14

The next morning, our paths diverged. Conveniently, Emelina decided to head to the northeast, while I knew that I had no choice but to continue to flee southwest.

"I'll never forget you, Emelina," I said solemnly, and Emelina replied matter-of-factly, and without any animosity, that she was quite sure she would eventually forget me completely. "But, after all," she added, "I have many more years ahead of me. Thousands of years. I can't be expected to remember everything. It really can't be helped, can it?"

I nodded.

"That's probably true," I admitted.

We sat there awkwardly, both of us on our horses, packed up and ready to go, the wind kicking up clouds of dust around us.

"I saw my little boy the day you were captured," she said.

"How?"

"I hovered invisible outside of his sod house. His father was dead. My little boy was drinking his father's whiskey. He'll do all right, I think. He'll work the land. Find his sister a husband in town who will sign up as a farm hand as part of the deal, maybe. Get himself a mail order bride in a couple of years. I'm quite certain that he'll do all right." After a little pause: "I hadn't expected his father to die like that, so suddenly. I had not seen that in his future."

I asked her how she felt about her husband's death, and Emelina replied, "Tell me how I'm supposed to feel, and that's how I'll feel."

After she rode off, I watched until she was just a tiny dot on the horizon. Then I turned and clicked my heels into my horse's side and galloped as fast as I could in the opposite direction.

CHAPTER 15

After Emelina left me, I worked my way south, straddling Colorado and Utah territory, keeping a watch out for bounty hunters and Pinkerton eyes, but with considerably less focus than before. I picked up some old habits. I fell into a few drunken card games along the way, and while I was losing a sizable chunk of Tang's money, some people got a good look at my face, though, in the sober light of morning, I calmed my addled brain by insisting to myself that this highly wanted mug was now bearded and haggard beyond recognition.

Hundreds of miles southeast of the territorial pen, in a slightly decrepit, slightly sad Colorado mining town that had seen better days, and would soon see worse, I sat in the dark and ramshackle Whitey's Saloon, buying my rotgut whiskey with yesterday's poker winnings. I'd been at it a few hours, and so the place was starting to look nice. Winnie, the saloon's one bar-girl, circulating among the town's grizzled old survivors - well, she still looked old and beaten down, but I was starting to see that as the natural order of things. In the corner of the saloon, the owner, a successful miner of yesteryear, pounded out a serviceable but uninspiring "Little Brown Jug" on a tinny piano.

A tidily dressed man in his mid-thirties sat down beside me. He had a big clean and white face, and, at the top of a long forehead, prettily feathered tufts of whitish-blond hair. His name was Tippens, he said.

"Mr. Watt O'Hugh?" he asked.

"I have nothing to say to you," I replied quickly, and stood.

He told me to sit down. That he'd have the law on me in five minutes unless I listened to his proposition. He was offering me a job on behalf of his boss, a wealthy Wyoming land baron – a fat cat I knew well during my years as a drag rider, a fellow with no real sense of civic obligation who was, as it happened, doomed to be murdered in his sleep within the decade, and everyone but the tycoon himself realized it.

"Some day, Mr. O'Hugh," he said, "you'll be a rich man, with more head of cattle than you can count, and more acres of land than you can count, and more money than you can count, so you'll hire someone to count it all for you."

Seeing my whiskey glass empty, he gestured to the bar-keep for another, which arrived quickly. I agreeably accepted the drink, if not his unlikely predictions of my future, and I downed the whiskey in one smooth gulp.

"It's a war out there," he said. "My employer owns the land, he owns the cattle, and he means to protect it."

I just nodded.

The baron had a "dead list" of fifty names, ranchers and their families allegedly infringing on his property rights and determined not to move. He was recruiting cattle inspectors and a sizable vigilance committee that would enforce the law of the West.

"Another whiskey?" Tippens asked cheerfully.

I nodded. I'd taken the worst room at the town's one hotel, I didn't know how I'd pay for tomorrow's rent, and, since I, having committed no crime, was nevertheless an outlaw with a bounty on my head, I'd started wondering whether I oughtn't to begin making some money at this villainy business. Tippens' offer wasn't a line of work that appealed to me, though the saloon and the near-full moon hovering outside its mud-coated window, the cartoonish denizens, the bearded bar girl, the dusty night and the bounty on my head all gave my situation an air of unreality. If this had been the 1950s, when tough-guy Western motion pictures were "in vogue" (as you might put it), I would have said that I felt as though I were in a movie. Dizzy, I looked down on myself from some other place, maybe the third row, balcony.

"This will be a quick surgical military strike," Tippens said, "and we will pay you handsomely."

"Not interested," I replied. "Thanks for the booze."

"You don't have a choice," Tippens said. "If you refuse, your name gets added to the dead list. If you accept, after you leave our employ, I promise you freedom. You'll have a new identity, a thriving dry goods business in a bustling Kansas town, as well as the protection of the local police."

A bottle, half-full, shattered over the piano player's right shoulder, the music stopped for a moment, and Winnie hurled an old whiskered drunk outside face first into a rising cloud of cold midnight dust. Now others stood, a few loaded old coots, one big fat guy with a beard down to his navel. They surrounded Winnie. The leathery, fuzzy old woman looked afraid, backed away. Whitey, over in the corner, kept playing as he glanced nervously at the proceedings, his rhythm slipping and warping like an old water-logged wooden house.

"Oh, for Christ's sake," I muttered, annoyed, and I stood.

"Not your business, Watt," Tippens said amiably. "Another drink?"

"Your killings can wait five minutes," I said, and I ran to the middle of the action. I asked, pleasantly enough, whether it really took all three of them to fight a woman. The fat guy turned around, I grabbed a drink from the bar, tossed it into his left eye, and from the way he blinked and yelped, fire practically leaping from his retina, I can only figure it must have stung. I swung with my left and crushed his nose in a couple of places with two heavy punches. His head snapped to the right and he staggered back a few paces; one of his friends drew a .45, stuck the gun up my nose and pulled the trigger. I felt little more than a slight tickle; the gun backfired, a blast shattered the ceiling and wooden shards cascaded down on all our heads. I silently thanked my ghosts, who, I fervently believed, had stuffed their resilient little fingers into the pistol's barrel, saving my sinuses. "Better late than never," I added, charging at the startled old gunman. I yanked his right arm behind his back until it snapped and bone ripped open his sleeve.

Well, I hadn't really expected that, but it did the trick, nonetheless. I teased the gun out of his fingers, he fell to the ground whimpering, and I guess he learned not to pick on women. But in the meantime, the saloon had erupted into chaos. Someone had thrown Tippens over the bar, and he lay prone on the floor, his eyes half open, in a puddle of moonshine. I figured I'd slip out the back way, but all the doors were blocked. I dusted off both fists and prepared to punch my way out.

At that moment, the piano took off, fingers pounding on the keys insistently, and I turned and saw a tall figure in the shadows at the corner of the room. Not the owner, but someone new. The piano player began to sing, loud and unrelenting, with a voice like a boxing match without gloves. I remember the song, too. It was a stupid little ditty called "Give It Back to the Indians," but which seemed somewhat appropriate, given that the performer was serenading an entire saloon of angry drunken white men on stolen Indian land who were prepared to kill each other without any of us having the slightest idea why, nor having thought about it, either. (For the record, "Give It Back to the Indians" was written by Rodgers and Hart – or maybe Rodgers and Hammerstein – but not for something like fifty years after that memorable night, a discomfiting fact that none of us drunken whities in Whitey's Saloon could have realized at the time.)

Everyone in the saloon turned, the piano player belted out the rest of the song, from time to time taking his hands off the keys to snap his fingers, pounding out harmony with his feet. Drunk as I was, I'll never forget that goddamn stupid-ass song, but I'll also never forget how that son-of-a-bitch could sing, like he was beating the crap out of a hundred happy men, every one of them loving it. The song ended, and he sang another punchy crowd-pleaser, this one about a vicious murderer (again, for the record, it was a number that wouldn't be composed until many decades later), then a morbid but high-energy show-stopper about a little orphan girl freezing to death in her windowless tenement apartment. Finally he stood, to whoops of joy and thunderous applause, and he hollered, "God bless you, you've been a marvelous audience!" The crowd was in a frenzy, but a frenzy that left them sated and drained them of their blood-lust. As the last screams died down, he shouted to the appreciative crowd, "End war; love each other; don't kill each other, brothers." He worked his way through the barroom, clasping hands, signing autographs, accepting kiss after kiss from the appreciative Winnie.

Today, as I write this, in the 1930s, one singing cowboy makes movies in which he melts his villain's heart with a gentle little song gently strummed on a guitar beside a campfire. By the time of the Millennium, that kind of hokum will have seen its day. Nobody will believe it anymore.

Maybe it takes three songs, not one, and maybe only a real Vegas showman could pull it off – even some seventy years before Vegas came into existence as a cultural phenomenon (as you, my readers, will know it in your day) – but I've seen the technique in action, and it can be done.

Tippens dusted off the glass shards, grabbed hold of the edge of the bar and unsteadily pulled himself back up, staggered to his seat at my table, smelling like three a.m.

"Now then," Tippens coughed, dispensing with any seamless segué. "About our range war."

My heart was thumping all over my body. I couldn't listen.

A dark figure sat down between us. I didn't look up. I knew who it was – Billy Golden, the hardest working guy in the business and the show-stopping savior of Whitey's Saloon.

"Hit the road, bad man," he said to my guest. "You want to kill people, kill them yourself, if you've got it in you. The Third's no murderer, in spite of what you've heard."

Out the door went my last chance at financial redemption. The singer ordered a sarsaparilla and made himself at home.

"He wasn't talking murder for hire," I argued lamely. "He needed soldiers for a precise little surgical extraction."

Billy didn't answer this, and I knew why.

"Eternal life, the fountain of youth, the love of a beautiful woman," he said smoothly, changing the subject. "Three for the price of one. Not offered to a man every day, you know." Then, after a suitable pause: "No wonder you're grumpy."

"Yeah," I said. "Blah blah blah."

I'd just made that up, but I thought it had a nice ring to it. *Blah blah blah.*

Billy plunked a hand on my shoulder.

"Passion killer," he said. *"Qu'est-ce que c'est?"*

"Goober Peas" rang, out-of-tune, in my ears.

"You let the guards die," I said. "Some plan."

Billy replied, a little shrug in his voice. "Don't worry about them," he said. "They're fine. I went back and fixed it in the editing room."

"Whatever that means." I looked up at him. He was older than I'd ever seen him, a man in his early seventies, and he looked tired, finally. As tired as I felt.

"You left *me* to die," I said. "After asking me to trust you."

"I didn't leave you to die," he said. "If I'd left you to die, you'd be dead, you ungrateful son-of-a-bitch."

"Yeah, well. Thanks."

"For a famous Western hero, you're dumb as a skunk. It's dark in here, but how long do you think it will be before someone recognizes you who can hurt you? I'm about a half hour ahead of the bounty hunters."

I was in no state to put up any real resistance, and, besides, I didn't want to. I liked Billy, and, in spite of everything, I still trusted him.

I stumbled after Billy through the mountain town, down a steep hill and past precariously leaning buildings, ramshackle and blasted to splinters by a hundred stray bullets over the years. A moth-eaten red curtain hung from the third floor window of a long-abandoned whorehouse, and one stage-coach sat at the town's perimeter, waiting for the morning, when, more likely than not, a few more distracted residents would flee its depleted mines.

The hotel's floorboards creaked loudly under our boots. Tang awaited us upstairs, sitting patiently in the seedy room's only chair. Her well-fitted man's suit freshly dusted, derby resting comfortably in her lap and her shotgun idle on the table beside her, she didn't match the surroundings, and she resembled nothing so much as a wealthy gentleman visiting either the poor relations he's left behind or a destitute hooker whose morphinic grip he can't quite break.

"Mr. Tang," I said, impressed and still drunk. "How handsome you look!"

Tang didn't acknowledge my wobbly attempt at humor. She barked a few orders at me. Bossed around by Madame Tang again, I felt like her infant son, and I wondered what had happened to her own children. Whether they had grown up and left home. Whether everything had worked out all right, for all the sacrifices she'd felt required to make on their behalf. Pack up, she commanded me, splash the face, prepare to ride out immediately. I explained that, having nothing to my name but the clothes left on my back when she deserted me in the Wyoming Rockies, I was already thoroughly packed up, and I wondered aloud what had become of the Great Proletarian Revolution, of Allen Jerome's glorious worker's paradise?

"Destiny," Tang said, "is like a hunk of clay. You can work with it, reshape it, mash it back into nothing and start from the beginning. Eventually it dries. At that time, so to speak, you either have a beautiful piece of art, or you don't." She gestured towards Billy. "He knows how to work the clay. Maybe he's the only one."

Billy nodded.

I must have seemed doubtful of this colloquy, because Tang suddenly screamed at me, as though I were quite blind, "Haven't you noticed that Billy keeps getting older and younger, day to day?"

"I thought, you know, that he has good days and bad days."

"One day," Tang yelled, incredulous, "he's sixty years old! The next day, twenty! Then fifty! Then *seventy!*"

I tried again. "I thought that, well, that he just ties one on, tries to kick the habit. Spends time in prayer. *'Sorry Jesus – one more chance?'* and all that sort of thing. Drinks a lot of vegetable juice or something. Then he's tempted all over again. Gambles and boozes, and maybe worse. All the rehabilitation for nothing. Back and forth. Over and over."

"He roams around in Time!" she bellowed at me, as though this were a more sensible explanation than the one I'd devised. "Pops in on us, every once in a while. One day, as a sixty year old. One day as a twenty year. He's roaming around in Time, trying to fix everything."

"I didn't think of that one," I admitted sheepishly.

"Can't you see what's right in front of your nose?"

Tang was so disgusted by my stupidity that she couldn't even look my way.

"How do you do all this?" I asked, trying, by showing some interest, to work my way back into their good graces. "How can you change the past, when the rest of us can't?"

"He has an utterly pure heart," Tang said.

"I have an unusual preponderance of oligodendroglia cells in my brain," Billy added.

"He was born," Tang added, "without a lateral fissure, and as a result, his inferior parietal lobe has grown quite large."

"But," Billy concluded, "we don't really know for sure."

I shook all of this jargon out of my head. I was drowning and confused.

"Listen," I went on. "This popping in and out of Time. I never even *tried* it before a few weeks ago. I didn't even know that this was such a popular pastime." I paused, feeling squarer than square (as you might say, if you're reading this in the 1960s), and I tried to compensate. "Don't get me wrong," I said. "I mean, I liked it. I liked it *okay.* I wouldn't want to make it my life's work, you know?"

"I keep hoping for Utopia," Billy said. *"That's my* life's work."

"He feels very strongly about them, Fawley and Jerome," Tang said. "He worked with them and tried to help them, in an alternate past –"

"And an alternate future," Billy added.

"And an alternate future," she said.

"Fawley and Jerome might have brought Utopia," Billy said. "But now they can't. By 'now,' I don't mean 1875. I mean Time circled around again and again and again, and a couple of roll-arounds ago, their destiny was set. Will they win or lose? I don't know. But they no longer have the potential to be good men. They will be great men of history. That's always been inevitable. But they will not be *good* men."

"Beware," Tang said, "of men preaching compassion. I don't think the man's been born who can envision Paradise and decide to share it with the world."

"I haven't given up," Billy said, but the sadness in his voice told me that he had come very close. "I'm working now on a guy named Mao who has some possibilities. I've nearly had some luck with a guy named Jesus Christ."

"You've heard of Him," Tang said. For the first time in my presence, she might have cracked a smile. But if so, it was a smile so brief that, after it vanished, and after her face settled again into a dispassionate stone mask, I could question my own memory and wonder anew if she had ever smiled in her life. Now I believe it to have been my imagination.

"I keep going back, trying again and again," Billy explained.

"He could have been the savior of Man," Tang said. "But his *hubris*. Billy's been through this with him maybe a dozen times. Every time, his hubris sinks him."

Billy held up a finger to silence my objections, although I had none.

"The New Testament was written in bits and pieces, every chapter composed many years after the fact," he said. "Only the apocryphal texts even come close, and even they're filled with gaping holes. *Believe* me, you don't know the full story."

He and Tang exchanged a brief, sad glance.

"Anyway," Billy said. "*Your* destiny is with us. And we don't want you to fall into the hands of the bounty hunters, and we don't want you shot to death in a bar fight."

"What if I don't accept this destiny?" I asked. "What if I don't go with you?"

"Then your legs will stop working," Tang said. "They will crack beneath you."

"And worse," Billy said. "Tang giveth, and Tang taketh away, but when she taketh away she tosses in a little vengeance. You know, it's only fair. You swore an oath. And she *did* give you a great gift."

Then he waved all this away, as though it were a silly misunderstanding between friends.

"O'Hugh," he said. "I have been working on your destiny, and on your past. It's not easy to do. You won't be a great man, I think. But a useful man. A worthwhile man. That's more than most people can aspire to. So come along for the ride, and don't be a troublesome boy."

I told you that we Roamers can visit the past and the future, but that it is not ours to change. An exception, as you've no doubt realized by now, is the great Billy Golden, a hero to all of us who parade back and forth from decade to decade. Maybe he's the *only* exception. I don't know how in the world he does what he does. To us, he's like Houdini to the illusionists.

The ability to change the past and to shape the future, of course, brings a great burdensome responsibility, which Billy, a man with two tons of social conscience to begin with, finds particularly consuming. We age more slowly in Other Time, so he's been able to spend more than a few lifetimes trying with varying degrees of semi-success to re-write the worst atrocities of history. Still, he's been known to take Time out from his busy saving-the-world schedule to drop in on the 1960s and early 1970s and play a few gigs in your Vegas, make an Ed Sullivan appearance or two. On your TV screen, sometimes he's a young guy singing rock 'n' roll, and sometimes he's an old bald guy belting out show tunes. For fun, in 1973, he assassinated an unproductive essence and faked his own death – newspaper reports indicated that he croaked due to complications from a routine dental cleaning – just to watch the young rock 'n' roll chicks cry. His old Vegas ladies cried much louder, and he felt guilty, tried to go back and turn it all around, but the cement had dried. The hoax was his legacy. By the time of the Millennium, old ladies still watched specials about him on PBS, dabbing Kleenex to their eyes. "It's good for them," Billy Golden figured with a sigh. "Catharsis. Psychically healthy."

Billy's tinkered with most every major social movement of the last few centuries, and some going back many more years. He admits to working with Jesus, but some Roamers insist that Billy is the Savior himself, and that one day we'll all awake to find that his first century fidgeting has paid off, our universal past has shifted and we're all living in a 2000-year-old Paradise governed by a scruffy and unshaven but hugely benevolent Messiah.

I hope so.

Not holding my breath, though.

CHAPTER 16

Billy accompanied us out of that little Colorado town, just to keep an eye on us and to see to it that we escaped the city's metaphorical walls alive and safe, but soon after he left us. We looked and he was there, and then we looked and there was nothing but sunlight shining through the dust in the air. Tang and I rode into Utah, where I took a job as a ranch hand, breaking horses, which I was good at. I assumed a new identity as a drifter named, oh, let's say, "Tom Shaw", and, what-the-hell, maybe I'm from Kansas. The boss was round and stout and bald, but solid and strong as a rock. I don't think he believed a word of my story, and I didn't try all that hard to convince him, but he probably didn't suspect that I was in fact Watt O'Hugh III. I now had a tangled beard, my brown hair was long and unkempt, my eyes bloodshot, my skin veiny and leathery from sun and drink, and so I didn't look much like my wanted posters. There was also, I figured, a good chance that the trail had just gone cold. The gang from the Wyoming prison had seen my dead body in the snow and ice, and I hoped the Pinkerton boys had heard the news too. The boss looked at me sideways, but he didn't ask me any particularly probing questions.

"I have a plan," Tang confided to me, as we bid temporary adieu at the ranch's front gate, she on her ageing stallion, and me on my bay gelding. The same horse that had carried me across the plains, a quiet, steadfast friend. "My plan," Tang went on, "is get a big, big army, plow through Idaho and central Montana." Then, at the nation's apex, she explained without much enthusiasm, she would ride into Sidonia, leading her troops like King David, "and we shoot everybody, bang bang, till everybody's dead!"

I patted my horse gently.

"This horse," I said, "is my only friend. The only friend I have left."

She shrugged.

"*I'm* not your friend, O'Hugh," she said. "Keep your horse close."

I guess that was a joke.

Though I was growing more and more puzzled about my ultimate role in her machinations, she promised me a retainer till she needed me again and warned me darkly not to try to escape her clutches. Then she rode off, and I watched her shrink into the vast Utah horizon until she was just a little speck bathed in a pretty sunset. I hoped I'd never hear from her again, even though I could use the dough. I was drinking pretty heavily at the time, and drinking that heavily costs a certain amount of money. By now I was what *you* would call an "alcoholic", though in my view I was a fellow reacting quite understandably to the slings and arrows of outrageous fortune. But I had not yet sunk so low that I would drink just *anything*. I still had my standards, after all. So when the salary she promised me arrived at the ranch for the first time, I greeted it with a mixture of horror and gratitude. The pay arrived the following week, and then again, week after week, regularly each week, and what she paid me for doing nothing, combined with my pay as a ranch hand, bought me enough smuggled Monongahela to let me drown my sorrows (of which I had many) each night, and to collapse into a fitful, restless sleep. I dreamed about Lucy invariably, and about my moment in the spotlight in New York, and I woke up sweating and shouting and wondering how my life had come to this.

Tang's plan, as she no doubt realized even better than I, was not a good one, but to be honest with you, my own plan was to drink myself into a stupor till I could figure out how to ditch Tang for good, without getting caught. Sure, she and Billy had cured me, and in exchange, I'd sworn an oath to them in the Wyoming prison, but I was sticking with her only out of fear, not obligation. Once I escaped, I planned to move south and team up with Tiburcio Vasquez. Vasquez was the only outlaw in the West who had ever actually offered me a job, though that had been some years earlier, and how I would find him, I couldn't tell you. In my sober moments, I realized that I didn't have it in me to join Vasquez, a horse thief, rustler, robber of trains, stagecoaches, ranches, inns and stores, and a dance-hall murderer.[*] But my sober moments were few and far between.

I worked at the ranch for a while, but I'm not sure exactly how long, because my journal entries, which by the week were growing

---

[*] As I write these lines now, I believe it to be the case that at the time of my employment at the ranch, my friend Tiburcio had already been captured and was well on his way to the gallows, though I hadn't heard the news. I'd fallen behind in my reading. Another good job opportunity out the window, I guess.

vaguer and more apathetic, here petered off into nothing. But I remember it a little. I did a good job with the horses, I think, because I cared less about staying alive than they did. The ranch was an expansive spread of cabins, corrals and pens that abutted a natural spring, ringed by a dark and snow-capped mountain range, which stared down at me, relentless, obdurate, day after day, night after night. My pitiless Heavenly judge and guardian.

And so on, till one sunny, bleary-eyed Sunday, when the ranch hands were summoned by the boss, who let us know that a couple of noted bounty hunters were spotted just west of town, and a Federal marshal was coming in on the Atchison Topeka from the east. Something big was happening, and two-bit wanted men might consider laying low for a few days, just to be safe. "But if I've got any notorious outlaws on my ranch," he added, "now's the time to flee to another state." Taking me aside afterwards, he put one foot up on the fence, looking out over his fields, at the horses grazing in the distance. "Mr. Tang is back in town," he said. "He arrived by coach last night from California, and he wants to see you right away." He unrolled a few bills. "I have the feeling I won't be seeing you again," he said, "and I owe you about half a month's pay. Good luck to you."

I found Tang in the parlor of her hotel suite in town, meeting with a couple of befuddled businessmen. The parlor itself was hot and stuffy and dim; the musty stench of mold drifted through the dusty air. My comrade herself, in a blue suit and vest, was in her "Mr. Tang" disguise, and the effect was stunning. When I entered that room, I entirely forgot that she wasn't a man. Her posture was sturdy and confident, her voice steady, deep and assured. Her arm was slung, informally, over the back of the chair, her legs spread carelessly before her.

"Ah!" she said, "Mr. O'Hugh! Sit down, please sit down."

She stood, slapped me firmly on the back, before she introduced the two men to me – the young one, the protégé, was Mr. Philips, and the older man, heavyset, with graying hair and worry lines etched in his forehead, was Mr. Choate. They had the shell-shocked demeanor of noblemen who one moment had been eating crumpets with the King of Prussia and the next moment, without warning, and without a chance even to loosen their ties, had found themselves dropped into the middle of the Sahara desert, breathing sand. Mr. Philips seemed to believe that he was on an important mission. Mr. Choate clearly understood that this job – meeting in a ramshackle western town with a Chinaman about a secret conspiracy – was some sort of demotion, a prank, a message from his employer that perhaps he should retire to the countryside.

She then introduced me, accurately, as a gunman she kept on retainer as she plotted the defeat of the Sidonistas. Philips, too eagerly, asked if I were "Watt O'Hugh, the famous Western hero turned outlaw?" I puffed up a bit with pride at this. Choate wondered aloud if Watt O'Hugh were not dead, shot through the head in the mountains after a violent prison break. Philips said he'd thought that Watt O'Hugh was "rather a younger man."

Tang explained it all at once.

"Getting shot in the mountains can age a man," she said. After a pause – a comedic-timing pause, it seemed to me – she added: "That is, getting shot in the *head* in the mountains. He's working for *us* now. To keep the West safe and orderly. Death was a hoax, so he can work secretly." Then, confidentially, she added, "O'Hugh's not really bad. He's good." Seeing me beaming like a happy puppy dog at all this attention, she explained, "This man has a nice smile, but he has teeth of iron."

They talked a while longer, two low-level hacks who purported to represent America's old money and a "Chinese businessman"[*] who claimed to speak for a secret global consortium of Eastern investors in New-West laundries and mines and other less reputable endeavors and who, like the bluebloods, was concerned from a business perspective about the destabilizing effect an insurrection from the far North might have on the flow of commerce across the states and territories, especially so soon after the civil war, the horse epizootic epidemic of 1872, the locust plague of 1874 and the great stock market collapse of 1873.

"We are living right on the edge, gentlemen," she said, clutching the brass handle of her walking stick. "Right on the edge of the abyss. I thank you for your support."

---

[*] This was a novel and maybe ridiculous idea at that time and in that place, but no mind: *I* (who didn't know any better) thought Tang was highly convincing. This concept – the Chinese businessman – may have its possibilities.

Once they had gone, she adjusted her posture just a bit, relaxed the muscles in her face, and once again she was tough old Madame Tang. Mr. Tang had left with the businessmen.

I said, "Do you think it was a good idea to tell them my name?" and she snapped, "They didn't believe any of it. Choate's going to drink himself to death, maybe today, and if he lives long enough to get back home to New York, he'll beat up his wife, *that*'s how humiliating this was for him. As far as he is concerned, the best evidence of your complete, total and irreversible death is that the Chinaman told him you're alive."

She grabbed her walking stick and marched into her bedroom, pulled her bag from the closet and began emptying her dresser drawers. "In San Francisco, Billy met with their bosses, and he was supposed to be here," she called to me. "I was just going to serve him drinks. Last minute, he doesn't show up, leaves a telegram for me. 'You'll be great, they'll love you,' he says – the crazy *lo fan* has been spending too much time in the 1980s, I think. Next time I do this, I need a disguise." She came out of the bedroom, her bag packed, a somewhat retrograde, wide-rimmed black hemisphere hat securely fixed upon her head, her tie impeccably, precisely vertical. "Next time, I go to the meeting as a big, fat, bald, old white man!"

She leaned against the wall and tightened her wooden foot.

"I need to buy myself a new one-of-these," she muttered, grimacing slightly.

I still sat there in the armchair. It was not the best armchair ever made, not by far, I am sure. But I'd been on the ranch for months, and the chair was soft and smooth, and stuffed with cotton or feathers (or something), and I thought I could sink into it and live there forever, inside the chair, and be a very happy man.

"I dunno," I said absently. "*I* thought it went pretty well."

Tang turned and glared at me, perhaps trying to choose the fierce profanity that would be most appropriate under the circumstances. Instead, after a moment of wrathy thought, she deflated, shrugged and gestured to me to get up off my ass.

"We're going to the settlement of Lervine up North a bit to meet Billy," she said. "We leave now."

"Why?"

"Because Billy told us to," she replied.

Tang had also gotten word of the unusual attention that bounty hunters and federal marshals were lavishing on southern Utah, and so Tang and I avoided the trails frequented by stagecoaches and respectable citizens traversing the state. Instead we cut West, and at times crisscrossed what came to be known as the Outlaw Trail, in that wild outback that bordered the Dirty Devil River. We hugged the cliffs by day and descended into a glowing maze of rock and dust to sleep at night. Sometimes we'd spot the speck of a rider or two on the distant trail, and once we even saw a Concord stagecoach, packed to bursting inside, with a dozen nervous lower-rent travelers balanced precariously on the flat roof. Tang and I would gallop nervously ahead, until they faded away into memory.

We rode through slot canyons, traversed an arch that joined two pink sandstone cliffs that the desert varnish had painted orange, green, gray and yellow, wandered fallow, desolate wastelands. The air danced like a ballerina in the hazy distance, and mountains floated like islands in an imaginary sea. At times, we would rise from the desert to a lush paradise of mountain streams and tenacious spruce and firs, mule deer, elk, marmots and raptors.

For all my trepidation about both the various villains hunting me, and the dangers that I felt sure awaited us in Lervine, the trip north was generally uneventful, with two absurdly extreme exceptions.

One afternoon, we were trudging through the desert heat. Coyote tracks stamped the wind-dimpled desert sand dunes ahead of us. Right in the middle of the narrow pass between two great sandstone peaks stood an old woman, dressed in rags, her skin dark and leathery from the fierce sun. She stood beneath a low stone arch, her bony hands grasping the two cliffs like columns. She had burst from the rocks and sand dust like a sickly stalk of corn.

Tang grunted in disgust.

"All the time this happens to me," she said.

She pulled on the reigns, and her stallion slowed to a halt.

"Get out of my way, old woman," Tang said.

"In a moment, my angry friend." She raised her arms, turned her palms upwards to the sun, and she said, "I will give you three pieces of wisdom, for three gold coins."

"Who do you think we are?" Tang said. "We're just about the poorest, worst outlaws in all of the West. We don't even have *one* gold coin. Tell you what, skip the wisdom, I'll skip the gold coins, I'll give you a strip of dried carrot to get the hell out of our way before we shoot you."

The old woman shut her eyes.

"It's a deal," she said. "But I will give you the three pieces of wisdom for free."

She cocked her head, shut her left eye, and stared intensely with her right eye straight at us. Her eye was green and pure, like an emerald.

"Piece of wisdom number one," she said, and she cleared her throat a bit. "What is seen, can be invisible. Piece of wisdom number two. Always thank those who have wronged you before you drink from the waters of eternity."

Her voice rose and fell in great rolling cadences, stirring and inspiring like a fine Shakespearean soliloquy.

I liked it, and I was happy for the break.

"Piece of wisdom number three," she concluded. "Pause twice before accepting the dispatches of a prince who is not a prince."

Tang impatiently tapped the side of her water flask.

"You'll get the hell out of the way now?"

The woman didn't budge.

"The wisdom was for free," she said. "Getting out of the way costs two strips of dried carrot."

"*One* strip of dried carrot," said Tang, as she fished around in her saddlebag, "and I promise not to shoot you in the ass."

"I hope you will bear the wisdom well," said the old woman, as she waited expectantly.

Tang looked up from her bag.

"You know what all that crap means?" she asked angrily.

"Yes," said the woman.

"Tell me what it means, then," Tang said, "if you're so god-damned wise."

Tang dangled the dried carrot over the woman's head.

"A second strip of carrot," Tang taunted, "if you tell me what your wisdom means. Easier to 'bear it well,' if I know what the hell it means. Otherwise, not so easy to bear it well."

"That I cannot do," the old woman replied gravely.

"Shut up, then," said Tang.

She threw the carrot strip to the old woman, who caught it deftly in her left hand.

"The meaning of the wisdom is something you must discover for yourself," the old woman said.

Tang rolled her eyes.

"You could tell me if you wanted to," she said. "But you have your dried carrot, so get out of my way."

The old woman stepped to one side. Her rags fluttered gently in the dry air.

"You may pass," she said, "with my blessings." Then, portentously: "Take heed."

The path ahead of us widened and we entered a broad canyon, populated by red sandstone statues that stood in formation before us like an army of terracotta goblin-warriors. After we'd gone a few yards, I asked, "Shouldn't we try to figure out what the old woman's riddles mean?"

Tang shook her head.

"Forget it. You'll find out too late – once you're drowning in the waters of eternity, you'll suddenly realize, *that old lady was smart*, as you go under for the third time. You'll accept the 'dispatches' of a man who will turn out to be a prince but not a prince, and you'll discover what that means just in time to lose your last nickel."

Ahead of us in the dust, a collared lizard, with a yellow head and green, spotted torso, stood up on its hind legs and ran.

"These people bother me all the time," she scoffed. "Oracles with their riddles. Always blocking my way when I've got someplace to go, demanding gold coins. If there is one thing I know, it's that every oracle alive talks in enigmas to drive people crazy and to try to feel better about herself. They're not nice people. They all think they're Elijah the Prophet."

"Who?" I asked.

I didn't remember that particular prophet from Randall's Island. I'd learned about Isaiah, who, according to my teacher, had prophesied the birth of Jesus. But no one had ever mentioned Elijah.

"Look behind you," Tang said. "She's probably turned into a bird. That's a little trick they all do."

I turned around. In the pass, where the woman had stood a few moments before, and silhouetted in the blazing midday sun, was a medium-sized white bird, with a slender, black bill, yellow feet supporting wiry black legs, and ostentatious plumes rising from its back.

"You're correct," I said, righting myself in the saddle.

"What kind of bird?"

"If I am not mistaken, a snowy egret."

Tang whistled through her teeth.

"Snowy egret," she marveled. "That's a new one."

The second notable event, in my view, is the following:

One night, we camped in a metropolis of winding empty avenues, carved into the rocks by a long-evaporated series of rivers. Tiered steps led up to red and white striped sandstone skyscrapers. It seemed a city filled with ghosts, and so I felt right at home. I lay there, in the middle of one of these streets, when, unheralded, a great lizard slithered across the night sky. It had hundreds of scales on its body, the head of a camel, a demon's eyes, a cow's ears, antlers like a deer, the neck of a snake, a clam's belly, a tiger's paws and an eagle's claws. The beast lit up the sky with its fury, and then, in a moment, it was gone.

I just stared at the sky, waiting for it to come back, to circle around and dive into our little rocky canyon and eat me for dinner.

"Did you see that?" I asked, just to be sure.

"It would have been hard to miss," Tang said, watching the sky, deep in thought. "It was a dragon, you know. I think it could be an omen. Something to do with the Red Eyebrows, maybe. Maybe not. Maybe not an omen. Could just be a dragon. But it had five claws. Did you notice that, O'Hugh? That was perhaps very notable."

I hadn't noticed that, but I believed her.

"Dragons are real?" I asked.

"A dragon just flew *over our heads*!" Tang exclaimed.

Tang went on to give me a brief and exasperated history lesson. Every society on earth, she told me, had documented its dragon sightings, many times over - China, each country in Europe, even the early nations described in the Bible. Only in the modern era was there even any doubt expressed about the existence of the great, noble lizards.

"There aren't many left," she continued, "and those that still live stay mostly out of sight. In China, by the turn of the Millennium, they were already so rare that whenever a dragon appeared, everyone thought it was auspicious. If a dragon appeared in your home village on the day of your birth, it sealed your future. Sometimes it was really an omen. Sometimes a dragon just wanted to stretch his wings."

"Real fire-breathing dragons?" I said, more than a little amazed.

She sat up and leaned back on her elbows.

"How could a dragon breathe fire?" she said. "This is real life, O'Hugh, not a bedtime story. If any reptile breathed fire, it would burn up its lungs and its mouth. Plus, reptiles by definition are cold-blooded – no mechanism for making fire, or even keeping warm. No, here's how that myth began: In the old days, dragons would often fly in thunderstorms – less likely to get a spear through the chest – and the next morning the crops and forests would be burning. Caused by lightning, but blamed on dragon. The *drachenmanner*[*] – dragon-slayers – found they could get better pay if they fought a fire-breathing dragon, so they had an incentive to propagate the rumor. More danger to it, the villagers were more worried, more eager to find an outsider to kill their dragons for them. So the traveling *drachenmanner* moved through Europe, and the stories grew through the years. I say Europe, because in China, we didn't kill our dragons. But no, dragons never breathed fire. They're just big flying lizards, dinosauria that didn't quite die out and that never evolved into birds. Didn't you ever study Darwin? Everybody knows about this."

"Tang," I said flatly. "Everybody does *not* know about this." A little rebelliously, I added, "And no, I never studied Darwin."

"Maybe not Randall's Island graduates. O'Hugh, sometimes talking to you is like talking to a child." Her voice grew a little quieter, a little more faraway: "Like talking to a little child," she said again.

"This seems amazing to me," I said. "A dragon in Utah territory."

"A dragon in North America," she replied gently, "is more unusual than unusual. That's why I think it has something to do with the Red Eyebrows."

Now I sat up too, realizing that I wouldn't sleep much tonight.

"You think this is an omen," I asked, "but a woman with three cryptic predictions who turns into a bird isn't an omen?"

Tang shook her head.

"Stop thinking about crazy old bird lady, O'Hugh," she said mildly. "The dragon, this is something different. Dragons are noble, intelligent animals, and very misunderstood."

"OK, and this is an omen of what?"

She blinked in the moonlight, thinking. The shadows wove deep creases on her much-burdened face.

"O'Hugh, can I trust you?

I said that she could.

---

[*] In German, a term that refers to a band of exceedingly brave, boastful, not entirely truthful and, for some reason (according to Tang) mostly Jewish dragon hunter-soldiers for hire.

She stared thoughtfully at me. Above us, a mountain lion was perched carefully on a boulder at the very edge of a cliff, staring down into the canyon below.

"No," she said. "I cannot trust you. But you have a right to know the truth. And whom will you tell? You have no one."

"So you will tell me?"

"Make us a pot of coffee, O'Hugh," she said. "And I will begin my tale."

CHAPTER 17

Tang told me a story of ancient and modern China. Was it true? I don't know. I still don't really believe that I even saw that dragon in the Utah night. Late in my life, I spoke to a lot of evolutionary biologists – after that night in the canyons, it became something of an obsession of mine – and none of them could confirm what Tang told me "everyone knows". A few of them laughed in my face; one of them called for security to eject an ageing old cowboy from his spiffy new research laboratory. So do I believe Tang's farfetched tale? I don't know.

It's complicated, so please pay attention. I don't have a lot of time – very soon I will die, as I believe I have mentioned – and so I have crammed a lot of information into a few pages. Also, this is the tale that Tang told me in the mountains of Utah, as we traveled north to Lervine, and she was trying to beat the dawn.

Here it is.

Tang told me of a poet who was born in 1838, and who grew up in the countryside in the middle of China. He was a terrible poet, but the governor of the realm favored him. Rumors were that the terrible poet was the governor's illegitimate son, which would explain his stipend in spite of his demonstrated lack of excellence. Maybe so. Maybe not – perhaps the governor saw a potential that wasn't clearly apparent to anyone else. But whatever the reason for his stroke of luck, the terrible poet had enough coin to write his bad poetry, and to drink, sometimes rice wine, and sometimes moutai when he could afford it, so he didn't really bother anyone. Although he didn't advertise it, he was aware that his poetry was not very good. Perhaps that was why he didn't write very much of it.

He was a handsome man, and charming, and unmarried and childless and terribly idle.

His name was pronounced *Yu Dai-Yung* in English, which, for what I hope are obvious reasons, I thought was a very unfortunate harbinger. Tang, however, told me that in Chinese, this could be considered quite a wonderful, auspicious name, summoning to one's mind both the elegance of a jade soldier and the simple wisdom of the countryside. "Or," she added, less enthusiastically, "a man who is second-rate, but who wears fancy clothes that do not fit him … and who, perhaps, is very effeminate and unintelligent, and who shrinks from a fight."

A few months ago, nearly finished with an epic poem, or so he claimed (in reality, he was thinking about beginning an epic poem, one of these days, that would tell of the terrible hostilities of the Warring Kingdoms period of China's distant past), and he was enjoying a stroll on the banks of the river, when a deputy of the governor summoned him to the governor's residence, where he was shoved into a rickety carriage which conducted him along pothole-filled paths and byways until he reached a dock on the river, where he boarded a river boat with both sails and oars, a great old wooden boat with many stories to tell, and which in turn transported him one hundred miles to the Tower of the Fragrance of Buddha at the Summer Palace on Longevity Hill. Palace ladies walked in the gardens, and overhead flew a red and black crowned hoopoe with delicately striped wings.

He climbed eleven flights of stairs. Upon reaching the very top, Hsu Li, an advisor to the Empress Dowager herself, greeted him. He was a stooped man, with a few sadly dignified tufts of hair above a wisely wizened face. He wore a purple robe. The room was small, of bare, spare stone, with an open window looking out over the courtyard, the forest, and the distant countryside. There were three chairs, two of simple wood, one more elegant and cushioned, made of polished mahogany and adorned with emeralds.

Over a cup of tea – the best tea he had ever enjoyed in his life, as it happened, come to think of it – the advisor and the bad poet talked about the weather, and about the orchids and peonies, which were just starting to bloom. They discussed this topic for what seemed to the bad poet an inadequately short length of time, considering the poetic beauty of the subject matter.

"Yu Dai-Yung," said Hsu Li. "According to a very wise seer, you are the reincarnation of Yang Hsiung."

"The great poet of the court of Emperor Wang Mang!" Master Yu exclaimed, but the old man shook his head.

"Not Wang Mang's great court poet," he said, "but his bastard son, who took his father's name upon the overthrow of the Hsin

Dynasty and the murder of his father, and who was a somewhat lesser poet, and who remained loyal to the memory of his father and of the Emperor Wang Mang till the end of his life and who longed for revenge." Confidentially, he leaned closer to Yu and, as though prying ears and eyes were on the other side of the wooden wall, he whispered, "Understand, there is a mention of this lesser Yang Hsiung neither in the official histories, nor in the unofficial histories (nor, for that matter, in any unofficial legends) but it has been prophesied, for what this is worth. More important, the Roamers have seen some sort of notable future for you, and have devised for you a great mission, a very great mission." He added quickly, "Never mind who the Roamers are, that's none of your business."

Yu, with what dignity he could muster, replied, "I would like to hear this from the lips of the Empress Dowager," and the advisor raised one shaggy, curly eyebrow in surprise.

"Of course you would," he said.

At that moment, the great wooden door creaked open and the room was bathed in sunlight.

"Apparently," Hsu Li said, with a slight smile, "Master Yu gets what Master Yu wants. May I introduce the Empress Dowager?"

She was only five feet tall, with six-inch heels, clownishly bright-red rouge cheeks on a pasty, whitened face. She had long fingernails, with which she was reputed to scratch the faces of those with whom she disagreed, when angry. Yu was relieved to see that she seemed to be in a good mood today. She wore a long orange robe decorated with some kind of flower, some kind of beautiful flower for which there was no word, because it was a flower that thrived only in Heaven.

Yu flung himself to the ground, his face on the stone floor, prostrate.

At this point in the story, I interrupted Tang and complained that she had lost me already. Tang sighed, and her story skipped back almost two millennia.

In the year 45 BC, she told me, a little baby was born in a provincial town in northern China, during the former Han dynasty. On his birth, dragons filled the sky.

"People sometimes say," Tang added, imparting a great secret, "that this was just a legend, made up many years later, but it *really* happened. Billy has seen it."

I told her that I believed her.

The little boy was named Wang Mang, and in the year 9 A.D., he ascended to the throne as Emperor and, as the dragons had intended, ushered in the new Hsin Dynasty.[*] The fiery phoenix flew overhead at his inauguration. During his reign, Chinese unicorns, known as *ch'i-lins*, appeared in the capital city. Later historians sought at the behest of the later Emperors whom they served to discredit Wang Mang, and so they described him as ugly and ridiculous. His chin was weak, they wrote, his eyes bulged like a fish, his voice was loud and unpleasant. But in reality, he was very handsome. His eyes were deep emerald green, and his voice was like poetry sung to the accompaniment of a four-stringed liuch'in. He ordered that every peasant should be a landowner; he freed the slaves; he decreed that the power of the moneylenders be broken. All of this was as predicted by an ancient scroll that he found, alone, on a walk in the mountains.

In the evenings, in the royal court, musicians played, lords and their ladies danced among sculptures of jade and ivory in a ballroom whose windows looked out on great forests and oceans, but Wang Mang's eyes were on the distant countryside, where he believed a beautiful change was taking place, heralding an age in which humankind's most noble spirit was soon to reign, forever and ever.

Frequently by his side was a diminutive court poet named 揚雄 (which is pronounced in English something like "Yang Hsiung"), a wise and ageing sage from the deep countryside, whose odes to Emperor Wang had led to his near-murder by remnants of the Han aristocracy, who spread vicious and dangerous lies of treason against the court poet. Falsely accused of plotting against the Emperor, Yang hurled himself from the highest tower of the imperial winter palace to prove his loyalty. Palace guards found his bent and broken old body in the ice

---

[*] While Tang liked the dynasty, she didn't like the name that Wang Mang had chosen. "Hsin" means "new", and she considered "the New Dynasty" a hopeless, uninspired and redundant name for a new dynasty, and especially faint praise for one that was to have changed the entire world forever.

and snow at the edge of the forest, terribly mangled and near-death, but still just barely alive. Upon hearing of this patriot's action, the Emperor awarded him a seat of honor in the royal court, and soon this balding and hunched, unnaturally baby-faced specter was haunting the hallways of the palace, jotting moist, adjective-laden paeans to the new Emperor, who gladly paid in gold. Now that the poet had become rich, honored, respected and powerful, albeit scarred and crooked after his terrible act of loyalty, it should be no surprise that a mistress came into the picture, a young, fresh, dewy-eyed girl who found the court poet irresistible, a girl with a smile like a beautiful emerald and dark hair as soft as silk, who even went so far as to bear him a child. In turn, he allowed her to play a noble role in some of his poems, and her fame began to spread.

The poet installed his mistress and their baby boy in an apartment half a mile from the Emperor's court.

(Did the young girl really love the poet? She did, with all her heart; her words were true. Did the poet really love the Emperor, as he claimed in his drizzly tributes? As Yang Hsiung's enemies wrote of him, behind his back: *Wanting purity, stillness/ He threw himself out of a tower/ Wanting solitude, quiet/ He composed a portent text.* His philosophy, for what it was worth, proclaimed that people were neither inherently good nor bad, and so was anyone, truly, worthy of his love?)

When the Emperor stared out his window at the distant countryside, he envisioned the great and noble changes that he believed were occurring, and because he believed himself Magical, he believed that everything he envisioned was truly happening. His perfidious advisors assured him of the truth of his visions. But in reality, vestiges of Han loyalty were strong in the countryside, and the landowners blocked Wang Mang's dreams for their peasants. Then something more terrible occurred. The land itself seemed to join the gentry in its rebellion. The Yellow River changed course twice in six years. Earthquakes devastated China. Fire poured from the sky. A revolution burst from the cracked, burning earth, led by boy-soldiers with red eyebrows. They carried bags of food. What could the starving peasants do but join the wave of human anger sweeping to Peking?

"Here was Wang Mang, the one for whom we'd been waiting," Tang sighed sadly, "the one for whom we still wait."

The one anointed by the dragons, by one thousand dragons, who had roused themselves from a great sleep to depart from their hidden caverns as though they shared a single mind and fly out into the night sky to herald the dawn of a glorious new era, an era that was to have united the world in peace and tranquility for a thousand years at least, and perhaps longer, if one were to believe the tea leaves and first drafts of the Roamer history, and the ancient scroll.

"The destruction of this dream," Tang told me sadly, "made the dragons very angry."

Disappointed in their expectations of a thousand years of dragon-inspired peace, they instead undertook a thousand-year rampage that spilled over a little bit into Europe (mostly Germany but also England), an era that was terrible for the farmers but which kept the *drachenmanner* gainfully employed and well-fed. At last, exhausted from their vengeance, the dragons descended to their watery caverns – Chinese dragons, Tang told me, live in the water, but fly in the sky – where they slept, ventured out rarely, and dreamed of what might have been, and what might still come to pass.

The dragons' love could not, did not, protect Wang Mang as the child-soldiers of the rebellion surrounded Peking. The Chinese unicorns fought for their benevolent ruler, but the soldiers hunted them down and ate them for dinner. The Red Eyebrows spilled into the Palace, where they found the Emperor, standing brave and stoic in a torch-lit corridor. He didn't struggle as the Eyebrows surrounded him and cut his throat. The Eyebrows attacked Yang, the court grandee, in the gardens, where he lay in hiding behind a rosebush. A boy crushed his skull. As for the poet's befuddled mistress, so suddenly and bafflingly beloved by millions, she was now just as suddenly and inexplicably despised in equal measure, and a small band of ten-year-old Eyebrows grabbed her on the road leading out of Peking and summarily disemboweled her.

But of their young son, no record exists.

Did he survive?; did he perish with his parents?; did he never exist at all? A great seer in China had found the answer, apparently.

"Now," Tang asked, "do you understand? Have I given you the necessary background? These are matters of history that one would have hoped you would have learned in fifth grade on Randall's Island."

She continued her story about the awful poet Yu Dai-Yung and his unlikely meeting with the Empress Dowager:

"Yu Dai-Yung," said the Empress Dowager. "For many years, the secret of the Red Eyebrows has remained hidden, this terrible secret that can change the course of mighty rivers and make the earth crack – and so much more, terrible things."

She stopped talking and drifted into thought, perhaps imagining those terrible things. Her eyes grew misty.

Hsu Li whispered: "Your Excellency?"

The Empress beckoned to the poet, and he followed her out of the room, onto a terrace, up another flight of stairs into a sky-garden that was hidden and sheltered from the world. They sat, each on a separate stone bench, separated by a suitable distance. Her Excellency's bench was slightly higher.

"In the depths of this building," the Empress said, "we keep many things. There is the body of an adult dragon, for example, and a live baby dragon, captured in the Himalayas." She arched an eyebrow. "Dragons are real, you know, Yu."

"I never doubted it," Yu replied.

A hoopoe alighted on the branch of a dark brown Chinaberry tree. Was this the same hoopoe? It had the same red and black head, and the same confident look on its beautiful face. It knew it was beautiful. Yu believed that it was the same hoopoe, and that it was here because it knew that this fierce little woman was the ruler of all China.

"Locked beneath this building," she said, "we keep, also, a tall man who was born on another planet. Sometimes he comes up here, to this sheltered garden, to drink tea with Hsu Li. He has greenish skin, very light green skin, just as today's writers of fantastic fictions would have it. He had told us many, many things. Nothing of value yet, but we continue to hope. We have had him only two hundred years."

She smiled. Although it might have been true, this was also a little joke. So Yu laughed.

"I can tell you all this," the Empress Dowager said, "because no one will believe you. *Because everyone thinks that you are crazy, Yu Dai-Yung! And so you will tell no one.*"

Yu breathed in the fragrance of the garden, let it all settle in his lungs and stay there for a little while. What poems a great poet could write about just the smells in this garden!

"I have lived an eccentric life of my own invention," he admitted to the most powerful woman on the continent. "I believed that it would make me a great poet."

"Has it?" she asked.

He shook his head.

"I lack something," he replied. "I lack the poetic voice. I have the poetic soul. I have the poetic mind. But not the poetic voice."

She nodded, not without sympathy.

"Well. Perhaps you *are* a great man of history after all," she concluded, "if our seer is correct. Just not the way you'd always planned it. The most important secret in this building is the secret of the Red Eyebrows, which can never be allowed out into the world. Never never. But it has been. We must get it back, before it destroys everything."

"And what do I do?" the poet asked. "What is my mission?"

"Ahah," said the Empress Dowager. "The mission is to *succeed*. In your mission."

"What is my mission?" Yu asked again, in a small voice, a little more plaintively.

"A very dangerous mission," the old woman said. "But one with great glory, should you succeed."

"And my mission," said the poet, trying unsuccessfully to clarify his question, "is *what?*"

"To go to America," said the Empress Dowager. "And to see what the future has planned for you."

The poet sat on the stone bench in the garden and stared at the ruler of China. He remained silent.

"And to be brave," the Empress Dowager concluded. "You will have to be brave."

The poet thought for a moment, and then he bowed, and he said, "好", which sounds like "How?", but which means, "OK." He would do it. He was up for anything, so long as it wasn't the wine-stained failure of his current life.

The hoopoe flew from the branch in the Chinaberry tree. It flew very high, and it disappeared into a cloud.

"The Red Eyebrows," I said. "Is all this true?"

"You may note," Tang said to me now, "that what happened back then, in those times, is happening today. The powers that could make the Yellow River jump its banks can make locusts descend on the plains and millions of horses die where they stand, as though they were a single beast. Why did you think that happened, O'Hugh? Did you think that was a coincidence?"

She stared at me as though she were waiting for some sort of response.

Yes, I thought it was a coincidence, I might have said. *I believe in ghosts*, I might have added, *but I believe in almost nothing else. Not in God. Not in forces that can change the weather, that can change nature. I lack belief. When horses die, it is because the horses die. I believe in ghosts only because I must.*

Tang looked into my eyes, and she shook her head, and she scoffed.

"It will only grow worse," she whispered. "The people who lived in the dirt turned on Wang Mang, who was their only true friend, in favor of the Red Eyebrows, who had summoned demons from the depths of the Earth to kill their mothers. So too, here, the people will join with Allen Jerome and Darryl Fawley, the men who have unleashed the forces that have nearly destroyed today's peasantry."

I stared absently at the beeplant flowers that grew incongruously from the cracks in the parched ground beneath my feet.

Tang said, "Even now, the nation and the world lurches closer to destruction, to a natural destruction that will make today's economic meltdown look like a Gilded Age by comparison."

I asked her what could be done.

"In most battles, you have your generals, your high level strategists and your troops, and the best thinkers leading the strongest men prevail. But the kind of situation we're facing today – a war between 'Good' and 'Evil', for want of a better way of describing it – is always very personality based. We've got our absolute evil unleashed in Montana, and if you listen to Billy Golden, there's our absolute good somewhere, hiding just out of view, waiting to fight."

I gulped, a little too audibly.

"Me?" I asked nervously.

Tang almost-laughed with almost-affection, which manifested as a grunt and a scowl.

"No, O'Hugh," she replied, "not you. Our hero will have a messiah complex as big as the Yarlung Zanbo canyon. You're like me – the best we can do is serve tea to the candidates."

I asked, in that case, what came next?

"In a month or two," Tang now told me, with a grimace that bordered on sheer hopelessness, "poet Yu will step off a steamer in San Francisco harbor. His job will be to stop the secret of the Red Eyebrows from destroying the world. This terrible weapon will spread like weeds if it is not stopped. First the nation of Sidonia gets it, and they take over America, and then a Sidonian spy sells it to Russia. Then China gets worried and gives it to Korea. Yes, we must worry about even little Korea. Eventually the anarchists get it, and we all unleash it on each other, and the world lies in flames."

"Will he succeed?" I asked stupidly. "Yu the poet?"

"He's a pretty good sharp-shooter, for a poet," she said. "But these genies, they don't go back in the bottle so easily.

"Especially," she added portentously, "the *evil* genies."

We slept a few hours. When the sun rose, we drank the rest of the coffee, now ice cold, we packed, and we rode off.

CHAPTER 18

The town of Lervine was flat, dusty and ramshackle. The watchmaker's shop and the hardware store that greeted us when we arrived were shacks that would collapse at the first good strong wind. But further along the principal business street were rows of saloons and gaming halls, all dark and deserted tonight. Kerosene lights blazed in the windows of the dance hall, in the very far distance.

Tang dismounted and tied her horse to a post near the entrance to town. I dismounted and followed her. In spite of the music and what seemed to be the forced gaiety of the voices at the end of the main artery, this was a town poised and waiting, and a nervous tension hung in the air. I could hear an out-of-tune piano and an out-of-tune banjo pounding out *Tramp Tramp Tramp*, and a lot of out-of-tune revelers singing along. The voices raised in song were strangely joyless and vigilant.

Tang marched purposefully toward the dance hall, her hand on the gun by her side. It was ten o'clock, and the night was growing darker. Clouds were covering over the stars.

Tang pushed the door open. The dance hall was broad and expansive and airy, and there was a festiveness that clung to it, in spite of the ominous mood of this particular evening. The kerosene lights gave the room a joyful orange glow. A few young women were there, standing near the window, prettily dressed in their best town clothes and smiling pretty smiles. A barman served drinks in the corner. A few couples danced the fandango.

Tang's shoulders grew broader, her face hardened, and when she spoke, her voice dropped an octave.

"Billy Golden!" she shouted, and our friend stood up from the middle of a little crowd that had gathered around his corner table.

"Mr. Tang!" he exclaimed. "Mr. O'Hugh!"

He gestured to us, smiling at the dispirited group.

"Two of the best shootists in the West!" he exclaimed. "Gentlemen, sit down."

"What are you doing?" I whispered.

"Fomentin' intrigue," he said with a cockeyed smile.

The crowd began to disperse, to drift away. "There's more of you than there are of them," Billy said. "Remember that. That means, in any firefight, *you* win." And then, patting a nervous young man on the back: "Just act normal. Dance, be happy. We've got snipers up on the rooftops. We're ready for McIntyre's army, so long as they're not ready for us."

"This doesn't look like much of a dance," Tang said, sounding every bit a disappointed gentleman. "Where are all the women?"

Billy said, "The few women here are just to make it look like a real dance from the street. They're all g'hals, kind of pretty and dainty when they want to be, but by their nature mostly tough and rambunctious. The rest of the town's women are in a safe house outside of town. Too bad. Men are idiots, always trying to protect women, when it should be the other way around. Womenfolk make the best shootists. You know why? Because they are entirely lacking in pity."

A lean, lanky young man lingered nearby. He had close-cropped, greasy hair and a sharply angular face. His eyes were haunted and wrathy. He cleared his throat, stared down at his drink. Billy summoned him, and the young man pulled up a chair and sat with us.

"This is Flip Tidwell," Billy said.

That's right: *Flip Tidwell*. A good name for a limerick, but not so good for a heroic Western paladin, which is how Billy, credulously or not, wanted me to see him.

"The last of the Tidwells," Billy continued, "whose brave, martyred family have brought us this chance, through the Grace of God."

Flip nodded.

"I know that Mr. Tang and Mr. O'Hugh are interested in hearing your sad, noble tale, Flip," Billy gently prodded.

Lervine was a new settlement, less than ten years old, developed by a few former Union Army officers and Presbyterian businessmen from Salt Lake City as a gentile outpost and forthright challenge to the

Mormon hegemony in the territory. They wanted to make money, but they also wanted to live in a town without any Mormons. (Lervine, incidentally, was named for the daughter of the first provisional mayor, who, upon turning eighteen, abandoned Utah, married a man of whom her family disapproved, and vanished into infamy in New York. Her name remained behind, a reminder of what might have been.) The settlement was designed to take advantage of its proximity to a projected railroad line out of Nevada, as well as hundreds of miles of not-bad and generally unclaimed grazing land that adjoined the new settlement. Flip's family had a strong desire to make money, shared a closed-minded suspicion of Mormonism, and longed for a good stiff drink, so they moved to Lervine from Salt Lake City at the very founding of the settlement. They built a little two-room cabin with their own hands with a couple of lean-to's out back, and they went into business herding sheep. After a few years, a local property owner named McIntyre sought to consolidate his control. When he leveled accusations of rustling against the area's small-time shepherds, including the Tidwells, the area exploded into a full-scale range war.

"The allegations were completely false, no truth to them whatsoever," Flip insisted redundantly and adamantly, but, it seemed to me, unconvincingly.

From the North, Sidonia sent guns and money to McIntyre and a little posse of new cattle barons, but Fawley and Jerome didn't yet trust them with Magic, or at least that's how it seemed, based on descriptions of the generally 19th century war McIntyre conducted.

One day, McIntyre's "soldiers" rode across the plains to the little Tidwell cabin and just opened fire. Flip fought alongside his brothers and his dad until there was no hope, then he escaped out the back way. His mother and sister were in town at the time of the attack and hadn't been seen since. McIntyre had organized a hunting party for the following morning to find young Flip and had promised tonight to buy a drink for everyone who had volunteered to help him.

"But we have a surprise planned for Mister Mac and his posse," Billy said, and he grasped Flip's arm collegially.

Flip smiled weakly, and he grasped Billy's arm in turn.

I asked for a moment of Billy's time alone. The Roamer nodded, tapped Flip and pointed to the other side of the room.

"Go give Linda Corey a dance," he said. "She needs something to occupy her thoughts while we wait."

"I don't understand," I whispered, once Flip was out of earshot. "Seems to me, someone comes around with money and supplies these days, you join him, you don't fight him."

Billy concurred. "Obviously," he said, "Lervine has flirted with Sidonian loyalties. The Great Depression is a year old, Watt."

Tang added, "Billy calls it 'The Long Depression of 1873 to 1896', which kind of worries me. That may be a joke. I hope so. Problem is, he says it as old Billy, then you ask him what he means, and he's middle-aged Billy suddenly, and he doesn't know what you're talking about."

I looked over at Billy, middle-aged Billy, whose face revealed nothing.

"But," Billy went on, "whether this thing lasts another year or another twenty years, people are panicking. Their horses die in the great equine influenza epidemic of 1872; then, because the horses die in the West, the money from the West stops flowing East, so the Eastern banks go bust, the Eastern factories close, cash from the East stops flowing West; little settlements like Lervine that are waiting for the railroad are going to wait forever, because the railroads are going under, and suddenly the rich think they need to conquer the county just to survive, and the poor risk going under for good. If you live in Lervine, a little town that thought it was just about to get rich before it got very poor, and Sidonia Joe comes around with Montana money, you're happy. Sidonia Joe offers you a job up North, you're happier still. You wake up in the morning, and your beautiful young daughter is feeding the goats, just as always, except that she died of malaria in 1871 and the beautiful girl feeding the goats is a deadling, here now, gone tomorrow. Maybe you're still willing to follow Joe anywhere, because you think he's an Angel of God. But maybe you've got your own God, and you think Sidonia Joe and his army of deadlings are agents of Satan. Or maybe you know there's no God at all, and then Sidonia Joe is something scarier. He's just a man with great power, who will only get stronger still, if he's not stopped."

"Sidonia is relatively weak here," Tang whispered. "This motley group might just have a chance against the sons-of-bitches. And Billy thinks that Flip may have a future, he may be a leader of the counter-revolution. Guys like this, we need to save them. We need to find them, and save them."

I listened to a doleful rendition of *My Pa's Waltz*, the banjo and piano, the smattering of voices, all sorrowful. As unconvincing a replica of a celebration as I'd ever witnessed.

"When the cattle barons ride into town with their guns drawn, hunting for Flip Tidwell, we'll be ready for them," Billy said. "But the rest of these guys, they're a little shaky with the firearms, a little nervous. We need one good sharp-shooter, a few guns, and" – here he shot a glance at Tang – "one woman of the dark arts. When this is over, if we're successful, we'll have a bulwark against the Sidonian army right at the Northern border of Utah and Idaho."

"OK," I said. "This is a better plan than most I've heard lately. But listen: why *should* I? Half your time you spend trying to find a messiah to save the world. The other half you're working to defeat the false messiahs you helped create. Well, my life is ruined. I have no reason to fight."

Billy leaned forward, deep concern in his eyes.

"Watt," he said gently. "I like you. But remember our bargain. If you betray *us*, your body betrays *you*. You crumple to the ground and die in a heap in the road."

Billy shrugged, as though it weren't his decision to make.

"Maybe you'd be doing me a favor," I said. "I don't have the will to fight here in Lervine. I'm catawamptiously chawed up, Golden. If I could die in the road with a little bit of roasted squirrel in my stomach, and a lot of whiskey, wouldn't that be better than dying at the hands of some Utah cattle baron?"

Billy Golden smiled. Now he was older, nearly eighty. It had taken him a long time to get this right. He had roamed back and forth in Time, tried it again and again, apparently, till he was an old, old man. Now Time was hardening, like a lump of clay that has been worked and re-worked, again and again. It was his last chance. His aged, weak, bloodshot eyes twinkled, just a little.

"You couldn't be more right, Third," he said. "If I want you to fight for me tonight, and if I want you to want to survive, then I need to give you something to live for. That's why your next stop is Weedville."

"And what's in Weedville?"

"A young woman named Lucy Billings," he said. Then he slapped his head, with an exaggerated show of penitence. "*I'm* sorry, Third. A young woman named Lucy *Fawley*."

I seethed, but I didn't get up and leave.

"Maybe not Fawley for long though," Billy continued. "She's lost the support of Sidonia, and she currently resides in a dirt floor jail in the little-nothing town of Weedville, Nebraska. You help me tonight, I give you full use of my troops in Slabtown, Colorado, you march in force to Weedville, and the woman you love is beside you forever."

"And then I'm out?"

"I hope not."

"But it's up to me. I do one job for you, you do one job for me, and then I'm out."

He smiled.

"You must do what you think is right, Watt, of course."

So what could I do? Tang, Billy and I spent the next half hour plotting strategy, checking our guns again and again, and pacing around, waiting for the action to start.

We stood by the window, watching the Lervine street.

"He's a cattle rustler," I said.

"He denies it," Billy said, keeping his gaze peeled on the scene outside, not looking at me.

"*You* think he is guilty."

"Sure," Billy agreed. "Sure I do. This is bigger than whether Flip Tidwell stole a few sheep. I know that, and you know that."

I considered this.

"I saw a dragon in the sky," I told him. "Right before we reached Lervine, the night before, there was a big dragon filling up the whole sky."

Billy nodded sagely.

"An omen?" I asked.

"Maybe."

"Maybe an omen about tonight? Of my impending death?"

Billy laughed.

"Not likely, Third," he said. "You seem sober. I don't think these clowns will outgun you."

"An omen of what then?"

"Red Eyebrows," Billy replied.

"That's what Tang says."

"Well, Tang would know. Wang Mang, he had some potential, that boy, before the Eyebrows got in the game. The *Eyebrows*." With a lopsided, sad-dreamy smile, Billy Golden whispered, "Alas, poor Wang Mang! I knew him, O'Hugh," and faded into a little reverie of memory, sang a few dramatic-sounding Chinese verses, which I wished I could understand, in a tune-that-wasn't-a-tune, but before I could ask him for a translation, a sentinel rushed from upstairs, a young boy, out of breath. Ten shadowy horsemen were a quarter mile from town, the sentinel announced. McIntyre and his posse were on the march.

The snipers maintained a careful watch from upstairs as the horsemen galloped into the center of town.

"Keep dancing!" Billy called, in an urgent stage whisper, and to rekindle the faux-gaiety, he moved to the center of the room and burst into a little ditty that the patrons probably believed he was improvising, but which I later recognized as a jazz tune that would become popular in 1927. It really moved, and Billy made it easier for the guests to pretend mirth. Soon the front door lurched open, and McIntyre stood before us, three-hundred pounds, confident, framed by two shaggy-haired henchmen. The other seven men stood behind him in the street. McIntyre wore a white hat, and he grinned a gold-toothed grin. He was ready to imbibe and then take over the county.

The music ground to a halt.

"Who wants a drink?" McIntyre called. "Who wants to go Flip-huntin' with me?"

He looked surprised at the dead silence that greeted his joyful invitation.

The crowd parted, and Billy, Tang and I stepped forward.

"Your Flip is over at the bar," Billy said.

McIntyre tilted his head to his left.

"Take care of this," he said.

The shaggy gunman on McIntyre's left drew, but I drew faster and shot him dead.

The shaggy gunman on McIntyre's right drew, but Tang drew faster and shot him dead.

Flip called out McIntyre's name. The big man drew, but Flip drew faster, albeit with something less than precise accuracy. Flip aimed carefully for McIntyre's chest, and he was more than startled when a big chip off the top of McIntyre's skull flew backwards into the street. McIntyre was still momentarily alive, and what was left of his face betrayed a mixture of surprise and genuine bafflement. All he had ever wanted was to earn a decent living in a lawless county and a difficult recessionary economic environment, to bring his wife flowers once a week, and to buy a few folks a drink at a town dance. The giant tried to regain his balance and grasped the doorframe in his great knuckles, steadying himself – as though there would truly be some hope, if he could just manage to stay vertical! – but he finally collapsed with a mighty crash to the wooden floor, where he lay, bent and broken.

Events grew less organized after that: more Law of the Jungle, less Robert's Rules of Order. I'm not particularly proud of any of it. This wasn't my fight. Some of McIntyre's guys in the street started shooting randomly, but the snipers cut them down in an instant. Two of the posse jumped on their horses. One shot at me and I shot back and he fell. The other rode out of town. Good for him.

So the fight was over, I'd killed two of their bastards, and our bastards lived to throw a party that lasted all night, while dead bodies sank into the mud in the street, as a dead body will do after you shoot a guy in a muddy Western town. Not to put too fine a point on it, but each corpse in the street was the dead body of some mother's son. You know.

I was relieved when we all rode a mile out of town to McIntyre's big house and found Flip's mother and sister tied up in the cellar, still alive and in good health. So the day wasn't a complete loss. Saving a life always makes me feel better than taking one.

CHAPTER 19

You may be wondering why federal agents and bounty hunters were suddenly on my trail again. It all goes back to J.P. Morgan, my first puppeteer. I had entered his mind once more, several months earlier, during what he found to be a particularly disconcerting evening.

Morgan's second wife, Fanny, was suffering from diarrhea, dyspepsia, flatulence, hysteria, anxiety, rashes, labored breathing, swelled ankles and cramps, and she needed fresh air, and so thirty-six hours earlier she had gone to Cragston and had taken with her the Morgan children, Jack, Anne, Juliet and Louisa. In the absence of Fanny and the children, Morgan felt abandoned. Not lonely, exactly, but angry. He was himself suffering from what he claimed were diseased lungs, but his primary complaint was desertion, and it wasn't *Fanny*'s desertion that pained him the most, though it was a reminder of an earlier desertion from which he still suffered. Truly, the only thing worse than Fanny at home (sinking disconsolately into the floors and gazing sadly at the walls) was Fanny anywhere else, fleeing his increasingly dutiful embrace and leaving Morgan alone to mourn all that he had lost. As the sun drew low in the sky, he still lingered in his emptying office at 23 Wall Street, that male-bastion of polished wooden assidity, writing a love letter to his wife. *I know you may not realize it*, he scribbled to her, *but I remain fond of you.*

He finished the letter and sealed it, held it sadly in his hands for a while. Then he walked across the sparkling cobblestones of the business district into his social club, where he loitered too long, angrily debating the Specie Resumption Act with anyone who would listen (I'm not entirely sure, but I think he was in favor of it), then insisted (too insistently) that Tony Drexel and Jim Goodwin would *love* to have a game of poker with him. The force of his personality was too much, and so Drexel and Goodwin – both married businessmen in their early 40s – returned to the Morgan mansion to play poker till midnight and argue about the Bland Bill (again, I am not sure, but I believe that the Morgan firm stood to lose money from the Bland Bill, and so he was against it). So they argued about the Bland Bill, among other things.

Drexel, his partner at the firm, was a short fat man with enormous nostrils and a deep resonant voice that brought to mind a professional opera singer. His eyebrows were blond, his hair was black, and his mustache was the color of a wild smoky horse. Goodwin, his distant cousin, friend, and business associate, was a pretty man, blond-haired and fine-skinned, who laughed like a little girl but cursed uncontrollably, almost involuntarily, as a man hiccupping.

Staring at the cards in his hand – at the Queen of Spades, specifically, who seemed to be plotting against him – Morgan insisted that his lungs were failing him, and remarked, too offhandedly it seemed to his companions, that his doctor believed he was imagining a bout of tuberculosis. Indeed, *willing* it.

"Do you know why I would will this?" he asked. "Can you guess why he believes that I would imagine that I was afflicted with such a disease?"

He coughed, a deep phlegm-filled cough, from the depths of his lungs; a very convincing cough, Morgan himself thought.

"Well?" he gasped.

Drexel nodded.

"I could guess," he said. "You want to witness a miracle, come back from the brink, maybe peer over the edge. Why would a man want such a thing? Wouldn't you rather play some poker?"

Goodwin agreed.

"I for one," he said, "would like to play some poker." He shook a finger in Morgan's direction. "I suggest you find another doctor, one more schooled in curing *real* illnesses, and ask him take a look at those lungs."

Morgan shrugged.

"And," Drexel added reproachfully (or so it seemed to Morgan), "you have Fanny now."

Morgan nodded again, and he remarked, as he frequently did these days, that he would soon retire from the world of finance, and that he didn't really want to be a banker. This elicited drunken hoots of derision. Drexel suggested that Morgan seek employment as a ballet dancer, and Goodwin gasped charmingly that Morgan could be a nude artist's model.

The laughter eventually died out, hastened perhaps by the image of a nude sculpture of J. P. Morgan (or of a nude J.P. Morgan, in the flesh), the three men each turned his attention to his cards, and the poker game continued until midnight, when Morgan expelled them both easily enough (neither Drexel nor Goodwin truly wanted to be there). Upon expelling them both, he ignored his wife's lingering perfume and portrait long enough to settle down in his den to a big fat Cuban stogie and a copy of *Une Saison en Enfer*, when he heard a woman's laughter on the Avenue, just outside his first floor window. He rose again, unlit cigar hanging from his lower lip. He recognized that voice, that laugh. He bounded from the room and ran into the street – a comical sight, he knew it, and he wasn't proud of it, but he wasn't ashamed either – and he ran down the block, following the laughter. At the corner of 36th Street, he saw her, a thin little figure in a green dress and a blue pelisse, twirling about in the mist, her light brown hair uncovered and billowing in the light midnight breeze. She stopped and stared at him, and she smiled, that pretty smile that he remembered so well. He drew nearer, now just a few feet away, her green-blue eyes a beacon in the night.

"Come with me, Pierpont," she called to him. "Join me, Johnny! It's a beautiful night. And I feel better than I have ever. I am cured, I think! Your doctors have cured me!"

Lights went on in the second floor of the mansion across the street. Nervous eyes peered through lace curtains.

He drew close. His hands folded over her dainty fingers, which were cool and soft. Her wedding ring glistened in the lamplight.

"I cannot follow you," he said, his great voice mournful, wracked with pain. "I cannot go where you are going."

"Then walk with me," she whispered. "Walk with me. Just down the street." Then, with the sort of utter warmth and affection that he had not heard for so many, many years, she whispered: "My husband …."

She walked a few steps ahead, and she turned her head to smile back at him fondly; a fond goodbye, as it happened, because then, without warning, she thoroughly vanished, and the great Morgan was again alone. Alone on the sidewalk, and in his life, again, unloved; all the love in his life had just dissolved into a night thick as coffee.

Did she actually disappear, did her physical body vanish, or was she just enveloped by a mist, which glowed only dimly in the gaslight? Had it even been her to begin with, or some terrible hoax? He didn't know the answer to any of these questions. At this moment, he didn't trust his eyes, which were blurry with tears.

Morgan summoned a cab, sank into the cushioned seat and listened to the horse's hoof beats clatter gently on the concrete streets, which increased in volume and rhythm whenever they crossed a patch that was still paved with cobblestones. The blindingly white home at 42 West 21st Street emerged like a ghost in the fog, this house that he had rented in 1862 for the bride who never returned from her honeymoon. Moments later, he found himself staring longingly at a lavish brick mansion on East 14th street, a great looming temple in the deep night, this home where Mimi had once lived, when she was a young woman and alive. The world was Mimi; her sweet smile lived on in every blade of grass, and each gust of wind carried within it still a touch of her honeyed breath.

Even when his lonely thoughts turned to family, he dwelled most on Little Louisa, with her brown hair parted in the middle and knotted at the neck and her smiling, shy face, the image of the other young woman, whom she had no right or reason to resemble, as though she had somehow been planted by a ghostly hand in Fanny's womb. This strange, unmentioned fact of life had made little Louisa, inevitably, Morgan's favorite.

He did not, he did not, he did not want this life, and he punched his armrest in frustration. He did not want to control the world economy, he did not want to own the railroads. All he wanted was to stand with Mimi on the deck of an ocean liner, to feel the cool spray of the sea on his face, to put his arm casually about Mimi's waist at a Parisian gallery, to look at a painting, to hear her voice.

At length the cab stopped on lower Broadway at Fourth Street. Morgan paid the driver, then ascended a flight of stairs to the midnight show at the Broadway Concert Lounge – a name intended to distinguish it from the "concert saloons" that were of a less reputable nature, or, anyway, of a lower quality of musical entertainment. Still, it was not entirely respectable for a man of Morgan's social status to sit in a candlelit room to watch a beautiful woman sing. The lounge was small, with brick walls and rough wooden floors. Windows displayed the great thoroughfare of Broadway, a dazzling comet that descended into darkness a few blocks to the south at Canal Street. The room was packed tightly. All the tables were occupied, and a crowd shoved each other at the back, near the bar. This romantically disorganized mood, either carelessly random or carefully cultivated, was entirely disrupted when a self-important fat man – *the* self-important fat man, come to think of it – burst into the room screaming.

The woman on the stage stopped her song, which, for the record, was *You Naughty, Naughty Men* (and a randyer version of that song has never been sung, either before or since, so the interruption was really quite unfortunate).

"Was it you?" he bellowed, his face red with fury, but it was a fury, the beautiful woman thought, that seemed entirely feigned. She smiled, with no little affection. In his moment of anguish, whatever had caused it, he had come to her. He had traveled all the way downtown, more than thirty blocks, to scream out his anguish to her – to no one else, to *her* – and she was happy.

No customer dared turn to look at the rich man. All eyes lowered, gazes drowned in their drinks.

"Whatever's put you in a pucker," she said, "I swan I'm not guilty. But thank you for joining us."

She was a little bit drunk, and her red dress slid off her shoulders. She looked gorgeous and daunting, adorable and unapproachable.

"Why don't you sit down and have a drink, listen to a song, Darling?" she asked.

Georgie (for the singer was, of course, Georgina de Louvre) nodded to her pianist and trumpeter.

"We know something that will make you feel better," she cooed. "Why don't you have a listen?"

Without waiting for a response, the great man's mistress began to sing, in a velvety voice designed to soothe, a ballad entitled *Someone Loves You When You Love Yourself*, a really lovely brainstorm that she improvised on the spot, thinking only of the crushed, cursed man she saw before her. (It was a song she never wrote down, neither music nor words, and which is lost to the moment.) The mood in the room calmed. Lovers held each other gently in the candlelight. The waitress roamed from table to table, pouring drinks, and tears glittered in the great man's eyes like diamonds. (Like the diamonds on little Mimi's engagement ring.)

A while later, a small group gathered in the Morgan mansion as the night began to wane and the sun prepared to rise.

The terrifying and formidable Mr. Sneed was there; dressed for the evening, he had clearly not yet taken to bed and seemed to consider a summons to the millionaire's mansion a suitably impressive way to end the night. His crooked smile was smug and subtly proud. Next to him, Mr. Filbank. If Georgina's later recollection can be trusted – and it usually can – his now-crooked nose gave him some level of authority and menace, which was my gift to him, I suppose, although he remained generally unprepossessing.

In the center of the room, groggy and irritable, sat W. Marley Talzek, counsel to the American Cigar Distribution Company, a shell company anonymously owned solely by the Morgan family, through which they executed their more questionable, shady transactions.

And Georgina sat to Pierpont's immediate left, her legs crossed, her smile mysterious. She was now dressed all in white for the dawn, and a parasol, closed and tied, leaned demurely against her armchair.

"Isn't anyone going to make any coffee?" Talzek groused. He was a bony man in his early fifties. He wore a suit that had once been a nice one, and he seemed disappointed in his life.

"All right," said Morgan. "I've got my secret police to break knuckles, I've got my Jew lawyer to do my dirty work." He gestured to Georgina. "And Miss de Louvre, of course." His voice trailed off into a general throat clearing, and the room was silent. "Because I need a sane brain," he added kindly. "Because I need someone in this room who can think straight, and who will tell me the truth."

"*Is* someone going to make coffee?" Talzek asked again.

Morgan shouted, "*C*offee!" and within a moment, white-gloved hands brought coffee. Hands shaking, Talzek filled the fine china cup to its golden brim, skipped the cream and sugar, and took a long desperate gulp. He settled back in his armchair, sighing with relief. Sneed poured himself a cup of coffee as well.

"Mr. Sneed," said Morgan. "Where is Allen Jerome? Where is my old golden boy?"

"Northern Montana, Mr. Morgan."

"And what is he doing in Northern Montana?"

"Gathering an army of outlaws," he said, "and plotting rebellion against the United States government."

Dishes clattered in the kitchen.

"As far as we can tell," Sneed added.

Morgan pounded on the coffee table.

"President Grant must send in the troops," he said with rising anger, "put down the rebellion, and deliver Allen Jerome *to me*."

Talzek cocked his head to one side, and he lowered his eyes.

Filbank tried to approach this delicately.

"I do not think that the President views the threat as – "

"There is an anti-government conspiracy in Northern Montana," Morgan insisted, incredulously. "And the President does nothing?"

"I think," Sneed added bluntly, "that the President believes and understands that this kind of thing is just what Northern Montana *does*. It's what it's there *for*. To attract this kind of thing, and to keep it off Wall Street."

"This is no small matter to me," Morgan said.

Why weren't these imbeciles more terrified? If there were any benefit to being ugly, fat, old-before-his-time and universally despised, Morgan thought, it should have been that he could easily terrify imbeciles.

"*Every*one," said Filbank, "is taking your concerns *very* seriously," in a tone of voice that inadvertently said, *No* one is taking your concerns very seriously.

"Contact President Grant," Morgan insisted slowly and solidly, "and tell the little lickfinger that if does not handle the security situation on the Canadian border and deliver Allen Jerome to me, I will make the U.S. economy collapse, and then I will make the world economy collapse."

Without waiting a beat, Sneed replied, "If we tell him that, he will assassinate you," to which Morgan said, "I wasn't aware that the United States government makes a habit of murdering its citizens for exercising their right to commerce, so I thank you for the warning. I will arrange to have *him* assassinated, *and* the U.S. economy destroyed, if anything happens to me that 'looks' to be an accident. How does that sound?"

Sneed nodded.

"We'll look into the military assault on Montana," he muttered. Smiling humorlessly, he added, "What's a military assault or two among friends? And you do make good coffee, so ...."

"And what about the cowboy?" Morgan asked. "The one who went to prison."

"Reliable sources have him dead in Wyoming after the prison break," said Filbank. "Other reliable sources have him alive in Colorado, drinking himself crazy."

"Which means what?" asked Morgan. "Both dead and alive....?"

Filbank shook his head.

"I don't think it means he's both dead and alive concurrently," he said, clearly befuddled and perplexed by the question. "*Rather*, I think it means that one of the sources is *wrong*, and the other is *right*. We just don't know which is which."

But Morgan was lost in his thoughts, staring moonily at his cigar. The first theory – "Both dead and alive," as Morgan whispered again – seemed to make some sense to him, seemed to warm his cold-white face like a little sunbeam of hope.

"Listen," Talzek said, "what is this about?"

Georgina replied for her patron.

"Allen Jerome stole his money. Where would Mr. Morgan be if employees could just steal his money and know that he wouldn't come after them? Why, I will tell you where, gentlemen. Nowhere. Out of business. He may lose money pursuing the nefarious Allen Jerome, but when Jerome is rotting in prison, it will be a (what's the word?) *detergent* against the next would-be thief."

She nodded at Morgan.

"Right, Darling?"

She knew that the correct word was *deterrent*. Georgina had a magnificent mind. But she believed (correctly, I think) that it would only damage her professional prospects if everyone knew it.

"*Is* this about the pilfered gold?" Filbank asked now, suddenly remembering Emelina's inscrutable insight. "Is this about money, or business, or revenge? Or is it about something else?"

Is the great man cracking up? And will he take what little is left of the world economy with him?

Morgan seemed to find the smoke from his cigar – drifting, disappearing, reappearing – endlessly fascinating.

"Why," Filbank asked, "do we care about the cowboy?"

Morgan sat forward, which took more effort and more time than he had apparently anticipated, and eventually, having righted himself in his armchair, he grunted decisively.

"Find O'Hugh. Tell him all charges will be dropped, if he can tell me how he can be alive and not-alive at the same time. And he can name his price. A million dollars, if he wants."

The room fell silent.

Georgina squeezed Morgan's hand, and she smiled sadly.

Outside, in a street bathed red by the fresh sunrise, Talzek said, to no one in particular, "I'm not actually Jewish. I'm a Prussian Catholic. Does Morgan realize this?"

"Miss de Louvre," Filbank said. "This isn't about the gold, is it? This is about …" Here he paused for emphasis: "*Love.*"

The group paused, each of them embarrassed.

But then Georgina filled in the void. She giggled with loopy, astonished joy, and she covered her mouth with one pink hand.

"Love, Mr. Filbank?" she gasped.

Filbank blushed, and he looked down at his shoes, his cheeks and ears burning.

"Whatever do you mean?" she asked him.

"I thought," Filbank muttered, less sure of himself now. "I thought it might not be the gold. I just thought, you know … maybe *love* has something to do with it. With all this."

Sneed took Filbank's doughy arm in his own strong grip.

"What Mr. Filbank means," he said to Georgina, "is that we've all had a long night, and we all have a lot of work ahead of us."

To the crisp morning air, Talzek said again, "I'm *not* a Jew, you know. Perhaps Morgan is confusing me with M. Warley Platzek, an attorney who *is* a Jew. But I'm not M. Warley Platzek, the *Jewish* attorney. I'm W. Marley Talzek, the *Prussian* attorney. I believe, for purposes of clarity and accuracy, that utilizing the correct terminology is so important, especially in the legal field."

Georgina de Louvre opened her delicate white parasol, just for effect (the morning sun was still dim), and she stepped south on Madison Avenue. Conversation stopped, and the three men watched her whirl off the Avenue onto 32nd Street and pass from view.

Some time later, many years later, Georgina and I were destined to have what you might call an "affair", a really crazy, wild affair, which is why I know all of these little details of Morgan's comings and goings. But my affair with Georgie is another story.

* * *

Months later, and across the country, the morning after the shootout in Lervine, Billy Golden stood at the stable door.

"Great work last night, O'Hugh," he said. "If you're ever in need of employment, I could certainly use you."

"Tang and I rescue Lucy with the help of your men, and then I am out," I said, chopping the air for emphasis. "That's our deal. I'm out."

"That's our deal," Billy said, and he shook my hand. "But my offer stays open. Forever."

"And my refusal stays final. Forever."

"Fair enough," he said. His smile, as always, charming.

On the road out of Lervine, I said to Tang:

"What happened to you in Sidonia? After all this, I have a right to know."

She just shrugged.

"Foolishness," she said. "That's all. There's nothing good in this world. I just learned not to hope anymore."

"Who did you murder?"

"No one."

"You were in prison for murder."

"I killed someone," she said. "I murdered no one."

"Are you like Emelina?"

"A little bit. In certain ways, yes. In other ways, no. Emelina is very skilled. I'm not as skilled."

"What can you do?"

"I can talk to dolphins," she replied, "which doesn't really come in handy out West."

"Can you read my thoughts?"

She grunted, *yes*.

"But I don't, most of the time." With a glance in my direction. "I don't want to die of boredom."

"Can you roam Time?" I asked.

"Of course. That's not hard. You want to roam a little bit, O'Hugh?"

I said I did.

She pulled on the reins lightly, and her horse stopped; my horse stopped beside her.

"I'll take you a little bit into the future. Maybe a hundred years. I warn you, though. Once you do it a few times, it gets easier and easier. It gets hard to resist. You may feel like doing it all the time. You need to remember a few rules. First, it is of no real value at all. It really cannot do you any good. You cannot escape from danger by roaming in Time, because you will always return to the same time and place from which you left. And unless you have an utterly pure heart, you can change neither the future nor the past."

I nodded my agreement.

"Do you need to hold my hand?" I asked.

She shook her head.

"Emelina held your hand for the effect of it," she explained. "For the romance, the support, the warmth. For the wild hope that you would fall in love with her." She looked over and her gaze met my eyes. "I won't hold your hand. I'll just take you."

Suddenly, the bright, cloudless sky was very slightly overcast, and the land was very slightly in shadow.

Looking up and down the deserted frontier, she said, "It's not so different, in a hundred years. A little hotter. But look there."

In the distance was a paved road, really the only difference in the barren landscape. Coming down the road was something I had never seen before, and which left me in awe at the time. But there's no need for me to be coy, and so I will tell you what it was: a 1971 Dodge Dart, long and dented and a little rusty. Smog poured out of its rear tailpipe, and it chugged and popped as it rolled along.

"Dodge Dart," Tang said contemptuously.

"What an amazing thing," I said.

"Horseless carriage, O'Hugh. Maybe *hopeless* carriage is more accurate, come to think of it. Exciting for you to see, but this is a real piece of crap car. Popular among a certain segment of the population, though, for a while."

We watched the Dodge Dart grow smaller and smaller until it was just a dot on the horizon. After a while, another vehicle came down the two-lane north-south highway, a car with a horse trailer behind it, tails flapping in the breeze. It, too, disappeared on the horizon, and a Volkswagen bug followed it.

"I wouldn't want to get in one of those," I said, whistling through my teeth.

The car horn beeped. Its horn was like the voice of an annoying little fat man.

"Why do you follow Billy?" I asked. "Why do you believe in his Cause?"

"I do not believe in his Cause," said Tang. "And his Cause is not what it seems, O'Hugh, although what it is, I can't tell you, not entirely. According to the evidence, his Cause seems foolish, but I do not think that Billy is a fool. He is unselfish, he does have an utterly pure heart, and he is smart. Therefore, his true Cause must be something other than what he presents. But as for Tang, I am selfish, and I help him for my own, selfish reasons, which have nothing to do with saving the world."

"Will you live for millennia, the way she will?" I asked. "Like Emelina?"

"No," Tang said. She pushed back her hemisphere hat and scratched the front of her white bald head. "I don't want to live for so long. I could not bear it. I will die. Maybe one day soon, and maybe next to you."

A battered and rusted blue car, long and wide and clunky, tried to pass a truck on the curve and almost hit a red convertible speeding in the opposite direction. The blue car ducked back behind the truck, and the two cars screamed at each other as they passed.

This is what will pass for danger, I guess, in 1975.

It must be nice.

CHAPTER 20

We arrived in Slabtown. The sun set over the great snow-capped peaks of the Sawatch Range in the west. The Mosquito Mountain Range sank into shadowy darkness in the east. We'd cut through the nearest pass, an improvised detour that took more than twenty-four hours, and now my head spun. I was dizzy up here, ten thousand feet in the heavens.

In front of us was not the dying gold town we had expected, but the noisiest place in the world. It was the noise of men growing rich. The streets were crowded with horses and miners. Pedestrians lugging suitcases and trunks dodged an eight-mule wagon, its driver screaming and cracking a bullwhip. A gang of six soaplocks galloped into town, waving their hats in the air. One fell off his horse into the mud. He sat up, wet and brown and laughing and shouting.

"Nat said to meet us in the saloon," Tang muttered. "I guess we've got a long night ahead of us, since there looks to be more than a dozen of them up this street alone."

"That's all right with me," I said.

"I thought it might be."

We needed a good army, but I also wanted a good drink, and the law of averages – which I had studied very briefly on Randall's Island – told me that to get a good army assembled, we'd have to visit a few dozen saloons, and so I said, "Let's go find ourselves some soldiers."

Tang frowned – well, she was always frowning, but this was a deeper frown – and the stars and the lights of the saloons danced on her face, making her look like a sad clown in a dark night.

"Something's wrong here," she said.

A little tangled mutt trotted gamely up to us, tongue hanging eagerly. I tossed him a strip of jerky, which he leaped up and caught in his mouth. I smiled, watching the little dog chewing hungrily.

"What's the story, buddy?" I asked, when he'd finally gobbled down the jerky.

The dog looked up at me with two sad, worried blue eyes.

"Things have gotten terrible strange, Watt O'Hugh," the dog replied. "It used to be a nice town. Poor, but nice. Watch out for yourself."

I blinked.

"How so?" I asked slowly. "What can you tell me?"

The dog nodded his head in the direction of the Coliseum, a large but squat brick building with awnings at street level, a commonplace building with an elegant name. A strikingly tall young man in a black tailcoat was exiting the building, surrounded by a group of generally happy miners, all shaking his hand, slapping him on the back, and talking excitedly.

"Ask Wilde," the dog replied. "I've got things to do."

The dog trotted away into the darkness of a narrow allow.

"Did you hear that?" I asked Tang.

"Yeah," she said, without much emotion or surprise. "Talking dog. That's an unusual thing. I've never seen anything like that before."

"So what do we do?" I asked her.

"What the talking dog said. Go ask Wilde."

We reached Wilde as he crossed Chestnut Street, beaming. The miners began to disperse.

"You're Wilde?" I asked.

"Oscar Wilde," he said.

He looked no more than twenty-five years of age. He was round-faced and gregarious, his voice was deep and friendly, as were his blue eyes. He had long curly hair, and he was dressed all in black, with a black silk tie, knickers and black stockings, and a silver walking stick which he didn't need. He was a student at Oxford, which I guess is some kind of a school in England, and he'd just attended an early evening lecture at the Coliseum, some culture for the pre-boozing hour. T.B. Walters, a famed author of dime novels, was the purported speaker, although Oscar Wilde, from the audience, had dominated the lecture.

"Not the finest lecture hall I have seen, when you compare it to Oxford, for example," he said, "but you can see that they are building an Opera House over on Harrison Avenue that should be something, when it is finished."

"What was the lecture about?"

"Oh," he said. "Something terribly uncultured, and I just asked a few questions and made a few comments about the practical application of Aesthetic Theory to exterior and interior house decoration with observations upon dress and personal ornaments. I told them about Benvenuto Cellini and how he cast his 'Perseus', and I bequeathed to them, I am sure of it, a real reverence for what is beautiful. Even the strong men wept like children, McKee Rankins of every color and dimension, large, blond-bearded, yellow-haired men in red shirts, with the beautiful clear complexions of those who work in silver mines. Imagine them marching through long galleries of silver-ore, looking so picturesque in the dim light as they swing the hammers and cleft the stone."

He smiled a charming smile, and I felt bad for Mr. Walters. He had once written a dime novel or two about me, though the miners were destined never to hear of it. Oscar sighed in the dark night as his poetic musings echoed through the town. I smiled at him, and Wilde smiled back, and Tang kicked a rock impatiently. Wilde was excited to be here, and I think that Tang understood why better than I could. The intensity of the attention that the miners lavished on him was something that he craved, like the attention that a zealot lavishes on society's golden calves. Maybe the Coliseum audience, today, was a microcosm of tomorrow's world, just a hint, a taste, of the universal adoration to which he might aspire. Here was a man who wanted to be liked and loved.

"A dog told us to talk to you about Slabtown," I said. "He warned us about it. Said you would know."

Wilde beamed.

"The dogs here *talk*!" he exclaimed. "This is something unexpected. Why, I had no idea before today that the dogs in America can talk!"

He grabbed my elbow.

"I am happy to say that I *can* help, that your dog was absolutely right. First of all, Cloud City is Slabtown no more, ever since the hills have burst with silver."

This was an unnerving development, and I cast a nervous glance at Tang.

Let's be inconspicuous, I heard her say, without moving her lips, *but remember where you parked the horses.*

I thought that being inconspicuous with Oscar Wilde at my side would be difficult.

"This was a failed gold mining town just a few months ago," Oscar continued, his voice rising, "and everyone told me to pass it by, but all of a sudden there was a little – oh, what's the word?" He rolled his eyes in concentration, held his right pointer finger to his lips. "A *buzz*. That's *it*."

From his jacket pocket he pulled a writing pad and a pencil, and he began scribbling.

"That's a good word," he said. "*Buzz*. It means excitement in the air, like bees, excited bees."

With the pencil, he stabbed his writing pad with finality, smiled, and announced, "I do believe that I have coined an *idiom*."

He put away his pad and pencil.

"We are trying to find a man named Nat Lewis," said Tang, "a resident of Slabtown since the beginning."

"I can help you find your friend," Wilde said. "Just follow me."

We walked on. Above the Coliseum entrance, standing on the roof, with one foot up on the cornice, was a bone-thin, black-robed figure. I turned and stared at him for just a moment, and he was gone. In that brief instant, I felt certain that he must be the killer from the Hippodrome. Then I shook that idea from my mind. What an unlikely coincidence that would be!

Now the town was changing, the darkness had arrived, and the last bit of the frenzied industry of the day had utterly dissolved into the sin of the night. The dance halls and variety theaters, gaming halls and saloons were all full to capacity, and I could hear some whooping and hollering, some joyful gunshots (I'll tell you, joyful gunshots sound different from angry ones), and at least three competing streams of music, *The Flying Trapeze* blending into *Silver Threads* and *Out of Work*, forming a sort of symphony of chaos, as each theater presented its own off-key band to compete for air space. We passed State Street, which even this early in its history looked like the Gates of Hell, already the infamous quarters of the City's gamblers, harlots, pickpockets (we called them "footpads" in those days), and scammers. We finally reached Harrison Avenue, which, Wilde told us, was fast arriving as Cloud City's primary thoroughfare. A canvas tent apparently housed a family of twelve. Dusty half-naked children aged two through ten ran in and out of the tent-flap, crying and laughing and punching each other, falling in the dirt, and being children in every way. (Ah, *children*!) Across the street, a wiry young man cooked a meal on a spit in front of a log cabin. Two doors down from the log cabin was a half-built mansion on which a dozen construction workers toiled, their sweat dripping onto the wooden side walk. Between the mansion and the log cabin was a small brick building with a sign over the door reading, *Bank and Saloon!*

"The exclamation point is a nice touch," I said.

"Shall we go in?" Oscar Wilde asked. "It's the Wild West, perhaps we should rob it," he added, and I thought to myself that this boy was not going to last too long out here.[*] Inside, miners lined up at cashier windows in the back with packs of silver ore, which they could deposit or exchange for chits to be used for drinks. At the front of the establishment was a bar of polished and elegant black walnut.

"And here is why the dog sent you to me," Wilde said. He gathered us both in close. "*I see what others do not!* Query, why are the mines suddenly bursting with silver, where a year ago, the miners will swear to you, there was none?" Before I could answer, or even wonder, he replied, "It is your worst nightmare, Watt O'Hugh. The Sidonian train has arrived. The hills are alive with Magic!" I opened my mouth to speak, but before I could respond, or even wonder, Wilde exclaimed to the room at large, "Ah! great canyons of red sandstone, and pine trees, and the tops of the mountains all snow-covered!" in a voice that nearly sang. The bartender laughed. Wilde ordered "A phlegm-cutter, my good man," which he quaffed without flinching, inspiring a burly, red-haired miner behind him to exclaim amiably, "He's a bullyboy with no glass eye, this one!", which in turn inspired Wilde to declare to the bar at large, "My simple friends, your artless untutored praise has touched me more than the pompous panegyrics of literary critics ever could!" which for some reason they all loved. Wilde hugged the bartender, and the bartender hugged him back.

Well, this seemed to be just about the friendliest possible time and place to start asking about Nat, and so once Oscar and the bartender broke their embrace, the young poet pointed to Tang and me and said, "These two gentlemen are trying to find a friend in this

---

[*] I bumped into him again in 1882 in Arizona, where I saw him take down four other men in a gunfight. The gentleman was good with witty repartee, but he could also shoot, and he could fight (and he could spit, for what it's worth). So while I understand him to have been skilled with your "comedy of manners", the guy was also pretty tough when he wanted to be.

teeming megalopolis," and at that point, all eyes were on us, and the bartender seemed for the first time to notice the pale foreign face that hid beneath the wide rim of Tang's hat, and his stare turned suspicious. All joy left his face.

I felt a tap on my shoulder, and Tang and I both turned. A fat young man with curly hair and a stubby nose introduced himself as a deputy of Cloud City. He explained that while his burg welcomed representatives of nearly every nation including Frenchmen, Irishmen, Jew pawnbrokers, and even a neighborhood of Coloreds, John Chinaman could not set foot within the city limits under any circumstances. "A Chinaman visited us once," he remarked matter-of-factly, "and we blew up his house."

Tang didn't budge. In a man's voice that was more conciliatory than I had ever heard her, she said, "I'm just here to do a little laundry. I thought the miners might need a good laundry."

To the dead silence that ensued, she added, almost cheerfully, "Who doesn't love a good Chinese laundry?"

I thought I could defuse the situation by changing the subject, and so I called out, "Does anyone here know Nat Lewis? He'll vouch for us," and the saloon fell completely silent.

"Now you've done it!" Oscar exclaimed with disheartening good cheer.

"A pillar of Slabtown," I insisted, against all the available evidence. "From the very beginning."

The bartender groaned.

The deputy's face darkened.

"Right?" I said, more than a little doubt creeping into my voice and my heart.

"Things change, I guess," the deputy said with regret. "Nat was a personal friend of mine, so I take no pleasure in telling you that his body hangs tonight from the half-built shell of the Tabor Grand Hotel, right across Harrison Avenue."

The miners formed a ring around us, their guns drawn.

"I'm going to have to ask you to give me your pistols," the deputy said.

Which didn't seem to be a particularly good idea.

After all, Nat, our good buddy (whom neither of us had ever actually met) was hanging by his neck from the rafters of a luxury hotel's banquet room, where one day, if Sidonia did its job properly, millionaires in tuxedoes would drink champagne with their gown-clad mistresses. What would keep us from suffering that same fate? (The rafters, that is, not the champagne or tuxedos or mistresses.) Our pistols, that's what.

My colleague, John Chinaman, had the same thought.

In an instant, she leapt into action; perched on her right foot, she spun about, and with her wooden left foot kicked the pistols out of the miners' hands. Two of their weapons smashed into the mirror over the barkeep's head, shattering it instantly, and the third crashed against the wall, discharging with a mighty blast and splintering the lovely wooden bar, but injuring no one. Tang leaped, hit the bar with both hands and flipped onto the deputy's shoulders, knocking him to the ground and sitting on his chest. "If you prick us," she said, landing a solid blow in the middle of his face, "do we not bleed?" Seeing the deputy unconscious, she turned, grabbed a glass from the table, threw it at one disarmed miner. The glass connected with his forehead, rendered him insensible as it bounced, then walloped the back of another miner's head, knocking him out cold in turn. "If you tickle us," she asked, "do we not laugh?" The bartender reached for his rifle below the bar, and in an instant, Tang had leapfrogged the bar, smashed his head against its walnut veneer, then smashed his bleeding head against the broken mirror, either to be safe, or just for fun. "If you poison us, do we not die?" she asked him, before letting him fall to the ground in the scattered shards of glass. Then, to the other patrons generally, she muttered, too quietly to be heard by anyone but Oscar and me, "And if you wrong us, shall we not revenge?"[*]

"Magnificent!" Oscar shouted, as we hurried out of the saloon, into a light rain. Oscar apparently did not realize that this hadn't been a theatrical presentation for the benefit of visiting European intellectuals. "Your use of Shylock's Act II Scene I soliloquy was inspired!"

---

[*] I will admit that I didn't recognize this recitation at all, and my journal that evening records only that Madame Tang made a "perhaps very strange speech about pricks and tickling, while punching and kicking – still able to clobber a crowd of burly thugs without getting too winded, and I note with relief that we are still alive as of this writing." A few years later I recognized her chop-socky soliloquy when I viewed *The Merchant of Venice* in Langtry, performed by a Shakespeare troupe that was touring the small-town West. Shakespeare was surprisingly popular, in those days, in those places.

"You don't have to come with us," I said, and Tang told him, "This is our fight, and we cannot promise to protect you."

We didn't manage to dissuade Oscar, who followed us, trampling through the mud and horseshit of Harrison Avenue in his patent leather shoes. We turned south, where we had tied our horses, but a crowd had gathered at the edge of town, and they were marching as one in our direction. Tang stopped in her tracks.

"Deadlings," she said.

She looked north, at the end of town, where another crowd had gathered.

"Deadlings?" Oscar asked, and Tang said, "A sure sign of Sidonian influence."

"Amazing," Oscar whispered, as the lurching figures drew closer.

Lightning flashed overhead, illuminating for just a moment three bodies – three dead men – hanging by their necks from crossbeams in the shell of a great building.

We rushed across Fourth Street and onto the less densely populated Poplar Street, but from all directions, new deadlings rose like weeds after a storm, in the cloudy, rainy moonlight, their faces lost and bewildered. A moment ago, they were nothing, floating unconscious through oblivion, bodiless, mindless, and now they were marching en masse through a muddy, unfamiliar town, angry with three strangers, for reasons they couldn't fathom.

We ducked between two buildings, running through alleys till we reached Elm Street, right at the border of town, but this too had its own triangle of deadlings. We were trapped. Tang kicked in the flimsy birch-wood door of a hardware store. Inside the store, we pushed a table flush up against the door.

I looked out the window.

The deadlings were a heterogeneous army, without any unifying elements to draw them together as friends or as soldiers. Their clothing was from all different recent eras, stretching back at least a hundred years, and they spoke a babble of languages. A young woman with soft features, beautiful and apparently happy, in a lime-green dress, held the hand of a thick, mournful old man, as they marched together across the street. But as they drew within a few yards of the door to the hardware store, the woman's face betrayed a muddled lack of concentration. Her lovely green eyes grew numb. Her body fizzed and popped, grew fuzzy at the edges. If you live in the 1960s or 1970s (before the advent of cable television), you would think this was all the result of *bad reception*, and you'd be up on the roof of your ranch house adjusting the antenna. A ghostly outline developed where the woman had stood and then dissolved with an almost inaudible sputter and hiss.

The old man found his hand empty, and he turned to look where the young woman had once stood. Finding her gone, he put his fingers to his temples, as though gripped suddenly with a moderate headache. Then his image wobbled, and very quickly he was gone as well.

"We need Time to think," Tang said. She turned to Oscar. "You coming with us, poet-boy?" and Oscar said, "Where?" and Tang replied, "To another Time. To devise a plan," and Oscar seemed to agree that this was a good idea. A moment later we were all sitting on a cliff at the edge of the mountain range, beneath a churning but not frighteningly active volcano, which spewed ash but not lava. Just before us were vast, arid desert sand dunes thousands of feet high, and in the shadow of the dunes a dark, murky swamp. A great lizard slogged through the ooze, thirty-feet tall, with a large skull, dozens of sharp teeth, and a long, powerful tail. Beyond the swamp, the shores of a shimmering ocean – not a mirage, this time – were guarded by a rather friendly looking, duck-billed lizard, about the size of a large man, which stood on two legs.

Tang was sitting cross-legged, her brow furrowed.

This was all more than Oscar could take in. Still trying to process the deadlings, he seemed not to have noticed the dinosauria. Oscar asked: "Are they real? The deadlings? Or are they the town's collective imagination?"

"Real," said Tang, "in a way. A deadling doesn't repossess his original body, which has molded away in the grave. But he is more than a hallucination or figment of the imagination of the bereaved. He repossesses his original consciousness, but not his original body."

"What's happening to them?" I asked. "Why do they vanish like that?"

"It takes a lot of concentration to stay in the physical world," Tang said, "if one is not *of* the physical world. It's like hanging onto the edge of a cliff with your fingertips. Eventually, you just … let go."

"Maybe," Oscar mused, "we should just wait. If we wait long enough, hold them off for long enough, maybe they'll all just vanish."

Tang shut her eyes and thought.

"I don't think so," she said at last. "I think more will keep coming. Each deadling will take a rest, then reappear, attack us and attack us in shifts."

Tang arched an eyebrow.

"O'Hugh, will you lose another essence?"

"How many have I got left?"

"Twenty."

"How many am I using?"

She squinted at me.

"Fourteen, now," she said. "You've activated two more since I last checked. One clicked on just now. You know how to roam Time on your own now, O'Hugh. Congratulations. You are a Roamer."

"And how many do I need?"

"Well, you need only *one*, technically, but that's a pretty empty existence for a gentleman who's figured out how to use twelve."

I nodded.

"If it's a choice between losing one and losing all of them, of course."

"We might need to give the deadlings two. OK?"

I nodded assent.

Off in the brackish distance, the great lizard roared.

"Wilde?" she asked.

"How many am I using?" he asked.

"Come on," she said. "Stop it. I know you well enough already to realize that whatever I tell you will be a crushing blow to your Oxford ego. I think for your own self-image, you need to tell yourself that you use eighteen, that no mortal has ever accessed so many, and that you can spare two of them. You know, the future is starving for its comedies of manners."

He cocked his head to one side.

"Is she making fun of me?" he asked me.

"Tang has no sense of fun," I replied, and Tang nodded in agreement.

"For the record," she said, "I consider *An Ideal Husband* your best work, which (*if* you survive this evening's adventure) you will write in 1895. Much better than *The Importance of Being Earnest*, which most critics will incorrectly choose as your masterpiece."

She looked at Oscar Wilde a little sadly, thinking about his pitiable future, which she'd apparently researched with some thoroughness since meeting him. You and I both know what was on her mind at that moment, looking at him here, on this cliff in pre-historic North America, and what made her so sad. Apparently, his fate, if he were to survive the night, was already written. With ink in a book, and sealed.

"All right, then," Oscar said.

Tang explained the plan. We had to make our struggle look believable. We would return to Cloud City Hardware, nail the door shut, board up the windows, and scream with fear at the hands and arms crashing through the glass. We would run up the stairs when the horde of deadlings crashed through the front door, taking half the wall with them. We would shut the door of the back room on the second floor and try to hold it shut for as long as we could, just three cornered souls battling an irrationally furious deadling mob bent on our extermination, until, at last, the door would crash against us, and the deadlings would carry us into the street and stomp us into dust.

Upon our return to 19th century Cloud City, we followed Tang's instructions, and the deadlings reacted as predicted. In the upper room, as the deadlings crashed through the house, Oscar said, "I feel that we should be fighting," and Tang replied, "The wallpaper and I are engaged in mortal combat." Looking at the room's shabby furnishings, Oscar exclaimed, "I wish I had said that!" to which Tang replied, "Don't worry Oscar. You will." We soon found ourselves watching our own deaths from the second floor window. Again, as in the Wyoming mountains, I bore witness to the spectacle of my forlorn, newly dead corpse.

We both turned expectantly to Tang.

"I think," she said, "that there is nothing to prevent our exit through the back door, into the side alley, which we follow till the town limit. We will retrieve our horses and escape. I recommend crossing Mosquito Pass by moonlight." To Wilde: "Oscar, I think that you should take the earliest train out of Denver. Telegraph your family as soon as you can to dispel any rumors of your death in Cloud City, then return to England at your soonest opportunity."

Hugging the shadows at the edge of town, we traversed the alleys and backstreets, until in the narrow space between a brick undertaker's shop and a wooden flophouse, we spied our horses, waiting nervously where we had left them. We ran to them. Tang and I leaped quickly onto our faithful friends. Doubling back around, Tang grabbed Oscar and tossed him behind her. As we galloped out of town, he held on tightly to her waist. In the center of the City, deadlings popped in and out of existence, all of them stamping on our bodies, dust rising into the starlit night. Unmourned, Nat Lewis's body still swung from the rafters, tugged gently by the Colorado night wind.

CHAPTER 21

The train pulled out of the station in Denver, puffing smoke, making a racket. A gleeful Oscar Wilde waved from his compartment in the third car, contagiously enthusiastic over what we had all just suffered. I was a bit rueful that he wouldn't accompany us to Weedville. I'm quite sure he could have done *something* to distract the gunmen there. And, anyway, I would miss him.

Tang, unsmiling, watched the train disappear in its own black smoke.

"Poor Oscar," she said, with a little actual emotion.

The problem with being a Roamer is that everyone you meet is a tragedy.

We lunched in a little grubshop near the train station. We were unwashed and shabby, but we weren't the worst there, and the rude smell of the customers almost overwhelmed the rude smell of the food. I was slurping down a bowl of potato soup with some sort of meat in it. *Potato Soup with Meat* was the official name of the food listed on the menu, and I had ordered it because I could afford it. Tang leaned forward, over her plate of hash.

"We need a plan, O'Hugh," she said.

"I have a plan," I said.

"We have some allies in Mexico," she said. "Well, not allies *yet.*"

She fidgeted inattentively with her fork.

"Every stranger is an ally waiting to join the Cause," she said, without much optimism. "We head south. Word of the rebellion is probably scaring people as far away as La Paz. Before too long, we'll just need to channel the fear. Then we'll come back up North, make a stop in Weedville with an army worthy of the name, which I could then bring North to Montana, when we're done with Nebraska."

She looked over at me hopefully.

I shook my head.

"We need a few brave soldiers," she said.

"I'm a brave soldier," I told her. "And my next stop is Weedville. I ride out tonight, with you or without you."

"It's a suicide mission, Watt," she said.

"So be it," I replied.

I sat there on a tree stump just outside of Denver. Our horses knew something was wrong. The sun was low in the sky and would soon be blocked by the mountains. I muttered, "Look, after my allegedly heroic exploits in Little Mount, I wound up in couple of dime novels that are probably still making their way through Kansas, and I'd like to be in a few more someday. If I keep following you back and forth across the country, doing whatever you say and not taking a stand and rescuing poor Lucy, then readers are apt to think I'm rather *passive* for a Western hero."

I stood up.

"Anyway," I went on, "that was supposed to be funny. If I don't leave now I never will, and I won't be worth anything to you or to myself."

Tang thought. Behind her, in the distance, Denver cranked along like a machine, the horses and riders clogging her streets, the trains rolling in and out of her station. The black smoke from the trains lingered in the air.

"We ride out tomorrow morning at dawn," she said with finality. "There's a lookout point above Weedville, where we can pitch camp. The next morning, we storm the town just before lunch. Catch them when they're distracted, thinking about chicken pot pie. We can't arrive at night and fight against gunslingers who know every hiding place in town."

"You don't have to go, Tang," I said.

"Of course I do," she said.

We were off trail for a while, passing through Northern Kansas and then crossing into Nebraska, where we arrived in the vicinity of Weedville late in the day, climbed the black cliffs and set up our camp. We tied the horses up a quarter mile from the cliff edge, so they wouldn't be visible from the town. Tang and I lay down on our stomachs and peered down at the town. Tang pulled out her field glasses and took a look, and then she handed them to me. I looked down at lifeless, boarded up shops, but a street that was oddly busy and lively. Far beyond the town, yellow fields, sandhills, scattered shrubs, like a torn, threadbare tapestry. Beyond that, the Loup River.

"What do you think?" I asked.

"No longer a 'town' in the typical sense of the term," she said. "No commerce, no business." She pointed east. "Warehouse at the end of the street, solid and locked-up." Then she pointed north. "Soldiers housed in the Weedville Hotel, fed in the mess hall across the street. Part of a weapon distribution network and militia recruitment scheme. Look at the little side alley that abuts the primary street. See the little jailhouse." She turned to me. "Not so many people here, though. Maybe a dozen, maybe two-dozen. Could it be that they're completely unprepared for our arrival? Did they not even imagine that the famous Watt O'Hugh III might attempt to break Mrs. Lucy Fawley out of jail?" She shook her head. "Again, something seems wrong here. This could just be a trap. The Sidonians dangle Lucy in front of you, and when you ride into town, they ambush you. No escape."

"Maybe we shed a few more essences?" I asked. "And just ride away?"

"That particular trick may work only on deadlings. I doubt it would fool those more fully attuned to the physical world."

"It worked in Wyoming."

"They found you dead in the ice, your skull blown off. They didn't watch it happen, and they didn't see you walk away. No, Watt, thanks for trying. Take my word for it."

She held her field glasses up to her eyes one more time. Something caught her attention.

"Monsieur Rasháh," she whispered.

I waited patiently for her explanation.

"An old enemy," she said. "It seems, O'Hugh, that I too have personal business in Weedville."

* * *

The sun was down and the stars were out, lighting the granite cliffs and the meadow below. Hoping not to telegraph our arrival, we didn't light a fire, and I lay under the stars, shivering a little in my bag, just breathing in the fresh air and trying not to worry about what was coming tomorrow.

I was more than startled when Tang emerged from the woods, aiming an 18-inch German flintlock pistol right at my head.

This was unexpected.

A few thoughts ran through my head: First of all, my gun was right by my side, and I was pretty sure I would have been able to shoot her and kill her in a moment, if she hadn't been skilled in Magic. But she was skilled in Magic, and so there was always that. Secondly, even if I could have shot her, I wasn't going to do it if I didn't have to. Finally, even then, with my life maybe at stake, I still couldn't help admiring the gun, its shiny, light brown wood and intricately carved silver handle. You don't see a gun like that every day.

Tang clenched her teeth, and her hands were trembling. She whispered a whisper that pounded in my head, drowning out the howling mountain wind, a threat of some ambiguous sort. She said that we could do this the *easy way*, or, if I insisted on making trouble .... And she just left it hanging in the air. Somewhere in the distance, a mountain lion roared. A catamount, if I wasn't mistaken. A magnificent, sleek hunter, not unlike Madame Tang. The wind whistled around us. I stared at Tang, and she stared back, fiercely.

"Um ...." I began hesitatingly. "Um. Are you robbing me, Mr. Tang?"

I didn't really have much money, I pointed out stupidly.

I blinked.

Now, I thought she had something in mind – thievery – and maybe you thought she had something else in mind, and maybe your guess was a *little* closer to the truth than mine was, but you and I were both substantially off the mark. By tomorrow morning, Tang would head with me into Weedville, guns blazing, and by noontime, either we'd both be dead or I'd be reunited with the woman I loved more than anything in the world. It was her last chance to be kissed for a while, maybe forever, and it had been a long time since Madame Tang had been kissed. With her somewhat but not-exactly youngish life about to come, maybe, to a bitter end – maybe a really painful bitter end – she requested, with a gun pointed at my head, a long, passionate, blast-her-to-the-Heavens kiss, under the full moon and the blazing stars.

Now then: when I was preparing my notes for these *Memoirs* and I came across my diary entry for that evening, I was at a little bit of a loss as to what I should tell all of you about it. I thought, well, readers of the late 20th century and the early 21st century will be very used to the deconstructed Westerns of the 1960s and 1970s, and they'll probably smirk. Some readers might think I was trying to make an unsympathetic character more likable, that maybe I thought I'd sell more books that way. So I thought I might just leave it all out. Just skip it, get my two main characters to sleep, and get them up in the morning in time for the shooting and cussing and spitting and dying that was sure to come in Weedville.

On the other hand, I considered spicing it up. I could make all manner of claims for my dexterity and manhood by writing something really filthy, and I do believe that you-all might appreciate some naked bodies and entwined limbs tumbling about in the mountain dust right about now, with blood and havoc right around the next bend in the trail. Some Hollywood movie producer might suddenly sit up and take notice. But as you read this I am cold as a wagon tire, maybe recent-dead, maybe long-dead, and I promised you the truth.

The truth was this: I knew that Madame Tang had somehow lost everything she'd ever owned and ever loved, and that she was about to walk into a hailstorm of bullets in middle Nebraska state to make sure that the same thing wouldn't happen to me. And if she survived that, then she intended to march into another hailstorm of bullets in Montana territory in an effort to save America from itself. So I figured she could have anything she wanted from me.

"A kiss?" I stammered.

"A kiss," she said, her gun still pointed at my head. "Or," she added, not very convincingly, "you get a bullet in the brain."

I smiled, half-disappointed, half-relieved.

"You didn't really need to aim a gun at me," I said.

My tone wasn't angry or hurt. Just matter-of-fact. Woman wants a kiss, I was usually happy to oblige, back then. Back in the 1870s. Gun really was never necessary.

She let her arm drop. She walked over to where I lay, and she crouched down beside me.

"I just thought it might make it all more interesting," she whispered. "I didn't mean to scare you."

She handed me the gun and I took it, flipped it over in my left hand.

"And look at it," she said. "It's a magnificent gun. It's not much good at killing. Still, a graceful, exquisite gun, like a flower."

She put a finger on the pistol's intricate silver handle and caressed it lovingly.

"This gun has a story," she sighed. "Like most guns, a beautiful and sad story. I will tell you someday, maybe, if we survive. But not now."

I handed her the gun, and she took it back, fondly.

Kissing those snarling lips was like putting my head into a lion's mouth. She wrapped her arms behind my neck, the gun handle whapped the back of my head, and her embrace was sad and fierce and angry-at-the-world; as we folded ourselves into each others' arms, I could feel another emotion rise from Madame Tang, which I would call *not-quite-hopelessness*, which made me feel not quite hopeless myself. It was a pretty good kiss for a man's last night on Earth, if a kiss was all a man could expect his last night on Earth.

One other thing you may be wondering, and which you may suspect I was now in a better position to discern: was Tang a woman pretending to be a man, or a man pretending to be a woman?

Well, she had been the sole inmate in the women's section of the Wyoming Territorial Prison, which gave me a bit of solace at the time. I knew that it was possible that the prison guards had been a little too intimidated to check to see if she truly belonged there, but, nevertheless, I thought that she was a strong, tough woman pretending to be a man, just as she always claimed.

But then again, I am a product of the 19th century, and given the events of that evening, that's what I would have to have thought, wouldn't I?

CHAPTER 22

I woke up before dawn, and by the time the sun rose, I was finishing up my first shave in months.

Then Tang cut my hair, a little sadly, I thought.

"What would you have done if I had grabbed my .45?" I asked her. "When you aimed the pistol at me?"

"You wouldn't have done that," she said.

"What if I had?"

She stopped cutting my hair for a moment.

"I suppose I would have blocked the bullet," she said. "Froze it in the barrel of your gun." She paused. "But you wouldn't have done that."

I looked myself over in the little mirror I carried in my pack. My eyes were red and tired, but my pallor was healthy enough, my jaw strong and daunting. Suitably tidy, I thought, for a little killin', then a little courtin'.

We rode down from the mountains, my bay gelding and I, Tang on her stallion, side by side.

"I hope your ghosts will help us today, O'Hugh," she said.

We approached a couple of guards who stood at the edge of the town. We rode through. I clopped the fellow on the left with the butt of my rifle, and Tang did the same to the fellow on the right, and we kept riding. No reason to kill a man if there's no reason to kill a man, and we galloped into Weedville, Tang and I. When men drew guns, we shot. When they didn't draw guns, but stood dumbfounded, we clopped them on their heads, and they folded. Though this was their town, with its own rules and laws which they sought only to uphold, our approach nevertheless seemed fair enough to me.

We cut right and wound past the jail; the guards ducked behind the brick building and began shooting, furiously but inaccurately. We jumped off our horses, and we dived between the deserted butcher shop and the deserted fresh fruit store. I kept my gun trained east, toward the jail and the little shrub of a forest. Tang watched the town.

"What's our plan now?" I asked, and Tang said, "This was your idea. I thought *you*'d have a plan."

This repartee – which could have had some potential for affectionate comedy in the face of danger if we'd had a moment to develop it – was cut short when, to my utter surprise, a dark man stepped into the center of town, the same one who had haunted my thoughts since that night at the Hippodrome. He was clothed as I remembered him in black robes that shrouded an almost impossibly bony body. His legs were no more than sticks. He narrowed his tiny eyes. He smiled a terrible smile with his blood red lips.

He shouted out Madame Tang's name, in a perfect Chinese accent.

"This is my old nemesis, Monsieur Rasháh," she told me. "I had not expected to find him in Weedville until I spotted him last night. We were bound to meet again, but I am disappointed that it has to be today."

"Do you want to see your children?" Rasháh called to her, in a quiet whispered hiss that somehow rang through the plains like a cannon blast. "If you want to see them, they're right here."

Now, the power of suggestion perhaps, he really seemed French. A villain who a moment before was just repellent and ugly had gained, in a breath, a certain *je ne sais quoi*. A flair. His creepiness had become *sang-froid.*

He pressed one black-gloved finger against his temple.

"They're here in my head, Tang ...." he whispered again, another deafening whisper.

The silence that ensued was so deadly I thought the town would explode. The black viper-man stood in the middle of the street, tapping the side of his head, smiling his blood-red smile.

"Let's both take this guy," I said. "Let's both go out there with our guns blazing."

She shook her head.

"Why?" she wondered. "Because you don't like him?"

I nodded. "That's right. Because I don't like him. I met him once before, you know."

"I know," she said.

"I didn't like him then, either."

She almost smiled, but then she didn't smile. I was disappointed, because I would have liked to see a smile grace Tang's grave face just once before we both died. She opened her barrel, dropped the bullets out, and reloaded.

"New bullets," she said. "Special Magic bullets for the dark man."

"On three?" I asked hopefully. "We both gallop out there, shooting together?"

"No, Watt, this is my fight. You can't just gun him down."

"I'm going out there with you," I said.

Tang sighed. She stared out at the street.

"What do we do?" she asked. "Look, there are three bad men guarding the jail, guarding Lucy, that is. There are two bad men at the bank." She pointed across the street. "A sniper above the barber shop, a sniper above the five-and-dime, and a sniper above the general store. Every one of them will be shooting at you if you go out into the middle of the street with me."

"Why don't you freeze their bullets in the barrels of their guns?" I asked.

"I don't know their guns," she said. "I don't know the gunmen. I cannot visualize the situation."

"You are not as good with black Magic as I had hoped."

"No," she agreed. "I can talk to dolphins."

I thought.

"Why don't you roam into the future to see how this all turns out, and what we should do to save ourselves?"

She shook her head.

"You can't change the past when you're roaming," she said. "If I go to my future to find out how to fix my present, I will be changing the past. I would be expelled from the interlinear Maze before I could take a good look at anything."

"You're giving me a headache," I muttered.

"I'll just have to meet you at the post office when all this is done with," she said. "This is impossible."

"It is not," I said decisively, suddenly getting an idea. "We fight him in other Time. He will surely follow us."

Around the corner, I could see the dark man, still standing in the middle of the street, calling to Tang with the voice of a small child, a scared, resigned singsongy voice, telling a long, childish story. Tang gritted her teeth; this was a voice she recognized well. Unfortunately for me, the little voice was speaking in Chinese, which at the moment I really wished I knew. Tang gave me six Magic bullets, I emptied my cylinder and reloaded. She gave me six more Magic bullets, which I put in my shirt pocket.

We looked at each other, just breathing.

"And now," Tang said, "Time stops."

The wind stopped blowing. The dark man kept speaking, kept taunting her, but otherwise, all was silence. Faces peered from the windows of the mess hall, unmoving, unseeing. The distant trees stopped waving, the birds stopped flapping their wings, and bees a hundred miles away stopped buzzing.

We jumped on our horses, galloped out into the center of town and began firing. The dark man caught our bullets effortlessly, with a clown's exaggerated red-lipped burlesque of mirth. He tossed our bullets (our special, extra-Magic bullets!) into his mouth, crunching on them like peanuts. We passed him and spun around at the end of town right in front of the warehouse and galloped ahead again, re-loading and shooting, with no better result. It was strange and despairing to gallop through a world in which the wind didn't blow. We felt dead, already dead.

Behind the dark man, a hole opened in the air, black in the middle, a glowing blue around the edges, tattered, rough-edged and not perfectly round, like a rip in a cowboy's denim shirt. Calmly the dark man put one foot behind him and into the void, which engulfed him instantly. Tang, who was ahead of me, furiously kicked her steed, which then executed a perfect vertical jump into this crater in space, pausing slightly at the lip, then speeding up, as though sucked through. I tried to follow, kicking my horse in turn and urging her onward, but the hole snapped elastically shut and vanished. Expecting to land in an unfamiliar setting, my horse and I instead tumbled onto the dusty Weedville street, where Time had begun again to flow, as always. The snipers began to fire.

And then I sensed them with me, my little ghosts, my long-lost ghosts. Bullets on a direct trajectory for my heart took a detour and cracked posts and splintered pillars, or dropped harmlessly to the dusty street. My right hand lifted and shot, and a gun flew from my holster into my left hand and shot, in each case with deadly accuracy. A gunman fell from above the five-and-dime. One shouted in shock as a bullet pierced his lung, and he crashed through the window of the apartment above the general store. A gunman jumped out from between the barber shop and the mess and I shot him with the gun in my left hand, without even really seeing him. Little feet kicked my steed and steered us out of harm's way, and before I knew it, I was in the stables, and a small group of gunmen were firing from the jailhouse. I thanked my little ghosts. I always try to thank my little ghosts.

The kids who live in this town – the town where I have chosen to live out the remaining months of my life – have asked me more than once whether I really believe that ghosts have saved my life, and saved my life again, over and over, through the years. Perhaps, they have mused, I am just a great shot, a better shot than I can even imagine, and that somehow in the midst of these extraordinary situations, I must believe that a force outside myself is protecting me. A woman with whom I once lived in Latin America, and who witnessed this phenomenon first-hand on two occasions, said that she felt more comforted believing that I was a delusional crack-shot who would protect her so long as I lived, and that she would be less confident in the attention span of little ghosts. I hear all these arguments, I understand that people question my sanity, and I even understand why. I once cracked open a book on abnormal psychology, just to see if they might be right. But I stand firm in my belief: little ghosts have protected me through my life, perhaps the little ghosts of the children that one day in 1863 I hopelessly and quixotically sought to save. I don't know them, but I love them.

The front of the stable collapsed from the gunfire, the horses ran screaming into the street, and I escaped out the back way. I crouched down by edge of the wall, trying to spot the gunmen. Apart from the roar of the terrified steeds, the town was wholly silent. I listened for footsteps; for the crack of twigs; for the click of a gun. All was silent.

Until I felt the warm barrel of a revolver nuzzle up against the back of my head.

"Drop your guns," came a voice, a nice rough-edged Brooklyn accent, a New Yorker like me. "And put your hands up."

I thought this was unsporting of my fellow Knickerbocker – he should have given me a fair shake - but what could I do? I dropped my guns, I put up my hands, and I waited for the ghosts to help me, although what even ghosts could have done at that point, I don't think I could have wagered a guess. Still, my ghosts have sometimes been resourceful.

"Now, turn around."

I turned.

Two gunmen faced me. The Brooklynite was a dark-haired smirker, with a crooked nose, and his big hogleg pistol was right in my face. The other gunman, heavyset and nervous, stood a few paces behind him, scanning the town and the stunted forests that bordered Weedville to the east.

"Crazy demons vanishing into the air," the fat gunman said, his hands shaking.

"One demon vanishing into the air," Brooklyn said. "One demon. It's important to get your facts straight. One demon and one Chinaman."

The fat gunman was trembling, waving his gun this way and that, jumping at shadows, jumping at emptiness. "Demon that vanished like that could just-as-easy unvanish itself."

"Better get this over with," Brooklyn said to me, as his friend shook violently in the weeds and grasses.

"I don't suppose you'd agree to a fair fight?" I asked, and he shook his head.

"I'm sorry," he replied, and he really did sound sorry.

"Good work, boys," came a voice from the side alley, and into my line of vision walked a man I remembered well: Monroe, the husky leader of the Wyoming Prison escapees. Monroe looked a little bit younger than he had back when I'd last met him. Still broad and hairy, but a little bit younger, as though the Sidonian air were having its intended effect.

He walked up to me, squinted into my eyes, up very close.

I expected him to smell like sweat, and piss, and shit, but he smelled like citrus, and pine needles, and cinnamon, and freshly fallen snow. He smelled beautiful, and his blue eyes were friendly and regretful.

"You a deadling, Watt O'Hugh?" he asked.

"Yes," I said.

"I ordered you killed, back in Wyoming," he said.

"I remember that," I said. My throat was dry. "I didn't like it much, and I remember it well. Being killed by your henchman, that is. Mr. Tang."

"Wasn't that Mr. Tang in the street with the demon-man?"

"That wasn't Mr. Tang," I replied. "That was Mr. Tang's brother, Mr. Tang."

"You're dead, then? Really dead?"

"You saw the body, right? Mr. Tang shot me in the forehead, not the face, so you'd be able to identify the body."

He grunted.

"Yeah," he said, acknowledging my point. "I saw the body. A real mess, but it was you."

Now squinting again, puzzled.

"You're a little too lucid," he said. "I've never seen a deadling so lucid."

"Can you think of any other explanation?" I asked, quite reasonably, I thought, and I hoped that Monroe could not, in fact, come up with another explanation.

He poked me in the chest.

"Solid as a rock," he said. "You're right here in the world. No flip-flip, no buzz-buzz. Deadlings, always they've got that little flip-flip, buzz-buzz."

Monroe looked over at Brooklyn.

"Right?" Monroe said. "You ever seen a deadling without that flip-flip, buzz-buzz thing going on?"

Brooklyn shook his head.

"I think he's a live one," Brooklyn said.

Monroe gave me one last look, and he shook his head.

"Look here," he said, pointing at my eyes, and Brooklyn looked closer.

The other gunman stood far away, still flipping his gun here and there, aiming at imaginary demons.

"What?" Brooklyn asked.

"His pupils," Monroe said. "Over-dilated, I think."

Monroe sighed with some relief.

"He's a deadling."

He stepped back.

"Plus, I saw the body," Monroe concluded. "Without much doubt, he's a deadling."

I tried not to show any emotion, and to hold my face and body steady. After all, why would a deadling care?

"Now that's settled," I said flatly, without any inflection. "So I will be on my way. Excuse me?"

Monroe put out a hand, flat against my chest.

"My men still have to shoot you," he said, not unkindly. "Just to be safe. It couldn't possibly make a difference to you, could it?"

I turned up my palms.

"The first time I got killed," I replied, "it hurt. It really hurt like a sonofabitch. So I'd prefer not to go through that again."

Monroe slapped me on the shoulder familiarly. This slap on the shoulder said it all: He liked me, didn't really want to make this unnecessarily adversarial, was glad I was already dead and that he didn't have to kill me, not *really*. This was nothing personal.

"That Chinaman shot you through the head," he said. "That's gotta hurt. We're more artful, O'Hugh. We'll all three of us aim at your chest. More instantaneous extermination," he went on, "and less pain. Maybe no pain. But, listen, O'Hugh, I gotta do this. How would it look if you didn't die in Wyoming, and somehow I let you slip through my fingers twice? How would it look?"

He had his career to think about, after all. The yearend bonus and whatnot.

He gestured to Brooklyn to step back, and he gestured to jitters-boy to step forward.

"We do this French firing squad style," he said. "An elegant execution for a more civilized age." To me, it just seemed like killing a poor sucker, but Monroe seemed awfully proud of his new European style, the style adopted, apparently, in Sidonia these days.

He asked me if I had any last wishes, and I said I'd been long-dead and buried now for – what was it? Years, maybe. So, no, I didn't have any goddam last wishes. Maybe he could have asked me this back when I was alive, goddamit.

A meadowlark fluttered across the low yellow Nebraska sky, alone, crying inconsolably.

I really started to feel dead.

Monroe wondered aloud whether he, Brooklyn and Jitters should shoot me "on three", or he should call out "Ready, Aim, Fire". He wondered aloud how they did things in France, and he asked Brooklyn and Jitters if they knew French. Neither one of them did.

As though someone else had, like me, grown tired of all this pontificating, a single shot of gunfire rang out. Monroe fell dead to the dust, and Jitters raised his pistol, shooting randomly and wildly until he was out of ammunition. Another single shot rang out, and Jitters fell dead to the dust.

Brooklyn just shrugged and cursed.

"Come out and show yourself, you coward," he shouted, exasperated, realizing there was no place to hide, and no hope. His only chance was to appeal to his executioner's sense of shame.

No luck. Another shot rang out, and Brooklyn fell dead to the dust.

Who in the town of Weedville would want to save me? Who else but the redoubtable Mrs. Fawley?

Where was she? I scanned the quiet town, the empty sky. I knocked on the window of the little jail cell, but it was empty. I scampered, head down, tripping across the clumps of wild needle grass, kicked in the back door of the long-abandoned dry goods store, brushed through dusty cobwebs which were as long-abandoned as the store, and I peered through the window into the street. I screamed Lucy's name, but I heard only silence. And then shooting; the window shattered and glass crashed into the store.

I shot back through the broken window. I didn't know what I was shooting at, but I reloaded fiercely, and I shot again, and I shot again.

At last, from behind the boarded-up windows of the dry goods store, I could see a man move into view. He was tall, lean and lanky; a scar disfigured his face from forehead to chin.

"O'Hugh!" he called. His voice was tinny and weak.

Simultaneously, a second figure moved out of the shadows, but I didn't have a clear view of him. This was because he held in front of him Mrs. Lucy Billings Fawley. She wore a man's denim shirt and rugged work pants. She was older; she was different; she was exactly the same. She was beautiful, and I loved her. A gun was at her head, a grimace on her face, tears in her blue eyes.

"Come out, O'Hugh!" Scarface called.

"If I come out, let Lucy go!" I shouted through the broken glass.

"That was our plan exactly!" Scarface shouted back. "If you come out, we'll let Mrs. Fawley go."

I winced, and I stepped through the front door. The second gunman tossed Lucy to one side. He was older, muscled, all horns and rattles, scowling and completely hairless – no beard, utterly bald, not even an eyebrow. Lucy ran off down the street sobbing, cut into an alley, vanished from sight. I couldn't see her but thought I could still hear her crying.

The two gunmen stood before me.

They drew their guns as one, and I drew both my pistols and fired before they did.

The gunmen fell, and the town of Weedville was silent. A turkey vulture sat on the top of the mess hall, observing the view, it seemed, with some anticipation.

At that moment, a figure darted from the open jailhouse doors, a small slender figure in the shadows. She moved like lightning, grabbed a chestnut quarterhorse, leapt onto its back and shot off into the horizon, kicking and shouting.

I didn't intend to let her get away this time.

Horse and mistress kicked up Nebraska dust as they veered south towards the black granite cliffs, climbing the rocks like a spider. But my horse was faster; I swept by Lucy and her now-panicked steed, grabbed her reins and slowed us all down.

"Are you really Watt?" she said in a panic. "Or are you a ghost? Are you a demon, dressed up like Watt O'Hugh?"

A wrinkle touched her lovely mouth. There was a new elegance to her, an aristocratic quality that mingled in her soul with the deepest pain.

I dismounted, and I helped her down. We were at the very edge of the black cliffs, and the Nebraska plains spread out below us. The air was cold up here. It was dusk, and the sky was growing overcast. A light rain-mist began to coat us. Her white face was wet and beautiful; her eyes filled with tears. I held her face between my hands.

"On July 13, 1863," I said, "you asked me to marry you. I couldn't accept then. I want you to understand why."

She nodded.

"Because you were visiting from the future," she said. "If you had accepted, you would have been blown back to the 1870s." To my stunned silence, she added, "I saw you on Friday, and then on Monday you were more than a decade older. I didn't know then about the Roamers, but I knew that you were visiting from the future. Anyone could have seen that."

She smiled.

"You wouldn't marry me, and the City exploded, and I escaped, looking for tranquility. I thought I was marrying into the English civil service and becoming conventional. I like tea biscuits, you know. Or is that tea and biscuits?" She wondered for a moment: Tea biscuits? Tea and biscuits? Which of these had lured her to Britain? Then Lucy concluded: "At any rate: silly me."

A hawk screamed like a terrified old woman and settled down on an adjacent cliff a few yards from us. The hawk eyed us quizzically.

"Well, I accept *now*," I said urgently. "You never withdrew your proposal, so it still stands, and I *accept*. I know that you are married to Darryl Fawley, but I've thought a lot about this. Given everything, I think we can declare him legally dead.

"I'll marry you, Lucy, and I will take you someplace far away from Sidonia and Darryl Fawley and all of this. We will have children and raise them and love them."

I held her in my arms – now she felt weightless, almost not there, but she hugged me back, and I could hear her whispering in my ears that she would marry me, and that she loved me. Every word was a struggle for her. I was happy, once again – happy, as I had been before, in the 1860s, during that brief stolen breath of joy, and my life, suddenly, was flowing like a little stream that emptied to a great and mighty ocean, where life is limitless and eternal, and love is infinite.

I know this is a story about a youngish man, and that at this moment in my story – as my story is coming to its conclusion – I think it looks as though something happy is about to happen, and that vistas of joy are spreading out before young Watt O'Hugh as far as the eye can see. While lives have happy moments – nearly *everyone's* life has happy moments – endings aren't happy. And as I think back on that moment, sitting beside Lucy Billings at the top of that cliff, that black cliff that in the plains of Nebraska felt like a mountain – well, thinking back on that moment, I want to yell and shout and slap my younger self. But I guess I was entitled to a moment of crazy optimism, even if it was only a moment.

Did I ever marry Lucy Billings? Did that crazy Chinese poet ever find the secret of the Red Eyebrows? To where did Madame Tang vanish, and what hold did M. Rasháh have over her? Who won the Battle of Sidonia? Why, come to think of it, didn't you ever study the

Battle of Sidonia in History class, back in 6th grade, if it was so blamed important? (On that last question, I posit: maybe you did. Can you really remember what you studied in History class back in 6th grade?)

As I write this, I still feel as healthy as a gopher in the Spring. (No, I don't know what that means either, but people seem to expect old Western cowboys to say things like that.) I still cannot really feel my health declining. Perhaps I have a hole in my left lung that a squirrel could crawl through; maybe a lump the size of a golf ball is growing in my brain, or in my cranial nerves. When I die, less than a year from now, no one will bother to figure out exactly what killed me, so I don't know now, and no one will ever know. Old guys die.

As I have said, I will die in early 1937, and now 1936 is more than halfway done. When I am dead, I will be nothing. I'm writing this story so maybe I can achieve a little bit of immortality. Maybe you've found this book, and maybe now you know that I did some things for which I deserve to be a little famous. But someday *you* will die, and then *everyone* you know will die. *No one* will remember you. And then the universe will collapse in on itself, and certainly the shoebox that held my little yellowed manuscript would not survive the collapse of the universe. So where is the point, I ask you? I am embraced by what feels like a brain seizure, then something that feels like a heart attack, and I ask you again. Still, somehow, I want you to know the answers to these questions. I want to tell you about my exploits in the Civil War, and I want you to know about my experiences with Tiburcio Vasquez, a really crazy 19th century outlaw, who really isn't mentioned enough when people talk about crazy 19th century outlaws. I mean, he really hasn't received the infamy he deserves, the infamy he sought out. Because Tiburcio Vasquez was a really crazy bastard.

So I think I will keep writing, and maybe you'll find more yellowed pages in the same attic where you found this manuscript. Or maybe you will never find it, and maybe you will spend your life searching for it, rummaging through "yard sales", "googling" my name on the "web"[*], trying to descry the answers to these questions. I wish you good luck.

---

[*] In my roamings, I have learned of something called the "web", and an activity known as "googling". As well as I can understand it, the "web" is magical lacework enveloping the universe that contains infinite wisdom and knowledge, and "googling" is a wizard's spell that can unlock that wisdom and knowledge for Seekers and Questers. I was happy to learn that the 21st century had rediscovered Magic, although much of this future is still murky and unformed.

Now, as for the early evening with Lucy on that cliff edge in the newly minted state of Nebraska. How long did my optimism last?

"Why did you run from me?" I asked.

"I thought you were a demon," she said, "or an illusion, or a ghost. I thought you had to be anything, other than you."

Now I knew why she had felt so weightless.

Now I knew what had frightened her, and why I hadn't been able to find her in the jail cell when I first arrived in Weedville.

"Why would you have run away from a ghost?" I asked sadly.

"Because you thought I was coming ...."

"To take me back...."

Now she grew a bit hazy, a little fuzzy around the edges, and the light in her eyes began to dim. With a look of supreme concentration and focus – as though she were *hanging onto the edge of a cliff with her fingertips* – she pulled herself into the world, so that she could stay with me, holding my hand, on the crest of that little valley.

I looked in her eyes.

I asked my Lucy, "When did you die?"

"Just last night," she said.

"So if I had skipped Cloud City ...."

"You would have saved my life," she agreed. "It's always the last thing we do that makes us late, you know."

She smiled. It wasn't a particularly sad smile, just one that recognized the irony of life.

"Have you *ever* noticed that, Watt O'Hugh?" she asked me. "For example, when I decide to have one more cup of tea, I *just* miss the El. It's a bit like that."

A bit like that, she said, with a little English accent, a little twinkle of Europe in her voice that I had never heard before. How long had she worked on that? Oh, Lucy Billings, my poor dead Lucy Billings .... Each moment was worth more than all the silver in Cloud City.

"Why are you here?" I asked.

"Maybe because you wanted me here?" she wondered. "After Sidonia squeezed the life out of me, you walked into their magic town, and your yearnings and expectations mixed with their faerie dust brought me back to life. *Maybe*? I don't know. What do I know? The overlords of Sidonia did not reveal the secrets of the Universe to me."

"You are alive now," I said. "You are alive and breathing."

"I don't breathe," she corrected me. "I suppose I am alive, in a way. For the moment."

"Where do you go, when you are not in the mortal world? What is the Afterlife like?"

"When I am *not* here, I go nowhere. There is no Afterlife, there is nothing, and I do not exist. It's oblivion, Watt. The oblivion that we fear our whole lives is real. Think back to what life was like for you before you were born, and that is what it will be like for you after you are dead. I don't know what rouses me from my black sleep."

"How long do we have?" I asked her.

"I can watch the sunset with you."

"Will you watch the sunrise with me too, Lucy?"

"No," she said. "I will be long gone by morning. It takes too much energy to stay here in the world. Darling, Watt. Hold my hand and watch the sunset."

"Will I ever see you alive again?"

"I will walk the Earth again, maybe for a moment or two, maybe sometimes for an entire hour. I'm your wife, after all. I'll miss you, won't I? I am sure I will find a way to come back." She furrowed her pretty brow. "I tried to love Darryl Fawley, Watt. I *liked* him from time to time. Sometimes I liked him a lot. But I never stopped loving you. No one ever pushed you out of my heart, Watt O'Hugh the Third."

This plan had worked out terribly. How could it have gone so wrong? Billy Golden was a guy who could see the future and the past, but he had worse timing than Billy Hayden.[*] He sent us into Slabtown a few months after it had turned into Cloud City, wasting a day in the planning and a day in the failure, plus the side trip over the mountains. Had we just skipped Slabtown, we'd have reached Weedville in time to save Lucy. So how could Billy have miscalculated so terribly? How awful he will feel, I thought, once he knows.

Here's the rub, my friends, something I am sure Billy had seen, over and over again, as he roamed Time: had we saved Lucy, I would have escaped with her to Mexico and left Billy's counterrevolution behind me, like the self-interested fence-straddler I'd become. But with Lucy dead, I wanted vengeance and would be ready to fight Sidonia like the good soldier I had been during the War Between the

---

[*] Some scholars of clown history will object to this characterization and tell you that Billy Hayden, a standup comic of the 1870s, in fact had very good comedic timing. I saw him perform in Lawrence, Kansas, and I beg to differ.

States. Suddenly, I had something to live for, and it wasn't pretty, but it better suited Billy's plans. He needed an angry Watt who would never stop fighting, and that's exactly what he got, and exactly what he had plotted, because for reasons I could not yet imagine, I had some predestined role to play in Billy Golden's historical re-write, and he could not and would not let me go.

When did I figure that out, when did this twisty conspiracy against me become clear, you ask?

Sometime in 1928, I awoke in the middle of the night, and it all made sense, all of a sudden. Billy Golden was responsible for all of this. He betrayed me, not in a moment of fear or weakness, but by careful, detached calculation and design. Our man with the messiah in his eyes, our white dove with an utterly pure heart.

Sitting on the Nebraska cliffs, I knew there would be more battles ahead, more victories and defeats to come. Morgan's army sought me from the East; the Sidonian army pursued me from the North; a crazy, fourth-rate Chinese poet approached from the San Francisco harbor in the West; and always always always, Billy Golden would watch me from his abode in some supernatural fog, plotting and weaving my future and maybe my past. But for now, I just held Lucy's warm hand tightly, because Lucy was all that existed in the world. The sun set into the stormy dark clouds on the far flat horizon, and the sky shattered in a great, black-orange blaze. Lucy groaned very gently, and her fingers slipped from my grasp, dissolving like a cube of sugar in a cup of tea. I looked where just a moment ago she had sat, and I was alone. Down the cliffs and across the plains, the bodies in the Weedville streets lay in the mud. During the night, they would slowly freeze, their faces locked, each one, in a clownish grimace. The clouds rolled in across the lowlands and collided with the cliffs; hailstones crashed out of the heavens like a slot machine jackpot, clattering to the valley below, and melted gently in the rain that bathed the quiet yellowing fields.

THE END

OF THE FIRST PART OF THE STRANGE AND ASTOUNDING MEMOIRS OF WATT O'HUGH THE THIRD

AUTHOR'S NOTE

In writing this book, I have tried to be as historically accurate as I could, given the demands of fiction and the fantastic nature of this yarn. My depiction of the details of New York life in the 1860s and 1870s are as precise as I could make them, as are the details of life in the Wyoming prison. There *was* a locust plague, and an epizootic epidemic that killed many horses, which may have contributed to the Great Depression that began in the 1870s, and so on – much in this book is accurate. But I've played around with details where the plot warranted it. The Draft Riots, for example, began in the morning on July 13, 1863, not the afternoon; I have put J. P. Morgan into his Madison Avenue mansion a few years early; Oscar Wilde probably didn't visit America in the 1870s; and Tony Drexel might not really have had unusually enormous nostrils. (But on the other hand, maybe he did.) I took other liberties as well.

Thanks to my wife, Lan, and my kids, Liana and Julianne, and to Fred Tippens and Raymond Kennedy for encouraging me to be a writer, wherever you are. Craig Eastland's original cover art is missing from this reissue, but I love it still. Mark Matcho's new front cover illustration is a masterpiece, which deserves to hang on a museum wall (and will, in February)! Jane Summers, Leslie Harris and Leslie Przybylek answered my questions on the history of the period and helped me with valuable leads. Finally, over the course of many many years, many many people read some version of this book and encouraged me, and since its publication, many more people have encouraged me some more. I really appreciate all the readers who have read this book since its publication, who will not read this author's note because they already own the book.

I thank you all.

Steven S. Drachman, November 2013